"What are you hiding, Kyle?"

When he didn't answer, she walked around him to the back corner of the room.

Leaning against the wall was the missing poster of her, performing on the ice in her skating costume from the World Junior Championship.

"Why...?" she asked him.

"Why didn't I throw it out?" he filled in the blanks dully.

Jessica nodded. "Yes. I asked you to."

He shrugged. "It's a good picture. Maybe I wanted to decorate my locker room with it."

"I don't get it, Kyle. It's an embarrassing picture. I was a stupid girl who did everything wrong back then—"

"Like hell you did." He uncrossed his arms and ran a hand through his hair. He wasn't looking at her. "I had a crush on you." In a lower voice, he added, "Maybe I still do."

She clutched her throat. "You *do*?"

"You think that kiss was by accident?" he shot at her.

She focused on his chest. His beautiful, muscular chest that she'd laid her cheek against less than a day ago. A small noise came from her throat. She didn't want it to be so, but that kiss had been a nicer kiss than the one her boyfriend—fiancé—had given her after he'd proposed to her. Her cheeks flamed.

Dear Reader,

Welcome to a new Wallis Point, New Hampshire, story, set in the fictional seaside town first described in *The Long Way Home*.

I've poured my love of the community of ice-skaters and ice-skating rinks into this story, as well as my deep respect for servicemen and women, particularly wounded veterans.

Kyle Northrup is a war-injured marine veteran with a secret that he's keeping. Jessica Hughes is a physical therapist who'd rather not think about her figure-skating past. When Kyle is summoned home for a reading of a will, he doesn't count on facing the former teen crush whose life he'd forever changed.

Now the two must work together to bring a dilapidated community ice rink back to life. They never expect to reconnect—and fall in love. But will their secrets ruin everything?

Thanks for reading! I hope you enjoy Kyle and Jessica's story.

All the best,

Cathryn Parry

CATHRYN PARRY

—

The Secret Between Them

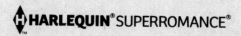

Recycling programs
for this product may
not exist in your area.

ISBN-13: 978-0-373-60952-9

The Secret Between Them

Copyright © 2016 by Cathryn Parry

Printed in U.S.A.

Cathryn Parry is the author of seven contemporary romance novels. Her books have received such honors as a Booksellers' Best Award, a CataRomance Reviewers' Choice Award and several readers' choice award nominations. Cathryn is also an adult figure skater and longtime fan of the sport. She lives in Massachusetts with her husband and her neighbor's cat, Otis. Please see her website at www.cathrynparry.com for information about upcoming releases or to sign up for her reader newsletter.

Books by Cathryn Parry

HARLEQUIN SUPERROMANCE

Something to Prove
The Long Way Home
Out of His League
The Sweetest Hours
Scotland for Christmas
Secret Garden

Other titles by this author available in ebook format.

To my readers.
I'm appreciative every day for your
support and goodwill. Thank you!

CHAPTER ONE

FROM THE MOMENT he'd left home, Kyle Northrup had fantasized about returning, triumphant, to Wallis Point.

Until that fantasy died two years ago on April 19. The day the Humvee he'd been driving had run over a roadside bomb in Afghanistan. After that, Kyle decided he would never go home again.

He thought nothing more about his discarded fantasy, until a call came in from a Wallis Point, New Hampshire, exchange.

Kyle gripped his phone in sweaty palms. He sat behind the desk at his new civilian job, staring at Navy procurement reports on a computer screen. The order-analyst position depressed him—he was more cut out for physical work, but that seemed off the table now that he was a wounded military veteran.

He listened as a lawyer back in his hometown spoke in hesitating, halting sentences.

"…Kyle, I'm calling about your stepfather," Natalie Kimball said. "I'm his attorney."

Kyle couldn't picture the face behind her name. A former classmate of his, she'd said, but he'd been gone from town too long to remember. "Yes, ma'am."

Natalie cleared her throat and continued. "I'm sorry to tell you this, but Joe passed away this afternoon. He wasn't in pain. All his funeral arrangements were completed, so there is nothing you need to do in that respect—"

"Wait, what? Joe is dead?" Kyle asked, struggling to catch up, reflexively gripping the edge of his desk.

How long had it been since he'd talked to his stepfather? Ten months? A year?

It's February now. I didn't talk to him at Christmas. It was the Christmas before that. He was irritated with me, as always.

"Joe had elective heart surgery just this morning," she answered. "He never came out of it. Kyle, I'm sorry."

Kyle pressed his lips together. He didn't know how he felt, or even what to say. Maybe he was in shock. He just knew that he wouldn't show any weakness about it, not to anyone.

"The funeral is on Saturday at ten o'clock at the Rogers Funeral Home," the lawyer continued. "I'm sure he'd want you to attend. He asked me to call you when the time came."

Kyle slowly exhaled. "I'll be there," he said quietly.

"Joe…had a will, which he named me as executor for. Could you stay in Wallis Point and meet with me about it on Monday?"

His heart feeling as if it was beating through his chest, Kyle sat up straighter. A will meant that Joe had left him something. There was only one thing Kyle had ever wanted, and Joe knew exactly what that was. Kyle was grateful he'd never told Joe he'd been injured because otherwise, knowing Joe, Kyle would have had no chance of getting what he'd hoped for.

What he'd always hoped for.

"I'll be there," Kyle said tersely. "I'll be there on Monday."

There was a pause. "Kyle, I really am sorry."

He stayed silent. He wasn't about to tell the lawyer this, but even before the final fight that had sent Kyle packing from Wallis Point for good, he and Joe had never really gotten along. Not since Kyle's mother died.

That day had hit them both hard.

"Well," the lawyer—Natalie—said, a forced cheeriness in her voice, "I'll look for you at the funeral. If you'd like to come early, my husband is a Navy vet. His name is Bruce Cole. I think that you two could talk—"

"I'm fine," Kyle interrupted. He knew what

she was attempting to do, but Kyle didn't need to "talk" to anyone about anything. He'd adjusted just fine to civilian life. "I'll see you on Saturday."

"Great. I also have a letter that Joe left for you. You were his only relative. He said that you're in the Marines—"

"I'm a veteran. Honorably discharged."

"Thank you for your service," she said.

Kyle felt his lips pressing together again. "You're welcome." Then, because he couldn't stand the awkwardness any longer, he asked, "What's Joe doing with the hockey rink?"

"I'm glad you asked," Natalie said in her gentle voice. She seemed excited. "Do you have an interest in it?"

Did he? Hell, yeah. Shakily, he pushed himself out of his chair. Joe barring him from the rink had been the last straw—the big blowup that had led Kyle to leave town. His main hope for returning to Wallis Point had been to reclaim his rightful position and run that hockey rink as he'd been brought up to do. As he'd *earned*. Of course, the one bad decision Kyle had made, the winter of his senior year, had ended the original promise from Joe.

But now was a fresh chance…

Kyle thought of his prosthetic left foot. Did he dare attempt it?

I have to. I can't sit in this office and stare at

this computer screen every day. This is not what I'm meant to do.

"Yes. Yes, I absolutely have an interest," he said firmly. He swallowed. "How soon until I can take it over?"

Natalie laughed. "Excellent—I'm relieved to hear you speak so enthusiastically. From a strictly personal perspective, Bruce and I are glad you're interested in keeping the facility open. But we'll talk more about it on Monday, of course."

Real hope filled him, for the first time in a long time. He *needed* this competency. Needed to be good at something again.

"That's great," he said softly. And oh, man, what he would do with the place. First thing, he'd track down some other wounded soldiers he knew. Some of them must have dispersed into Maine and New Hampshire. Maybe they could set up a wounded warrior hockey league. A similar program had been the main thing that had gotten him through the two years of rehab in Maryland after he'd been flown back from Germany—

"Kyle," Natalie said, interrupting his thoughts. "Jessica Hughes is invited to the will reading as well. Do you know her?"

Kyle couldn't speak. Slowly he sank back into his chair.

"She didn't go to high school with us," Natalie

said. "She was home-schooled while she trained in figure skating at Joe's rink. Jessa Hughes, she was known as then."

Kyle wiped his hand over his face, trying to regain his composure. "Jessa is back in town?" he asked, as steadily as he could.

"Yes, but she goes by Jessica now."

Didn't matter what she called herself, she would always be the famous *Jessa* that everybody loved. The sweetheart of Wallis Point.

The great ache of his teenage years.

Kyle exhaled and stared at the ceiling. The last time he'd seen her, he'd inadvertently hurt her. Physically, but not emotionally—on the contrary, she'd had no problem breaking off all contact with him. And Joe's decision to bar Kyle from the rink had been based on that one stupid mistake that he'd always regretted.

In retrospect, Jessa—Jessica—was also a big part of the reason he'd left Wallis Point after high school to impulsively join the Marines.

"Joe left her something, too?" Kyle asked. If Joe had, it would've been to rub it in Kyle's face. That was the only reason he could think of.

"She's…my next call," Natalie said. "Jessica works as a physical therapist at a clinic in town. Joe mentioned that she helped him after he went through knee surgery last year and needed rehabilitation."

Kyle caught himself shaking his head. There was so much irony in that job choice, both for her and for him.

Don't dwell on her. She has no use for you. Never really has.

"So, I'll see you Saturday, then?" Natalie asked.

In practical matters, Kyle didn't care what money or other physical property Joe had willed to Jessica. She could have everything else Joe owned and be welcome to it. All that Kyle cared about was getting his rink…and avoiding speaking to her at all.

He stared at his foot again. Physical therapist, huh? No way would he be telling Jessa—*Jessica*—about his physical problems.

"I'll be there," he said.

THREE DAYS LATER, Kyle was back in New Hampshire. Friday night, in the dark and cold.

He was glad he'd practiced walking with his prosthetic leg so many times in the rehab center that it had become second nature to him. Because in mid-February, the sidewalk in Wallis Point was mounded on either side with snow and ice. The wind from the crashing ocean at high tide body slammed him and threatened to knock him off kilter.

He'd forgotten his gloves, so he kept his fists

balled inside his coat pockets. Hunched his shoulders in the thick navy wool coat.

His boot slipped, and for a moment fear gripped him, but he stayed upright. Trained his gaze on the dark sidewalk, gritty from rock salt and sprinkled dirt.

He was a tough New Englander born and bred. He could handle a bit of snow.

With renewed determination, he headed back toward the one establishment open on the boardwalk. The Grand Beachfront Hotel, where he'd just finished checking in.

Kyle had always liked the place. Had even worked a second job washing dishes at the hotel one summer, when he'd been sixteen and saving money for hockey camp.

The turn-of-the-century hotel had been so busy and popular that an army of teen workers had been employed as valet-parking attendants, bellboys and lobby help. That was during the high season from Memorial Day to Labor Day. Now, in February, the arcades on the boardwalk were closed, the fried dough stands shuttered. In the dead of winter it was usually a ghost town.

Not tonight, though. The hotel lobby had even been fairly busy. Kyle had left his truck idling out front while he'd checked in with his single suitcase. But when he'd gone back outside to park his truck, he'd discovered that the hotel parking lot was full and valet parking closed for the season. He'd been forced to squeeze his truck into a spot on the street about six blocks away.

Maybe Wallis Point had become more popular since he left. As he approached the rear of the hotel beside the attached restaurant, he heard noise inside from a large crowd of patrons.

He flinched, but he didn't know where else to go. He'd kept in touch with no one here. He'd blown out of town on a hot summer night, the week after high school graduation, and no one had come after him.

Other than Joe, Kyle had no living relatives. Nobody he knew of, anyway. Kyle's friends… old platoon mates…they were scattered over the country. He just wasn't big on staying in contact with people.

After he left the Marines Kyle hadn't known what he was going to do, just that desk work wasn't for him. He'd kill to be manager of a hockey rink, especially this one. Now, if he didn't screw it up, he had his chance.

Trudging along, slow and careful, he made it to the hotel entrance, opened the door to the lobby and went inside. The plan was to order takeout food from the restaurant and then hide out in his room for a quiet dinner. He needed to mentally prepare for the funeral tomorrow. Get his head together. Figure out how he was going to handle public perceptions of his below-the-knee left leg amputation.

It still made Kyle sick to think about it. In the military world, with other wounded warriors, it was one thing. In the civilian world…frankly, the thought of their reactions terrified him.

Kyle had never even told Joe what had happened to him.

Swallowing, Kyle followed the familiar path past the concierge desk and down the hallway toward the restaurant. But within a hundred feet, he knew that the situation was worse than he'd realized.

The place was packed. As in waiting-for-tables packed. The crowd was so thick in front of the bar that people could barely pass through to the hostess table.

Kyle stood in the middle of it, overwhelmed. A harried waiter pushed past him, moving Kyle ever so slightly off balance. Kyle caught himself and widened his stance.

Another guy brushed past carrying one of those black plastic squares that flashed red lights and sent off an alarm when the table was ready.

Kyle moved carefully to a pillar and backed against it. This place was nuts.

And then he noticed, *really* noticed his surroundings… Red heart-shaped balloons at the hostess station. Pink bunting edging the doorway leading into the dining room.

It was Valentine's Day.

Kyle groaned. *Just great.* The biggest date night of the year.

He stood pressed against the wall, painfully cognizant of his left foot beneath his pants leg and stiff new boot.

Everyone was coupled up.

He closed his eyes. He had not touched a woman since he'd left for his last tour in Afghanistan. He doubted he would touch one again.

Frankly, like this, he didn't want to.

He edged away. His palms were itching. He had to get out of here. But instead of escaping, he heard the voice of the one woman he most wanted to avoid—Jessica Hughes.

He'd been thinking about her since the lawyer had mentioned her, even though Kyle hadn't wanted to remember. But the laughter and lightness in her voice as she spoke was so uniquely hers. She was conversing with someone in the crowd nearby, hidden from view by the coatrack. Judging by her tone, she seemed happy and hopeful, though he couldn't catch what she was saying.

He could have left right then without her seeing him, but curiosity got the better of him. Kyle edged closer.

If he hadn't heard her first, he would never have recognized her.

She was…heavier than she'd been when he last saw her. She'd taken her coat off and was hanging it up, and he could see she was wearing leggings with a baggy tunic on top. Was she pregnant?

She lifted her hand, and he could see she had a big, pink, glittery rock on her ring finger. His heart sank.

Ridiculous, he told himself. Why shouldn't Jessa—*Jessica*—be married? Or have kids? Or be happy?

She'd never been his, not really. He'd never even kissed her.

Still, his feet seemed rooted. She'd always had the most expressive brown eyes. A way of looking at people with her head tilted, as if she was really paying attention to them—really seeing them.

He'd seen between the cracks, though. God, he'd *ached* for her. Disgusted with himself, he shook his head.

He should leave. Make his retreat while he still could. Ultimately, he'd been the one responsible for injuring this girl—he'd flooded the ice with water when he'd been angry at Joe, and even though Kyle hadn't personally seen it, as soon as his Zamboni had left the ice, she'd fallen, injuring her knee. He'd tried to talk to her about it afterward, but she was nowhere to be found.

She hadn't recovered in time to compete for a slot in the Olympic Games. The incident had gotten so much media attention that she'd gone underground. Kyle never talked to her again, had never known for sure if she blamed him, but Joe had. So, he was certain, had her mother.

Damn—her mother. Kyle would probably bump into her, too, at Joe's funeral tomorrow. It might be less painful to get an initial meeting with Jessica done and over with now.

Girding himself, he stepped toward her...

He knew the moment she sighted him. She gazed at him with confusion in her eyes, which slowly dawned into recognition.

Yeah. He no longer looked like Kyle-the-high-school-hockey-star, either.

He had a beard now, as well as a couple dozen extra pounds, which he liked to pride himself was all muscle.

He didn't get a smile from her.

A man stood beside her, chatting with the hostess, oblivious to the fact that Kyle was staring at his date. What did Jessica see in this smooth-looking player of a guy wearing an expensive business suit and overcoat? *Fancy-pants*, even for a Valentine's Day date.

Or maybe Kyle was just jealous. But he couldn't

bug out now even if he wanted to. He was itching to reach down and adjust the sleeve that covered the top of his prosthetic leg, beneath his pants, but he couldn't. No way. Not in front of Jessica.

He walked over to her, as carefully and confidently as he could. As he approached her and her date, she placed a hand on the guy's arm and he turned to her briefly, smiling at her before turning back to the hostess stand. Jessica gazed at the guy longingly, biting her lip before facing Kyle again.

Kyle felt slayed. From the day she'd moved to Wallis Point when he'd been fourteen years old, he'd been drawn to this girl—now woman—and he thought she had been drawn to him, too. Until she just *left*.

"Kyle Northrup?" she asked, squinting up at him.

He nodded at her. Once. Sharply.

She gave him a smile, but it seemed forced. Her hand stayed on her date, though he was still engaged in an earnest conversation with the hostess, and now, a server. Something about him wanting a booth in a quiet room by the window and that nothing else would do.

"You're…in town for Joe's funeral?" Jessica asked Kyle in a low voice.

She didn't seem angry, just…reserved. Cautious, he nodded again. "Did the lawyer call you about the will reading?"

"Yes." She glanced down, licking her lips and looking guilty. "It's nothing, really. While Joe was in for a therapy session, I made the mistake of complimenting his onyx ring. He said he would leave it to me in his will. I thought he was joking."

That onyx ring had been important to Joe. He'd never taken it off. "He didn't joke," Kyle said.

"I'm not…horning in on anything that's yours," Jessica murmured, still not looking at him. "You're his only living relative. I'll give it to you if you want."

Strange, but *she* was the one who seemed guilty. "I don't want it," Kyle said, more sharply than he'd planned. But he didn't care about the ring. He was here for the *rink*.

The guy she had her hand latched onto turned back to her and winked. "You ready, babe? They're setting up a table for us."

She smiled at him, looking relieved. "Sebastien, this is Kyle Northrup."

Sebastien? Kyle thought. What kind of name was that? They'd never had any *Sebastiens* in Wallis Point.

Sebastien gave Kyle a questioning half smile, but made no move to shake his hand, and that was fine with Kyle.

"Kyle is Joe Mansell's stepson," Jessica explained. "He's here for the funeral."

"I'm sorry for your loss," Sebastien said, looking genuinely concerned.

"Thanks," Kyle conceded.

Jessica turned to Kyle, smiling harder now. This was her "on" face, her way of smoothing social niceties. He remembered that about her.

The last time he'd seen her she'd been seventeen. To the world, she always came off as poised, confident in her talent. She'd always been friendly and chatty toward other people and the media. She knew how to shine brightly, make everyone around her feel better.

But Kyle had seen beneath the cracks in her facade. So often, she'd been in closed-rink sessions—he'd see her sometimes when she left, and she rarely looked happy. He'd privately thought her mother was a viper. Pressured her just as hard as Joe had pressured him. Jessa also had her hiding spots in the old rink. The ballet room in early mornings, for one. Kyle used to come in, catch her alone when he could, bring her coffee to cheer her up…

He snapped back to reality. There'd been a long, pointedly awkward silence, and he needed to say something. But now sure wasn't the time for an apology for ending her great career. Not with *Sebastien* looking on.

Kyle stared at her glittery pink engagement ring. He felt her staring at him silently. Sebastien, too.

Kyle's gaze moved over to her stomach, beneath the baggy top. Back to her ring again.

"Congratulations," he muttered, nodding at the ring. Then he cleared his throat.

Without looking at Jessica again, without trying to see or judge if there were still any more cracks beneath the facade or even feelings of commiseration with him, as in days of old, he turned and left. After the funeral and the will reading, he hoped he'd never see her again.

JESSICA TURNED TO SEBASTIEN. "I need to visit the ladies' room. I'll be right back."

Without waiting for a response, she pushed into the bathroom before she lost it.

Kyle is back.

Feeling dizzy and off balance, she slipped off the cheap metal-and-glass ring Kyle had been staring at and tucked it inside her pocket. Kyle had always noticed things about her that others didn't. If Sebastien had noticed the ring, he would've laughed. It was just a child's gift from her client, little Benjamin Davis, in honor of Valentine's Day.

Once inside the bathroom, shaking, she headed for the sink and a cold compress, glad she no longer wore eye makeup—hadn't for years. She no longer did a lot of things since her skating days, but Kyle didn't know that, either.

She put a paper towel under the faucet and ran cool water over it, then pressed it to her forehead. She should have prepared herself. It wasn't surprising that Kyle would show up at the Grand Beachfront Hotel tonight. The tall, broad-shouldered Marine. She'd been expecting him at any time, all week long, and dreading it. It was like a churning in her gut. She had so much guilt where Kyle was concerned.

The stall door opened and Maureen Cole stepped out. "Jessica!" she said. Maureen was a real estate agent in town. She'd helped Sebastien with the paperwork for his rented beach house. Someday Jessica hoped they would use her services for a permanent home belonging to both of them.

"Hi, Maureen." Through the mirror, Jessica gave Maureen her warmest smile. Keeping in control of her emotions was the most important thing.

"You look so beautiful," Maureen said.

I don't. I'm fat. Kyle had said so with his eyes. He'd stared at her stomach as if he thought she was pregnant. She wasn't—no chance of that, though someday it would be an absolute dream to have a family of her own.

"Thanks, Maureen. You do, too."

Maureen really did look beautiful, with her hair done up and wearing a sexy black dress. Smiling at Jessica, she turned on the faucet and began to soap up her hands.

Jessica turned back to the mirror, swallowing the lump in her throat. She'd wanted so much to look pretty tonight. She glanced at her blouse, her most beautiful garment, exquisitely constructed and embroidered. It was her favorite top and it flattered her face and coloring, but now, if she looked at herself through what she imagined as Kyle's eyes, all she saw was a chubby, pale woman, no longer young.

The last time Kyle had seen her she'd been a figure-skating princess. Fit and thin to the point of being ethereal.

She squeezed her eyes shut. Looks were such an illusion. In reality, back then she'd been dealing with the hell of her mother's pressure, coupled with bulimia and control issues. Nobody knew. Kyle had maybe guessed, but—no. She wouldn't go down that road. Since she'd last seen him, Jessica had been for a long time fighting her own battles, breaking free, struggling through her recovery. Now here she was, a survivor. With a place of her own. A job of her own.

And Sebastien.

She pressed the paper towel to her eyes one

last time, as if cleaning a speck from her vision. She was acutely aware of Maureen's gaze on her. She had to regain control of herself.

Maureen turned off the faucet and reached for a paper towel. "Was that Kyle Northrup you were talking to?" she asked, seeming casual. Jessica assumed there was an agenda. She always assumed that, because it was so often true with people who approached her.

"Yes," Jessica answered carefully.

"I didn't recognize him at first with that beard."

"No." She wasn't one for beards, herself. Sebastien was clean-shaven. Never even had scruff, and she liked it that way.

"He still has those beautiful green eyes," Maureen mused. "I remember him from high school. He graduated in my class year. The hockey captain. Other kids gave me a hard time because of my brother Bruce and his legal troubles, but Kyle never did. He was sort of geeky, shy with girls, but I always thought he was a good guy."

"Umm," Jessica said noncommittally. She hadn't gone to the public high school and wasn't sure what Maureen was talking about. She just knew that she didn't want to gossip, about anybody. For years she'd been the topic of gossip herself.

Maureen fished a lipstick out of her bag, still sending sideways glances at Jessica. "He got really big, didn't he? Filled out. Kyle was in the Marines, right?"

Joined the service because of Jessica's lie. It still made her feel queasy. For years, she'd dreaded that if something happened to him, it would be on her conscience.

"I...don't know," Jessica said. "Kyle and I didn't keep in touch."

Maureen cocked her head. Gazed through the mirror with the sort of calculating glance that Jessica, as someone who'd been well-known, had gotten used to spotting. "Do you think he's the one who stands to inherit the old twin rinks property?"

That must be Maureen's angle—seeing if prime beachside property will soon be on the market.

"I honestly don't know," Jessica replied.

Natalie Kimball, Joe's lawyer, was also Maureen's sister-in-law. Maureen could ask Natalie about the twin rinks if she was interested in its fate. Because Jessica was not interested at all. If she had a vote in the matter, they'd tear down the place and repurpose it. She made it a point never to drive past it these days.

"Well, we'll have to wait and see what happens," Maureen said, tossing her lipstick tube inside her purse. She smiled again at Jessica. "Enjoy your Valentine's Day dinner."

"Thanks. Happy Valentine's Day to you, too."

Jessica *had* been looking forward to this dinner all week. Sebastien so often traveled. But he was her boyfriend and this was their one-year anniversary, and he was out in the dining room waiting for her.

Taking a deep breath, she tossed the wet paper towels and pushed her way out the door. The restaurant was bustling. Busiest day of the year, according to a client who waitressed here. Sebastien was leaning casually against the hostess stand, the most handsome man she'd ever seen.

He bent down and kissed her on the cheek. Then he took her hand and led her through the bar area and to a back room, much quieter, with a row of secluded, leather booths near the window. Tables were also set up throughout the space, but the voices were low murmurs, not part of their private world for two. She heard only a quiet tinkling of cutlery as other people dined, and the faint rattle of ice buckets as champagne glasses were filled and refilled.

Now was her moment. The tension in Jessica's neck subsided. Just before Christmas, Sebastien had casually asked her what kind of engagement rings she liked. She'd thought maybe he would propose to her at Christmas, but he hadn't. New Year's Eve passed without a proposal, too. Valentine's Day—their anniversary—was the most logical day…

Relaxing into the booth, she accepted a goblet of wine from Sebastien.

Over the candlelight, he lifted his glass. His eyes looked deeply into hers.

Usually, she let her gaze drift away. It was embarrassing to let people stare into her eyes for too long. Off-putting. But Sebastien seemed so insistent that this time, she didn't look away.

"I need to ask you something," he said.

Her heart was pounding. Would this be the moment she'd been waiting for? Her gaze flicked to the pocket of his suit jacket. No telltale bulge from a jeweler's box.

She glanced back to his eyes, holding her breath…

"Is everything okay with you?" he asked.

"Of course!"

"You were in the bathroom a long time. I was concerned."

"Was I? Please don't be."

Just then, a loud gasp went up from the table behind her. It sounded like a feminine expression of happiness.

Jessica turned in her booth. The couple behind them were hugging and kissing. The woman had teary eyes. She was glancing with pleasure at a new round solitaire with a platinum band settled around her beautifully manicured ring finger.

Jessica couldn't lie, her first emotion was bone-deep envy. A longing for what she didn't have, so familiar from the emptiness of her childhood. But she fixed her smile and turned back to Sebastien. "Isn't that nice?"

Sebastien's gaze had shuttered. He'd put down his wineglass. Whatever had been between them in those earlier moments when they'd first sat down, had somehow broken.

Sebastien picked up his menu. "Good for them," was all he said about it.

CHAPTER TWO

JOE MANSELL'S WAKE was in Wallis Point's sole funeral parlor, a refurbished Victorian mansion that, one hundred years ago, had been built by Wallis Point's wealthiest citizen.

Kyle stood in the back, away from as much of the action as possible, feeling suffocated in his suit and tie. He'd wanted to cut out early, but as the only family member, he couldn't. The funeral director had tagged him the moment he'd walked in the door and pulled him aside, giving Kyle the day's agenda.

Evidently, Kyle had duties. Joe had planned the whole thing, and Kyle was to stay for the prayer service to speak his part.

He was in hell.

Kyle shifted onto his good leg. Maybe he had a bad attitude where Joe was concerned, but Kyle still hadn't forgotten years of his stepfather's verbal abuse. Joe had been like a drill sergeant. The fact that Joe had been a Vietnam veteran might have explained it, but didn't excuse it, in Kyle's opinion. Still, after Kyle had attended boot camp himself he'd understood Joe a little more.

Joe had always needed that sense of order and discipline. A world where the rules were clear and the consequences for breaking them were set out.

But Kyle had always thought Joe had taken it too far. He'd been rude and angry most days, and Kyle didn't want to be angry, not like him.

He shifted his weight to his other side.

A lot of people had shown up for the service, and Kyle was taken aback by the show of love and support for the cranky old man. Then again, Joe had behaved like a good guy to mostly everybody else. He'd liked to sit in his office in the front of the rink and listen to anybody who came to him with a problem. Jessa Hughes, for one.

"He wanted to be cremated," Kyle heard one of the mourners say. "Didn't want people seeing him in a casket."

Joe's ashes were in a gold urn on a central table covered with a maroon cloth. A photo of Joe, a candid, taken at the rink about thirty years ago judging by the haircut and his youth, sat beside it. It was a good shot, and it captured what a good guy Joe *could* be. A lump formed in Kyle's throat.

The funeral director, Henry, brought over Reverend Ellsworth to introduce them both.

"Joe chose two scripture readings and a song," the reverend informed Kyle. "He asked if you would please read the Twenty-third Psalm. Are you comfortable with that?"

Kyle stiffened. He hadn't been to church since his mom had made him when he was young. After she'd died, he'd sort of been against it. Joe had, too. Kyle was lost, and he wasn't ever going to be found.

"Reverend Ellsworth will be giving the eulogy," Henry said.

"Fine," Kyle replied. "I'll do the psalm reading." Psalms were short, after all.

"Then we'll be ending the service with a song that Joe chose. Are you familiar with the Byrd's *Turn! Turn! Turn!* Lyrics taken almost verbatim from the Book of Ecclesiastes."

To everything there is a season, and a time to every purpose under the heaven, Kyle thought.

He hadn't known that Joe had embraced religion again. Kyle just wanted to get through this day. Honestly, he'd been through too many military funerals these past years, and each of those had been a special kind of suck, but this one...it reminded him of being a kid at his mom's funeral. Twelve years old. Standing beside Joe. Joe had arranged that one, too. Kyle had been too devastated to be of much use. He'd thought his life had ended. In a sense, it had.

Henry led him to stand before Joe's gold urn. Henry was a tall, polite man who was good at his funeral director job. His demeanor was calm and peaceful, so composed at dealing with bereavement. Comfortable with death.

Kyle gritted his teeth.

People that Kyle had forgotten approached him to offer their condolences. Mostly these were people from his old rink world. Guys who'd run the Zamboni, the snack bar. Lots of skaters and hockey players. They all shook Kyle's hand.

There were a bunch of mourners Kyle didn't recognize, too, but they looked like figure-skating people. Joe's rink had two ice surfaces. Technically, the place was called the Wallis Point Twin Rinks. One rink had been mostly used by the local figure skating club. Periodically they hosted competitions and then they would take over both rinks. And when there were hockey tournaments they took both rinks, too. That was Kyle's world back then. He'd wanted nothing more than to be an NHL player, but once he'd joined the Marines, it had pretty much been out of the question to pursue anything like that.

Where *was* Jessa—Jessica? Or her mother? Kyle had forgotten to ask about her when he'd seen Jessica yesterday.

"Hey, Kyle. It's good to see you," one of Joe's former employees said to him. Johnny David was his name. "What have you been up to?"

"Marines," Kyle said.

"Wow. You still active duty?"

Kyle shook his head. "I work for the DoD now. Department of Defense."

"I heard you live in Florida."

"No. Maryland."

"You still play hockey?"

His pulse sped up. He was especially cognizant of his leg. "Yes."

He did play hockey, in a wounded veterans league.

But that rink was an hour's drive from his job. To run a league here, at his own ice rink, would be heaven. And he was quickly realizing that he'd never fit in here, except on the ice. And now, only on the ice with other guys who knew what it was like. What he was going through.

Johnny David prepared to ask Kyle another question, but Kyle was saved by the touch of a hand on his shoulder.

"Kyle?" A slender woman smiled at him, a pretty blonde he vaguely recognized. "I'm Natalie Kimball. We spoke on the phone."

Natalie seemed nothing like any lawyer he'd ever pictured—she was sweet-faced, thin and slight, soft-spoken. He shook her outstretched hand and nodded at her, saying nothing.

With her other hand, she curled her hair back over her ear. Natalie wore a hearing aid.

He felt himself relaxing.

"This is my husband, Bruce Cole."

Bruce reached over and shook Kyle's hand, too. Bruce was older than Kyle; his face wasn't familiar, though Kyle remembered the name—he'd been blamed for the tragedy of his best friend's automobile death.

Kyle noticed the heavy gold ring Bruce wore. "You went to the Naval Academy?" he asked without thinking.

Bruce nodded. "I'm inactive. I work in IT now, at the Portsmouth Navy Yard."

Kyle guessed that Bruce hadn't seen combat. Still, Bruce was military. He understood. Kyle nodded back at him.

Get through this, Kyle thought. *Just get through this.* If it weren't for the will, he probably would've skipped town already.

"I, ah, don't see Jessica Hughes here," Kyle commented to Natalie.

Natalie glanced over the crowd. "You're right. Maybe she stopped by earlier."

Kyle had been here since before the doors had opened. Jessica hadn't come earlier. "Maybe she's not feeling well."

Natalie tilted her head at him. "Do you know something I don't?"

"I saw her last night, I thought maybe she was pregnant."

"Really?" Natalie looked surprised. "Did you say that to her?"

Oh, hell. Had he screwed up? "She had a ring on her finger. A guy was with her. She was wearing a baggy top and..."

"Trust me, she's not pregnant," said an authoritative-sounding blonde who popped her head into their three-person circle.

"That's my sister Maureen," Bruce said, nodding to the blonde. Kyle remembered Maureen Cole. They'd been in a lot of the same classes in high school.

"Jessica's not married or engaged, either," Maureen said to Kyle. "I know, because I leased a beach house to her boyfriend, and I ask about these things. *If* you're interested."

"No," he said flatly. "I'm not interested."

They all looked at each other. *Great.*

But Natalie smiled at him. "Don't worry, Kyle. Things will be fine on Monday."

He shook his head. He'd just made their appointed meeting at her law office that much more awkward.

"Where are you staying?" Natalie asked him, taking him aside.

"The Grand Beachfront Hotel."

"Would you like me to give you a ride on Monday?"

"That's okay, I have my truck."

"You drove up from Maryland?" Natalie asked.

He stared at her. "I wanted to be ready in case there's anything I need to move to or from the rink to take it over quicker."

Natalie's eyes widened. "Have you given notice on your job down in Maryland?"

"I'm hoping to do that on Monday, ma'am."

Natalie gazed at him for a long time. Then she smiled. "That's really good to know, Marine."

JESSICA HAD MEANT to go to the funeral.

She'd dressed in funeral clothes: a black skirt with boots and a long dark coat. But when the street had forked and it had come to a choice between steering her little orange Volkswagen toward the funeral parlor and taking the road that led to Sebastien's house, she'd chosen Sebastien.

She parked in his driveway, not exactly sure what she was doing. She felt knocked off-kilter about their Valentine's Day dinner. After she'd turned around to watch the couple behind them getting engaged, it had been as if a switch had shut off in Sebastien. And for the rest of their dinner, he had been disconnected from her. Oh, he'd kept up polite conversation—he was a corporate marketing professional, after all, great with making small talk—but when he'd driven her home, he'd been quiet and pensive. And he'd begged off coming in for coffee. He had a full day on Saturday, he'd said.

So had she. The funeral, for one thing. She owed it to Joe to attend. But…this thing with Sebastien was bugging her. He was her hope for her future. Her dream, her safe place. She hoped that Joe would understand she needed to set things right with Sebastien before she paid her respects to him.

She stared at Sebastien's black Nissan, parked in his driveway in front of her. She and Sebastien had never had a misunderstanding or a fight before. He was usually so easy and laid-back. He never asked her about her old life as Jessa Hughes and she didn't ask him about his past, either. She'd thought that had been a great part of their relationship.

Suddenly queasy, she turned her rearview mirror toward herself. She looked terrible, pale and drawn. She pinched color into her cheeks. Found her tube of lip gloss in her purse and smeared it on.

She glanced at Sebastien's front door. Since his car was in the driveway, he very likely was home. She was sort of hoping he'd see her out here in the cold and come outside and kiss her. Act as though everything was okay, as usual.

But it wasn't. She was the one who would have to be brave, who had to face whatever it was that had gone wrong. She got out and knocked on his door. She didn't even have a key.

He answered, dressed, a coffee mug in his hand. "Jess? Don't you have a funeral to go to?"

She nodded, miserable, standing on the doorstep feeling more alone than ever. "I'd rather talk to you."

Immediately, he opened the door. "Come in." Instead of his normally easy smile, he wore a quizzical expression. He was in his bare feet, and she gazed down at them as she walked in.

He took her coat and draped it over a leather couch. She never got over how spectacular his rental house was. On the beach, it had views of the surf. The ceilings were high, and in the kitchen, everything was gleaming modern stainless steel and white marble and real wood. The complete opposite of her dingy little winter rental in a drafty apartment beside a gas station.

Without asking, Sebastien went into the kitchen and came back, pressing a warm mug of coffee into her hands.

"I'm…sorry about last night," she said. "It's pretty obvious there's something wrong between us. It feels like there's a big distance, and it's scaring me."

He sat at right angles to her on the leather loveseat, so close his knees brushed her skirt. "Yeah, I've been thinking about it, too." He frowned into his coffee. "Honestly, Jess, I wonder if I even know you sometimes. You get so closed up tight that I have no idea what you're thinking."

She expelled a breath. She'd been hearing that most of her adult life. She made a small laugh. "I don't want to be like that with…the man I hope to marry."

Sebastien froze for a moment.

"You did make hints," Jessica said gently, setting down the mug. "At Christmas. You asked what kind of engagement rings I preferred."

Sebastien nodded. She couldn't read his face exactly, but he took her hand in his.

"I don't want to be a controlling person," she continued, "so I didn't push. I know better than most what it's like to be pushed. My mother…" She paused.

"It's pretty obvious this funeral is stirring something up in you. That's all I wanted to know about last night."

She removed her hand from his and smoothed her skirt. It was more than Joe's death and Kyle's presence that was bothering her. It was as if she'd been propelled into the past, feeling helpless and broken again.

"You never explained this Joe person to me," Sebastien said. "And there's a will reading? Are you inheriting something from him?"

"I don't know." She stood and paced, irritated

with herself. "I'm sorry. I'm just…I don't like to talk about the past or my family." She glanced at him. "Honestly, you don't like to talk about yours, either. And I've never pushed you about it. I assumed that was part of why we get along so well."

He smiled gently. "I'll tell you anything you want to know about them. Later."

Okay. She couldn't get out of this conversation. She had to go there and trust that he'd be fine with it.

"So…you know how I used to be a figure skater?" she said. "Well, I trained at the Wallis Point Twin Rinks. Did you know that?"

He grinned at her. "It's on your Wikipedia page, Jess. Your skating career is pretty much an open book."

She winced. She hadn't ever thought about that, though she supposed it made sense. The big thing she'd loved about Sebastien was that he never pressed her about those days, specifically that one incident that strangers still occasionally came up to her and offered sympathy for.

"You were America's sweetheart," Sebastien said. "You got injured and had to pull out of your final competition just before the Olympic Games. When you cried on live television, everybody in the country cried along with you."

Jessica sat down again. "That was a really bad time in my life, Sebastien."

"I can imagine. It's why I never asked you about it." He sipped his coffee and gazed at her over the rim of his mug. "I thought you were over it. You never bring it up, so I assumed..."

She'd honestly thought the pain and guilt had dissolved, too. Until Joe had shown up in her physical therapy office and then had written her into his will. Kyle coming home had been her tipping point.

She closed her eyes, overcome with guilt so sharp it stabbed into her solar plexus. She felt dragged right back to age seventeen. Crushed. Under everyone's thumb, panicked and alone, and handling the situation all wrong. She'd better pull herself out of that place if she hoped to salvage all that she'd so painstakingly built for herself since then.

Sebastien eyed her. "What's wrong?"

"I...need to tell you about something that probably isn't on my Wikipedia page." She took a deep breath. Her hands were trembling just anticipating telling him.

Sebastien set down his coffee mug. All his attention—love and concern—on her.

That gave her the courage she needed. "People don't know this...and I actually promised myself to never tell anyone, but..." She *had* to do this. Had to bring Sebastien back to her again. "I went to a lawyer shortly after my injury, when

I was still seventeen, to look into being legally emancipated from my mother." She wiped her eyes with her thumb. "You have to understand, Sebastien, my mother was my only family. She and I were…well, I was exhausted and I couldn't please her anymore. For a lot of reasons I had to separate myself from her, and that one drastic step changed my whole life and not necessarily in the best way."

She stared at her black skirt, hoping her Wikipedia page wasn't specific enough to clue Sebastien into what was missing. *Kyle's role.* Which would only lead to a secret she could never divulge to anyone.

Instead, she reached for the other, lesser thing that bothered her. "I think I'm kind of screwed up because I have to go back into that same law firm again on Monday. I think it's messing with my head. That's all," she finished.

"Why? Why are you getting an inheritance from this rink owner? Is he your secret father or something?"

"No!" She laughed aloud, relieved. "He was a client. Like you were," she teased. "That's how I connected with him again after so long. He mentioned a ring he wanted to give me—an inexpensive onyx ring. Maybe he was just sentimental about the old ice rink days, but like you, I'm not." She shivered. "Anyway, I'm considering not going to the will reading. I don't want to go back into that law office. I know it's silly, I know the law firm is run by the daughter and not the father anymore, but still—"

"Do you want me to take off work, go with you to see the lawyer on Monday?" Sebastien asked. "For moral support?"

"You would do that?" she asked, surprised. Sebastien's job always came first.

"Of course."

"I…yeah." She smiled at him, grateful. "Please do come to the lawyer's office."

"Great. It's settled." He patted the seat beside him. "You want to hang out today?"

"I thought you had to work?"

"It can wait. I'd rather spend the day with you."

That was a change. She felt so much better. "Thanks for not giving up on me."

"No worries," Sebastien said. "You know you can trust me."

She hoped she could. She really did.

Because if she couldn't, she didn't have anyone else.

CHAPTER THREE

THE KIMBALL FAMILY Law Firm was in the same old brick building that Kyle remembered from his youth. Natalie's father, Asa, had run the law firm back then. Now he was retired and spent the winters in Florida, leaving Natalie in charge.

A receptionist in heavy-framed glasses met Kyle in the lobby and offered him water or coffee while he waited. Kyle chose water. The receptionist—Zena—settled him in an empty conference room at a glossy conference table so big a person could play Ping-Pong on it. Sun from a skylight lit up the room, and several large floor plants thrived. The walls were covered with framed postcards. Wallis Point in the past.

Kyle had always wanted to be rooted, to belong somewhere, and this room gave him the feeling of history. His mom had grown up in Wallis Point, and even though there weren't any close relatives left, it comforted him that there were people in town who remembered her. It had never sat well with him that Joe had, in effect, kicked him out of the rink and forced him to leave town as an eighteen-year-old.

He was home now.

He peeled at the label of the water bottle that Zena had given him. He opened it and took a long, refreshing swig.

Natalie came into the room. Her heels clicked on the old wood floor, which had been restored to a bright sheen. Her hair was up and she wore a high-necked blouse under a gray business jacket. He might have been intimidated by the lawyer look except for the Disney *Beauty and the Beast* bandage she had wrapped around her thumb.

She put a stack of folders on the table and sat at the corner beside him. "Thanks for coming in today." She gave him a smile that helped the stiffness in his back relax a bit. "How are you doing?"

"Fine," he said politely, "m—" He choked back the word *ma'am*. He needed to remember this wasn't the military.

Natalie smiled gently at him. "Joe met with me several times over the past month. I got to know him better. I remember him from skating at the twin rinks as a kid, of course, but..." Natalie tapped the folders. "Kyle, he wanted you to have this." She opened the top folder, and Kyle felt himself holding his breath.

She slid a key across the table toward him. "This is the key to 18 Linden Lane."

Not the key to the rink. Kyle deflated. This was something he hadn't expected at all.

"Joe's house," he said. From the age of ten to almost eighteen, Kyle had lived there. He knew this key well. Somewhere, tucked away in a duffel bag in his apartment in Maryland, he had a copy.

Natalie also took a letter from the folder and handed it to him. "This is from Joe, to you."

She'd mentioned it during her initial phone call, but Kyle had forgotten. Frowning, he placed the letter on the table, but he didn't open it.

His hands were shaking. He didn't know how he felt about this. "If Joe was thinking about me so much, why didn't he call me? You found me on the internet easily enough."

Natalie smiled sadly. "I don't know, Kyle. I'm hoping he might have answered some of your questions in his letter. I don't know for a fact because, of course, I didn't read the letter—though I admit to wanting to."

"Why did you want to?"

"Because Wallis Point is a small town. I care very much about what happens here. The rink is a community rink."

He glanced at the Disney bandage on her thumb. "You have kids?"

Natalie nodded. "A daughter. She's three.

She's in her princess stage. A future ice princess, she hopes."

"So…what about the rink?" he asked, his heart beating hard. "Where are the keys for that?"

"That's a good question." Natalie sat up straighter, took in a breath. He got the impression she was struggling to keep the smile on her face.

"Joe *did* want you to run the hockey rink…"

But. There was a *but* there.

"There's a stipulation," she added.

He squeezed his palm around the thin metal house key. "What kind of stipulation?"

Before she could answer, a commotion sounded outside. Both he and Natalie turned toward the open door. Zena's loud voice was greeting people in the lobby.

"Jessica's here?" he asked.

"Maybe." Natalie got up and shut the door, then sat back down, facing him.

"Isn't she joining us for the will reading?" Kyle asked.

"All things considered, I decided it's best I talk with you both separately."

"Why?"

"As I said, Joe did want you to run the hockey rink. I believe it was his intention that you come home permanently and take over ownership and management of the Wallis Point Twin Rinks."

"Yeah, that's what I want, too. But what does that have to do with Jessica?"

There was a soft knock on the door. "Come in," Natalie called.

Zena stuck her head in. "You've got a phone call you'll want to take. Also, I've got Ms. Hughes and her friend settled in the small conference room."

And her friend. Hell, that has to be Sebastien.

"Thank you," Natalie said to Zena.

Kyle was gripping the water bottle so hard it crumpled. After Zena left, he said, "Is *Jessica* part of the rink deal with me?"

"Yes, she is," Natalie said. "You see, it was Joe's intention that you both work together to bring the rink back up to speed."

"You've got to be kidding."

"You might want to read Joe's letter."

That was the last thing he wanted. If he could go beyond the grave to see Joe now, he would punch him.

"Does *she* know about this?" Kyle asked.

"No, not yet."

"I doubt she'll go for it," Kyle said matter-of-factly. The thought calmed him. Yeah, Jessica would definitely turn this down. He doubted she'd want to run the rink with him.

He met Natalie's gaze. "Can I make Jessica an

offer and buy her out?" he asked. "It's better that I do this on my own."

"Technically, you can't. At least, not yet."

Kyle didn't like the sounds of this. It wasn't the lawyer's fault that this deal was so insane— that was Joe's doing. Likely, Natalie had no idea that Joe blamed Kyle for killing Jessica's Olympic chances. "Give it to me straight and simple, no legal jargon, please."

"Before you can buy her out, both of you, together, need to put forth a good faith effort into restoring and running the twin rinks profitably for six months, at which point the facility will belong to you both equally. *Then* you can make your own agreement as to whether to buy or sell."

"Six months?" With Jessica? Cripes, he thought. "What if I don't ever want to sell and she does?"

"I'll help you through those questions when the time comes." Natalie leaned forward and tapped her papers. "But, Kyle, that's not the part of the will that I'm concerned about right now."

"It gets worse?"

"First things first. You both need to agree to work together. If either of you refuses the opportunity, then the property will be sold outright and the money given to charity."

"What the hell kind of inheritance is that?" Kyle demanded.

"I'm sorry." Natalie sighed. "I tried to talk Joe

out of it, but he said he had very strong reasons for setting up the arrangement this way. I mitigated it as best I could. I warned him about the importance of discussing it with you in advance, but his response was to write the letter that I gave you. Jessica will receive one, as well."

Natalie stood. "Kyle, please read his letter, plus the will on the table, and I'll be back in a few minutes. I have a quick phone call to return, and then I'll be back to discuss your concerns and desired course of action before I see Jessica. Please sit tight."

Natalie left, closing the door behind her.

Kyle pinched the bridge of his nose between thumb and finger. He should have known that Joe would pull something like this on him.

Under the table, Kyle moved his leg. He should also be thankful that Joe hadn't known about his injury. If he had, Kyle doubted he would've wanted him managing the place at all. Joe had no patience for people who didn't show full competence at their job.

Kyle put his head in his hands. Until these last few days, he'd never thought too much about his relationship—or lack thereof—with his stepfather, but in truth, Kyle probably *had* joined the military just because Joe had been so down on it. A Vietnam vet, Joe hadn't had a good experience, or so Kyle assumed. He really didn't know much, because Joe refused to talk about it. Joe just raged. Foul moods. Brooding. With Kyle, he'd been brutal.

With women—Kyle's mom, with Jessica and Jessica's mom—he'd been the perfect gentleman. It was all an act, though.

Kyle had never known his own father. He'd died in a snowmobile accident when Kyle had been a baby. His sled had fallen through lake ice up in Maine. Kyle's grandmother, before she'd passed away, had told Kyle that the authorities hadn't found the body until the spring thaw. Kyle's mother had met Joe when Kyle was really little. His mom had doted on Kyle. Her life was wrapped around his. It had actually taken her a few years of grieving for her deceased husband and then careful, platonic dating before she'd trusted Joe enough to marry him.

Those first years had been great. But Joe's darkness came out after Kyle's mom died.

He felt a lump in his throat. He remembered his mom as gentle and fragile. When he'd lost his leg, he'd felt glad that she wasn't around to see it. It would've devastated her. Still, he had no doubt she would've supported him no matter what he did with his life. He'd supported his mom, too, in all her decisions. He remembered the day she had asked him what he thought about her marrying Joe.

"He has an ice rink. Marry him, Mom."

So she had. And for a while everything had been good. But after his mom got sick and passed away, everything about Joe turned bitter.

If it weren't for the rink, who knew what would've happened to Kyle? He'd always felt the rink had saved him after his mom's death. Now he wanted it to save him after losing his leg.

Natalie returned, shuffling her folders. Busy and official, she sat and looked brightly at him. "So, after reading the documents, tell me what you think?"

Kyle hadn't touched Joe's letter, still on the table. He hadn't even glanced at the will.

Kyle leaned forward to face the lawyer. "I don't care what you have to do, Natalie. Whatever you have to promise Jessica to make this deal happen, please just do it."

"You don't have any questions for me?"

"No. Get Jessica on board any way you have to."

"All right." Natalie nodded as she pushed back her chair. "Let me talk with her and I'll get back to you in a few minutes."

Kyle nodded. He had a good idea of Jessica's thoughts regarding partnering with him. "You've got your work cut out for you."

Natalie tilted her head. "Why do you say that?"

He couldn't explain years of history to her, ending with the guilty fact that he had caused

Jessica's career-ending injury. He just shook his head. "Honestly, it would be a lot easier if you could help me put together a deal now to buy the rink behind the scenes. Somehow that has to be possible."

Natalie shook her head. "No, it's not viable, Kyle, because at this point, if the rink goes up for sale you'd be competing with land developers with deep pockets. The land alone is what makes the property quite valuable. And at this point, I'm bound to take the highest bidder. That isn't the case in six months. In six months, if the business is profitable, then we can arrange for you to achieve financing and buy out Jessica's share. But first you need to partner effectively with her."

Partner effectively with her? Frustrated, he sighed. "Maybe you should just let me talk to the bank?"

Natalie reached over and put a hand on his arm. "As a member of this community, and one with a child who I hope will someday use the skating rinks, I'm heartened that you want to keep the facility open. However, without a track record of running a business, I don't see the bank giving you such a large loan, under any circumstance." She smiled. "Let me talk with Jessica. I'd like to hear what she has to say before we make any plans."

Kyle shut his eyes. He was doomed.

JESSICA UNZIPPED HER coat and unwound her woolen scarf from her neck. The law office felt stifling. Sebastien seemed comfortable, though, strolling around, hands in his pockets, checking out the framed old postcards on the walls. They'd been in the conference room for twenty minutes now.

"Do you still think this will is about you getting a nothing piece of jewelry?" Sebastien asked. "This seems like too much of a production, asking you to show up here, then waiting like this. Maybe you're inheriting something that's worth some money?"

"I honestly don't know." Jessica sighed. She was starting to feel guilty about not attending Joe's funeral. Once he'd been the closest thing to a father figure that she'd had. Then, after she'd left skating, she hadn't even wanted to see him. He reminded her of those other, more painful times. And she hadn't wanted to be his physical therapist at first, either. "I don't know why he even chose me."

"Joe never said anything to you? Never a hint?"

"No. He just made that offhand comment about his ring that one time."

"Well, did he have a lot of money? Because this law firm doesn't look cheap."

Jessica had to admit, she liked the vibe of it more now, with the daughter running it, than when she'd consulted with the father. Today, the decor was homey and inviting, a mixture of modern and antique, but with renovated and restored architectural features. Really, this whole town had so much historical character—she'd fallen in love with it at first sight.

She and her mother had shown up one cold February, similar to this one, and they, too, had taken a winter rental near the beach. Not as nice a place as where Sebastien lived, but the raw beauty of the New England beach in winter had made an impression on Jessica. She'd wanted to stay in Wallis Point forever. She'd begged her mom. She'd been so tired of moving around.

Natalie came into the room, a folder in her hand. She wore a cute light-gray suit and black pumps. Jessica rarely got to dress up anymore. As a physical therapist, she wore a T-shirt, jeans and sneakers—the uniform of her trade.

Natalie smiled at her. "Hi, Jessica. Thanks so much for coming today. I'm sorry I left you waiting."

"This is my friend, Sebastien. Sebastien, this is Natalie Kimball."

"I was admiring your postcards," Sebastien said.

"Thanks," Natalie replied. "I collect them. I love learning about the local history."

"It's interesting that the beachfront arcades

look nearly the same a hundred years later," Sebastien remarked.

"Take a look at the panels with the turn-of-the-century citizens strolling the boardwalk."

"I saw them." Sebastien smiled. "Great old bathing suits."

"I sometimes wonder what people back then would think if they were transported here to modern times," Natalie mused. "Bikinis. Flip-flops."

"Tattoos," Sebastien added, laughing.

Natalie smiled. Jessica sincerely doubted that Natalie had any tattoos. Jessica had a small one, well hidden. She wanted another, but it seemed as though Sebastien was sort of horrified by the idea.

"Well, I'm sure you've wondered why I asked you here," Natalie said, seating herself at the table across from Jessica. "The reason is that Joe Mansell has left you a half share in the twin ice rinks, together with Kyle Northrup, and—"

"No, thank you." Jessica pushed back her chair and stood. "Kyle can have the ice rinks. I'm not interested."

But Sebastien gave her a look. He glanced at Natalie and raised a brow.

"Joe left you a letter," Natalie said kindly. "Would you like to read it before you make your final decision?"

"No, thank you," Jessica repeated. She looked at Sebastien to back her up on this.

"I'll read it," Sebastien replied, seating himself at the table.

"No." Jessica took the letter that Natalie offered and stuffed it in her purse.

"Why, Jess?" Sebastien asked, turning in his chair. "Is there something you're not telling me? You're not even willing to listen."

Tears pricked in her eyes. It was wrong that her boyfriend thought that of her. She'd assumed after their conversation yesterday that he'd understood how painful this topic was for her. She'd told him she'd been here before. Literally here, in this room. She'd been seventeen years old. Jessica had read in the newspaper about young athletes who'd emancipated themselves from their parents. Her mother was…well, she was figure-skating royalty. She'd won a gold medal in the Olympics, and she wanted her daughter to follow in her footsteps. Jessica had wanted to please her. In the beginning, it had been fun. But in the end, she was suffocating with the pressure and expectations.

"Sebastien, could I talk with the lawyer alone, please? I don't want to work in an ice rink. I thought you understood this."

"Do you *realize* how much that property is worth? I'm saving you from yourself here. Trust me, you'll thank me later." Sebastien turned to Natalie. "Tell Jessica what it's worth."

Natalie pressed her lips together. "Close to two million dollars," she admitted.

"Jess, don't you understand what kind of money that is? How much work it takes to earn that outright? How many hours I have to spend traveling and not even come close to that?"

"Technically," Natalie said, directly to Jessica, "you would be required to work with Kyle for six months to try to make the business a success, in good faith, before you'd get your half. In addition, if you don't agree to this term, then the land and the rinks will be sold, immediately, and the money given to charity."

"There you go—please do give it to charity. I prefer a children's charity, if at all possible." Jessica said it with a deadly calm. Then she looked pointedly at Natalie. "I talked with your father once. He knew about my past history and my concerns."

"Jess, be reasonable," Sebastien murmured.

She gritted her teeth. Her mother used to talk to her this way. And Jessica had listened, coming as close to being destroyed as she ever wanted to come again.

She'd had thoughts of suicide at the time, which had terrified her. Her mother had icily told her there would be no legal emancipation, but that Jessica could do whatever she wanted, her mother was going back to the West Coast, convinced Jessica would never make it in Wallis Point on her own.

But Jessica had. She'd cut her hair and changed her looks. Stopped the training regimen, the diet. In the early summer she'd moved herself into a cheap studio apartment in an old motor inn near the center of town. She'd waitressed at a busy beach restaurant. People didn't recognize her. She'd felt free. She felt herself healing. In the autumn she'd gone to community college, taking whatever courses interested her. And because she really had sustained injuries over the years and she wanted to understand her body, how to stretch and heal, she had studied physical therapy. Eventually that led to her current career.

She hadn't wanted to come to this office today—Sebastien had convinced her. The first time she'd come here, Asa Kimball, of the Kimball Family Law Firm, had convinced her to start with a simple conversation with her mother instead of filing emancipation papers. So they'd both come in and he'd mediated a discussion between them. Her mother had been furious with her but a verbal deal had been struck. Her mother never reneged on it and neither had Jessica.

And they hadn't spoken since.

"*Why* did Joe Mansell leave the ice rink to Jessica?" Sebastien asked Natalie.

The young lawyer took a deep breath, but her smile stayed on her face. "Why don't we review the terms together and then we can talk about that?"

Jessica covered her solar plexus with her arms and leaned forward. She was developing her own suspicions regarding Joe. She hadn't quite understood when he'd first come in, insisting that she be his physical therapist after his knee operation. She'd tried to refuse, but her boss believed that clients should choose the therapist they felt most comfortable with, and Joe had remained adamant that his therapist should be Jessica.

"Why?" she'd asked him.

"Kyle was responsible for your injury when he deliberately flooded the ice that day," Joe had said. "It's his fault you were hurt and left skating."

Her blood had turned cold. Kyle had had nothing to do with her injury or her decision to pull out of skating.

She pulled Joe's letter from her purse, took her time opening it, drawing one finger inside a crease in the envelope flap, making a long, slow, jagged tear in the heavy paper as she eased it open.

"What are the terms?" Sebastien was asking

Natalie. He drummed his fingers on the table. "May I read the will?"

"Yes, of course, if Jessica would like." Natalie nodded at Jessica. "First, though, let me give you an overview, in layman's terms."

"Great." Sebastien crossed his arms. "We're listening."

Natalie pursed her lips. "As I explained to Kyle Northrup, his stepfather's intent was to keep the skating rink open to the community. As such, he believed it best that Kyle have assistance from Jessica. Jessica, he believed, had knowledge from the figure skating community and Kyle from hockey. It's a twin rink facility, and, in that business, the love, knowledge and understanding of both worlds is important for success. Joe believed that you two were his best hope."

"I don't have love for ice rinks," Jessica said flatly.

"What are the terms?" Sebastien asked Natalie.

"If Jessica agrees to participate, then in six months an assessment of the business will be completed. If it's profitable, then half the business is Jessica's."

"Can she force the sale of the business at that point?" Sebastien asked, cutting to the chase.

"If she chooses to sell at that point, then Kyle will have first option of purchase," Natalie said quietly.

"He gets to set the price?"

"No, an independent assessor sets the price based on the rink's business value."

"Will they take into consideration the value of the land?" Sebastien asked. "Because let's not kid ourselves. The land attached to the rink is the valuable part. I wouldn't be surprised if there weren't developers chomping at the bit to purchase it, tear down the old rink, and build something a lot more profitable, like condos or a modern hotel."

Silence filled the room, as Jessica stared at the half-torn envelope, her thumb still.

"I've always found that the bank assessors take all factors into consideration," Natalie said calmly.

Jessica glanced up at her. She gave the lawyer credit for poise.

Natalie looked her square in the eye. "I won't pretend this isn't unorthodox. Believe me, I consulted with other specialists in estate law before agreeing to go forward with it. His will may be irregular, but it is legal."

Sebastien put a hand on Jessica's. But the strange thing was, instead of comforting her, it made her seize up inside. Warning bells were going off all over.

"What if the rink isn't profitable?" Sebastien asked. "What then?"

"Then it's sold to the highest bidder and Jessica gets half."

"So…Jessica has to participate for six months to get the deal," Sebastien said. "What exactly does *participate* mean?"

Jessica felt like throwing up. She'd made a conscious decision never to *participate* in anything related to that world again. The loss of control she'd suffered—the manipulation—had nearly destroyed her. She'd had to lie to get out of it, and that lie was the reason Joe blamed Kyle for her injury, which then led to Kyle leaving Wallis Point.

And the fact that Sebastien was even asking this stuff when he knew how upset she was… She clenched her hand into a fist and put it in her lap.

Natalie was answering him. "It means…" The lawyer glanced at her as she spoke. "It means that Jessica needs to put in a good faith effort, specified as attendance at the rink at least thirty hours per week."

"I can't do that," she blurted. "I have a job, commitments." *I have dreams.* She gritted her teeth and stared at Sebastien.

After their talk on Saturday morning, they'd had a great weekend at his place. They'd walked on the beach, watched movies in bed, cooked. She'd never felt happier with him.

But now…after what she'd told him about her

mom and her, he could just *do* this? Sentence her back to those days?

Sebastien turned to Natalie. "Thirty hours per week is a lot. Will she be compensated for those hours?"

It was as if she was watching from outside her body. A feeling of betrayal came over her. Her heart felt as if it had stopped in her chest. She was sure her mouth had dropped open.

Natalie smiled sadly at Jessica, and Jessica felt her face heating. Natalie saw her embarrassment, but Sebastien apparently didn't.

"The agreement doesn't specify a payment," Natalie said gently. "I'm sorry." She stood. "I'll leave a copy of the will here on the table. Perhaps you'd like to read it, along with Joe's letter, and I'll be back in twenty minutes to discuss it further."

"Yeah," Sebastien said, glancing at Jessica for the first time, and giving her a "buck up" smile. "I need to talk with Jess."

Natalie set the document on the table, then shut the door on her way out.

Jessica's hands were still clenched in fists in her lap. She stared down at Joe's letter. Halfway opened. The jagged rip she'd made but couldn't finish.

"Jess," Sebastien said softly.

"Jessica," she said woodenly. "I'm Jessica."

"Jessica, I know you don't want to do this. Honestly…do you think I like being on the road all the time? I don't. But, Jess, I do it. I do it because it pays well."

She swallowed. Gazed at her thumb, the cuticles ragged. "I know about not having money." She'd supported herself, all that time. All those years, alone, away from her mother. "I did it…" *To save my soul.* "…because I was being destroyed, and destroying other people in turn. It needed to stop. I needed to keep myself safe."

I'm not a machine, she added silently.

He took her hand, smoothing over the jagged cuticle with his thumb. "I care about you, Jessica… I really do want to marry you," he said quietly. "But I don't…I never wanted to get married without being in the right financial place to support a family. I've been saving, but it's not happening the way I'd hoped. I won't lie, it's tough out there. The economy is lousy, and this inheritance of yours is easy money. If you did this, if you sacrificed for us the way I've been sacrificing for us, then we'll be able to get married. Don't you see?"

She stared at him. "You *want* to marry me? Still?"

"Of course. Isn't that what we talked about?"

Not exactly. She wasn't sure. All she knew was that her heart was pounding and her throat felt dry. She fumbled for the bottle of water on the table.

"All I'm saying, Jess, is that we can use the money from the sale of the rink to go through with it. We could afford to buy a home in Wallis Point, a real nice place together. We could afford to have kids."

Her head was reeling. This was exactly what she wanted, too.

"Well, Jess? Jessica," he corrected himself. "What do you think?"

Just then there was a knock and the door opened. Natalie again. She sat down and smiled at Jessica. "I've spoken with Kyle. He'd like to go ahead, if you would."

"I…" Jessica was acutely aware of Sebastien, staring at her. He'd offered to give her all her dreams.

"Why don't you let me know what your reservations are," Natalie said to Jessica. "I'll talk to Kyle and see if we can smooth anything out."

"She's worried about losing income," Sebastien said to Natalie. "If she works thirty hours a week at the rink, then she won't be able to work at her real job much more than a few hours a week."

"Is that correct?" Natalie asked Jessica, politely. "Is the loss of income your *only* reservation?"

Jessica gazed over at Sebastien. She really,

really wanted to marry him and have a family of her own. Children she could love and give a happy childhood to, the kind she hadn't experienced. She could take care of them, nest in her own home with them. She wouldn't have to move back and forth from her beach rental to her summer studio rental at the change of seasons. She'd have a home that was hers.

Then everything would be fine.

She wanted that life more than anything.

Hesitantly, she nodded to Natalie. "It's true, I can't afford to work for free or to lose my physical therapy job."

"You're not worried about Kyle working with you?" Natalie asked.

Jessica shook her head. It was sort of a lie. But more than the guilt of having to face Kyle again, and more than the worry that she'd been a source of estrangement between him and Joe, she didn't want to have to explain that history to Sebastien.

Sebastien was her safe place—her hope for the future. She didn't want to ruin that any more than she already had.

Natalie stood. "Very well. Let me talk with Kyle and see what can be done."

KYLE PACED THE ROOM. He couldn't sit still. He had no idea what was going on with Jessica, but he could guess.

The door opened, and a little girl toddled inside. She had sturdy legs and plump fists. She tilted her head up at Kyle, clearly unafraid of him. Her blond curls bobbed as she spoke. "Hi! Who are you?"

"Kyle," he answered.

"Hi, Kyle."

"Oops, sorry about that!" Natalie stepped inside, picked up the girl and kissed her forehead. "Mommy's working. I told you to stay with Daddy," she said gently. She and the girl disappeared from sight.

Finally, she came back into the room. "Again, I'm sorry for the wait. I've spoken with Jessica." She sat at the table and placed her palms flat.

Kyle tried to read her expression. "What did she say? Is it good or bad?"

"Frankly, I believe she can be swayed," Natalie said. "There's one point she's uncomfortable with, and if you're willing, I recommend you negotiate."

Wow. That was a shock. He sat, nodding. "Okay, I'm listening."

"She's concerned about losing salary. She's a physical therapist and is worried about cutting her hours."

"*Money* is her sticking point?" he asked, flabbergasted.

"It is."

"She's not mad about working with me? She didn't say anything personal about me?"

"No, she did not."

He shook his head. Maybe things with her weren't as bad as he thought. Maybe she'd forgiven him for their history. Maybe she hadn't noticed that he'd assumed she was pregnant when he'd seen her on Valentine's Day.

"So…what do you suggest I do now?" he asked the lawyer.

Natalie was silent for a moment. "As the will document notes, you received a substantial cash inheritance from Joe, as part of the estate. Jessica didn't receive any such thing. I'm guessing you'd intended that money for living expenses while you get the rink online, but if we can't get Jessica to work with you to begin with, then it won't do much good there."

Kyle slowly nodded. "Right. I could give her part of that."

Natalie looked relieved that he'd suggested it. "I believe an offer to her is the best course. On the other hand, you could offer nothing and take your chances. But honestly, Kyle, she might walk."

He didn't want that. "Make her an offer on my behalf. Go in strong." A Marine on a mission, he was prepared to do whatever it took to make the rink his place.

Natalie nodded and stood. She left the room, leaving the door ajar this time.

While he waited, pacing again, he faintly heard Natalie's soft voice speaking from a room down the hall. She must have forgotten to shut the door. The words were a low murmur rather than anything clear.

This was torture. He stuck his head into the hallway, and noticing no one, he headed toward Natalie's voice. His leg wasn't cooperating that well—phantom pains, maybe because he'd been sitting for so long. But he was in his old, familiar "walking leg" prosthetic. He didn't make a sound with it as he passed two offices, a small kitchen and a watercooler.

He stopped outside the open door of a smaller conference room. Natalie was making his offer, just as they'd discussed.

Please, Jessica, Kyle thought. *Take it.*

"That's not enough," a male voice—Sebastien—answered. "She'll need more money than that."

What the hell? Was the boyfriend negotiating for her?

"How much more?" Natalie asked. "Because Kyle has offered you half of the cash he inherited from Joe. That's an extremely generous offer on his part, and not what he was required to do."

Damn straight. Kyle was debating walking in

there and telling them so himself, when suddenly Natalie exited the door, nearly bumping into him.

"Oh!" Natalie said. "Were you listening?"

"Yeah," he murmured. And then he didn't think, he just marched into the open conference room, intending to face Jessica.

But Jessica and her boyfriend had their heads together, sharing what looked like a romantic moment. She was leaned in close to him, and he was murmuring something into her ear.

For a moment, Kyle lost his breath. Stupid of him. It shouldn't hurt to see her like that. Kyle wasn't meant to be with anyone romantically. He was fine with that state of affairs.

Jessica glanced up. She sucked in her breath when she saw Kyle. Her eyes widened.

Kyle focused only on her. The rest of the room seemed to melt away.

"I won't take your career away from you, Jessica. Whenever you have time, all I ask is that you squeeze in your hours at the rink. You won't have to do anything you don't want to do there. I'll take care of everything that needs doing. You can sit in Joe's old office, away from everybody, doing whatever pleases you. I just want you in this partnership with me, however you need to do it to make it work for both of us—so that we both get what we want."

Her mouth dropped open. For a moment, no one made a sound.

Kyle figured he'd screwed up. He probably should have gotten on his knees and begged her forgiveness.

Well, dammit, his knees were tired. It was best she made her decision soon, because his leg wasn't going to allow him to stand here all day.

A PARTNERSHIP. THAT would make both of them happy.

Kyle understood her better than her own boyfriend did. Then again, Kyle had lived her history with her. He'd been in that rink with her for most of her time training. He'd seen what she'd gone through. And vice versa.

Maybe she was crazy, but something about Kyle drew her…enough to overlook her guilt. Enough to be curious about him.

He seemed fine. He'd come back from his tours of duty unscathed. He didn't seem to blame her for the fact that his relationship with Joe had suffered.

"All right," she said, her eyes lowered. Because Sebastien was present, she forced herself to stand and cross her arms, acting more businesslike than she felt. "You have a deal, Kyle. I'll do this under the terms that you and Natalie specified."

Kyle stared at her, directly into her eyes. Again,

that silliness—her knees felt weak. He'd bulked up so much—it was apparent now with him standing there in a wool sweater. And his beard was so bushy and full. He looked nothing like the wiry, defiant teenager he'd once been. But he still seemed capable and honest.

He tilted his head and looked at her, almost as if he was reading her mind. As if he saw something in her that nobody else did. Maybe she should have been worried, but she wasn't.

In a flash, the moment was over.

"Kyle, may I see you a moment, in private?" Natalie murmured to him.

He nodded, and with deliberate steps he left the room.

Jessica gazed back at Sebastien. He was fiddling with his phone, scrolling through his messages.

I'm alone in this, she thought. *Six months. I have to do six months in that rink without him, on my own.*

She tucked the half-opened envelope with Joe's letter back into her purse, too dispirited to read it just now.

"Kyle, I hope you understand there's more to making your business successful than just paying Jessica to show up and doing everything else yourself," Natalie said, her soft voice filled with concern.

"Yes, ma'am," he answered, and without breaking stride he swiped Joe's envelope off the table and stuck it in his back pocket. He also pocketed the key to Joe's house.

He wasn't concerned about doing all the work, whatever needed to be done. Based on their past history, he fully assumed Jessica would be avoiding him most of the time. He was prepared for that.

"Where's the key to the rink?" he asked Natalie.

She exhaled. "I can't give it to you just yet. I'll need to walk both you and Jessica through the facility on the first Monday in March. That will give you two weeks to give your notice on your job and to settle your affairs in Maryland. Is that acceptable to you?"

It made sense, actually. But his mind couldn't help racing ahead, to the important stuff. "What's going on with the rink? I drove over yesterday, but it was closed. It looked deserted."

"It's been closed for most of the winter, except for weekday afternoons when the high school hockey team holds their practices."

"What about the kids' leagues at night?" Kyle asked. "And the high school games on Saturday? And...public skating in the morning?"

Natalie shook her head. "Joe had to cut back. His poor health necessitated it."

Wow. Kyle swiped a hand over his face. "Do I have any employees to work with?"

"I spoke with several of them, and there are three who want to come back."

A skeleton crew. Shit. "Do I know any of them?" Kyle asked.

"Carol from the office, plus Patrick and Mike who do maintenance work and operate the Zambonis."

Kyle had no idea who any of them were. His heart was sinking fast. What did he expect? That this would be a walk in the park with two good legs? *Right.*

"Let's not worry about that for now," Natalie said. "You and Jessica will figure it out together."

He refrained from snorting. Natalie didn't need to doubt his attitude. Instead, he nodded at her. "Thanks. Those three employees will be good for me to start with."

"And *Jessica*," Natalie repeated. "You'll have *Jessica.*"

No, he would never have Jessica. If anyone had Jessica, it was her boyfriend. The two of them were close enough that he'd accompanied her to Natalie's office and had done a lot of the negotiating for her, too, it seemed.

Kyle sighed. What he had from Jessica was

strictly a business agreement to sign on with him for Joe's crazy deal, just long enough to meet the insane six-month waiting period to make sure that the rink ended up in Kyle's hands.

He had no doubt he'd be required to buy her out at the end of the summer. That was fine with him. Preferable, even. She was welcome to Kyle's money until then—that wasn't a problem in his mind, either.

The only thing he did care about was that the rink wasn't being sold to a stranger. Torn down so some rich developer could get even richer putting up more condos. Taking away what had meant most to Kyle.

Kyle shook off the worries. He'd gotten Jessica to agree to Joe's terms. That was all he needed to start his new life.

Well, he hoped that was all he needed, because in no way did he deceive himself that Jessica Hughes would ever really be his partner.

CHAPTER FOUR

KYLE HAD A long list of plans for his new life. Before the first week was out, he gave notice to his landlord and packed up what few clothes and personal items he'd accumulated.

He also announced his intention to close out his Maryland employment commitments. Nobody in his office was surprised, least of all his manager. He asked Kyle where he planned to go, and Kyle replied, "Home."

The Wallis Point Twin Rinks had always been Kyle's real home. And now he was so close to running it that he could taste the excitement in his mouth—he could barely wait.

By the time he drove back to New Hampshire— seven-plus hours of motoring northeast up turnpikes surrounded by darkness—he still had another ten days before his Monday morning meeting with Natalie. Then he would finally have the keys to the rink pressed into his hands. He wasn't ever letting them go.

Antsy, impatient, he aimed for the rinks, rather than 18 Linden Lane, his childhood home, to crash in his old bed. He wasn't eager to check out how Joe had changed the digs. Even in the zero-dark-hundred hours, he was reminded that the terrain on this side of town looked different from when he'd lived here.

The road had been widened to accommodate more local traffic. They'd squeezed in a new convenience store between the old pizzeria and the landscape and gardening center. And, they'd put up a traffic light.

But the strangeness disappeared when Kyle turned into the twin rinks' lot. Security beacons illuminated the familiar concrete building with the low, flat roof. The parking spaces were freshly plowed—a good first sign that things were being taken care of.

Eager to do some interior reconnoitering, Kyle scanned for the handicap spaces. He was grateful for the installed ramp that ran the length of the building leading to the glassed-in entranceway. It meant that Kyle could avoid the awkwardness of using the stairs. He'd spent much time practicing climbing stairs in rehab, but he hadn't completely rid himself of the limp, and occasionally he still had a slip.

He didn't want to slip—and definitely not fall—in front of Jessica. Just the thought made his heart stop in his chest.

Jessica would be present during the rink walk-through and key exchange with Natalie. No way could Kyle risk her seeing him having any difficulties getting around.

Long ago, he'd decided he'd let no civilian form prejudices against him based on his being weak. That went double for Jessica, or anyone else he worked with.

He parked in the closest unmarked spot beside the ten handicapped spaces, and then hoofed it as fast he dared along the barely lit, shoveled-and-sanded ramp that led to the front doors.

Once there, he blew on his bare hands in the cold, frosty, dark morning and cupped them between his face and the glass.

He couldn't see anything inside. And the entrance doors were both locked and chained. Still, he was home. One step closer in a long and winding journey that was fast closing in a circle, bringing him back to the place he'd started.

Older and, hopefully, wiser.

JESSICA ROARED INTO the parking lot of the Wallis Point Twin Rinks with a well-thought-out action plan in mind: *Tell Kyle the truth so we can survive these six months together without feeling guilty all the time.*

She had to tell him—her conscience was bothering her. Her past mistake was tormenting her thoughts, keeping her up at night and driving a new, uncomfortable rift between her and Sebastien because of her refusal to discuss it with him.

And her guilt had only gotten worse since reading Joe's letter.

Her neck muscles tightened as she faced the familiar building. Gripping the steering wheel, she aimed toward the only two cars in the lot, on the farthest edge beside the handicapped spaces. As a physical therapist, she appreciated these aids for people who needed them, like her clients. She slowed to a stop and parked beside what she assumed was Kyle's big, black pickup truck with the Maryland plates.

Her little orange Volkswagen seemed so beat-up and old beside the hulking, gleaming monster. Her car was used. Ten years old, with over two hundred thousand miles on the odometer. It broke down all the time, and on cold days it didn't always start. Like today.

Outside, she secured her tote bag across her shoulder and wrapped her scarf more tightly around her neck. She was freezing. Worse than that, dread swirled in the pit of her stomach.

She pulled open the double glass doors to the rink lobby. Kyle stood there, big and gruff, wearing a poker face. He didn't meet her eyes—not good.

She swallowed, focusing on Natalie, all dressed up in a long wool coat and high-heeled boots, with a smart skirt-suit beneath it. Very lawyerly looking.

But it was the sleepy child in Natalie's arms that made Jessica truly relax.

"Aren't you a sweetie?" Jessica smiled at the toddler, bundled into a pink snowsuit and wearing cute boots with princess decals.

"Sorry I had to bring Hannah along to the walk-through." Natalie shifted the child to her other hip. "I'm dropping her off at my mother's house before I head into court this morning, but seven o'clock was a bit early, even for Mom to take her."

Kyle glanced at his watch. Jessica knew she was twenty minutes late. Her cranky car had needed a jump start from her neighbor.

"I'm sorry I couldn't be here on time," she said.

"That's all right." Natalie pulled out a huge key ring, with what seemed like dozens of keys on it, and handed it to Kyle. "How about if you do the honors, Kyle? We'll head into the receptionist's office and I'll get you both started with the paperwork."

Kyle froze for a moment, staring at the keys in his hands as if he couldn't quite believe he was holding them. He was in awe, like a kid at Christmas.

Another reminder of how sad it was that she'd been responsible for unfairly poisoning Joe toward Kyle. Jessica dipped her chin inside her wool scarf, her heart sinking.

"Hi!" the toddler suddenly said. "Who are you?"

Jessica glanced up. The toddler was speaking to her.

"I'm Jessica. And you're Hannah, right?"

"Hi, Jessica."

She smiled at little Hannah. As she followed Natalie into the rink, Hannah grinned at Jessica from her position over her mom's shoulder. Jessica winked at her, and the toddler giggled, her chubby fingers over small pink lips. Sweet.

Once they were in the office, Jessica found it helpful to watch Hannah while Natalie gave them the rules of the road, so to speak.

"Even though I've passed over a set of keys to Kyle," Natalie said, "I have the master set in my office because, technically, I'm acting as executor until the terms of the agreement are fulfilled. I've made up sign-in sheets for both of you to record your hours." Natalie leaned over, reaching into her bag for a blue notebook, and in doing so she set Hannah on her feet.

"Do you mind if I hold her?" Jessica asked.

Natalie straightened, glancing first at her daughter and then Jessica. "Sure, go ahead."

Jessica lifted Hannah into her arms. The child was heavier than she looked. Immediately, she

reached for Jessica's necklace, which was swing-
ing free over Jessica's turtleneck.

"I wear this?" Hannah asked, holding the pendant between thumb and forefinger.

"Hannah, we don't ask people for their things,"
Natalie said gently to her daughter.

Jessica laughed. "It's just an abalone shell I
picked up at a crafts fair." A yard sale, actually. And the shell was encased in sterling silver, which Jessica had cleaned and polished. "Of
course, honey, I'll let you try it on if you'd like."

Hannah put her chubby arms around Jessica's
neck and buried her cheek inside Jessica's unzipped jacket.

Jessica lowered her nose to Hannah's wispy-
fine curls. She smelled like talc and baby shampoo. It was the most comforting, heartwarming
scent she could imagine.

The room turned quiet. Jessica glanced up and
noticed Kyle staring at her with a strange look on
his face. Natalie just seemed pensive.

Natalie cleared her throat. "Kyle, why don't
you sign yourself and Jessica in, since she has
her hands full?" She turned to Jessica. "Every
time you come in, I'll need you each to clock in
and out on this sheet. We'll leave it on the honor
system. Don't worry, I trust you—the paperwork
is for your safety, in case anyone ever challenges
that you kept to your bargain. It will be proof you

were here when you said you were. Then, every few weeks, I'll come and pick it up. I need to file a report with the court every month as part of the trusteeship, and we want to make sure our records are unimpeachable. Does that sound all right to you both?"

"Fine," Kyle gritted out.

"Great," Jessica said, smoothing Hannah's curls.

"I'd like to see the rest of the rink," Kyle said. His gaze was looking everywhere around the office except at Jessica and Hannah. Up at the ceiling. Down at the floor. Studying the faded Formica countertops.

"Well, I do need to warn you again," Natalie said, picking up her bag. "Since the facility was partially shut down during Joe's illness, it's in rough shape."

"That's okay," Kyle said gruffly. "I'll fix it."

Jessica had no doubt that he would. She gently rocked the toddler in her arms, which helped Jessica stay calm. Except for the present conversation, she'd barely noticed she was back in the rink she'd sworn never to set foot inside again. She'd been dreading this day since the meeting in Natalie's office.

If she could keep Hannah with her every day for six months, she might be okay. She laughed softly to herself. Yeah, Natalie would love that, she thought, shaking her head at her silliness.

"I'm not going to sugarcoat it," Natalie was saying. "As I understand it from the assessors, the rink is in crisis. Much of the old machinery is falling apart. The second Zamboni isn't working. The compressor in the big rink is on the fritz. That's a direct quote from Joe. The small rink— the figure-skating rink—isn't working at all..."

Jessica tried to tune out what Natalie was saying. She had no intention of having anything to do with any of it. She thought she was doing pretty damn great as it was. She felt calm, no longer filled with anxiety and guilt. Hannah quietly played with Jessica's abalone pendant, chattering to it in sweet toddler talk, distracting Jessica and settling her nerves.

"...in addition, two of the toilets are inoperative and one of the sinks is cracked. A plumber needs to be consulted."

"I'll do it," Kyle said in his quiet, authoritative voice. "I'll fix all the equipment."

He actually seemed happy about the challenge, and it was the one thing about this whole scenario that Jessica was grateful for—that Kyle was happy. It helped ease her guilt. Somewhat. She still needed to talk to him about her letter. To get it off her chest...

Natalie unlocked a door beside the desk clerk's

counter, and a musty odor filled the room. Jessica wrinkled her nose.

"The place just needs a good, deep cleaning," Kyle said, not to Jessica but to Natalie, who was standing stoically by. "I washed this place from top to bottom every season as a kid."

Jessica remembered that. The rink used to shut down for a week in June. One time she'd been inside with her mother, meeting with Joe, and she'd noticed that Kyle had seemed to be assigned a lot of the messy janitorial duties. Painting, cleaning rubber matting, disinfecting the locker rooms, shining exterior windows...

"I'll take care of it," he repeated.

Jessica swallowed. Her guilt was kicking in again.

"Why don't we take that walk-through?" Natalie suggested, glancing at her watch. "I have about ten minutes before I have to leave if I want to make it in time for court."

Jessica's heart sped up. She had no intention of venturing past this entry area, certainly not into the heart of the rink with the ice surfaces or locker rooms.

She hugged Hannah, but the toddler squirmed and Jessica set her down on her feet.

Jessica glanced through the glass doors and across the hallway. Joe's old office was located there, and it was where Jessica planned to stake out her thirty hours per week for the next twenty weeks or so. That was their agreement, and she was sticking to it.

"I'll stay here, in Joe's old office and watch your little girl for you," she said to Natalie.

"Are you okay?" Natalie asked, peering into her face.

Jessica nodded, glancing away. Once she'd been prone to panic attacks, and she well knew how they started. Flushed cheeks. Rapid breathing. Fixation on an unwanted result.

"I'm fine," she insisted, more to herself than to Natalie. She opened the glass door and prepared to head out to the hallway again. "Where's the key to Joe's old office?" she asked, turning...

And as she turned, she saw a bare, rectangular spot of faded paint on the old concrete wall above the double doors that led to the twin rinks.

The office door closed behind her. Jessica froze, alone in the hallway, staring at the wall above the double doors. *This* was where her poster-sized portrait had been. Her smiling image had greeted everyone who'd entered the Wallis Point Twin Rinks during all the years she'd trained here.

The office door clicked open and shut behind her, and she heard the heaviness of Kyle's work boots on the rubber matting beside her.

From the corner of her eye, she saw him gazing at the empty spot, too, and then at her. He'd worked and played at the rink during the same time she had. He would remember that poster. He would be thinking exactly what she was thinking, except that he wouldn't know that her smiling face had been a lie.

He exhaled, darting a glance her way. Maybe he did suspect she'd been lying back then. Sometimes the way he used to meet her eyes when they'd had a rare moment alone had made her wonder what he thought. But he'd never said a word about any suspicions he might have had regarding her real feelings. He'd made kind gestures—a small favor here or there, a cup of coffee or a kind look. Actions, but not words.

That's who Kyle was—the strong and silent type. He didn't avoid unpleasant situations, as Sebastien tended to, but he didn't dwell on things, either.

She turned her back on the rectangle of faded paint, breathed slowly in and out. Focused her attention on the lobby floor. On the peeling rubber mats that had seen better days. The dirty, scuffed interior walls and a limp plant, dead in its pot.

She felt a gentle pressure on her shoulder, a comforting human touch.

Kyle. She wasn't prepared for him to touch her—he'd barely glanced at her all morning—but when she looked into his face, she saw *un-*

derstanding, the gaze of someone who'd known and remembered her.

In all the years of their awkward teen acquaintance, she'd never been physically close to him before. They'd never touched skin.

She reached across her chest and pressed the back of his knuckles with the palm of her hand. She meant it as a thank-you, but the shock of his heat and strength struck her at once.

Her heart made a trembling pitter-patter in her chest.

"It will be okay," he murmured.

Her breathing sounded loud, even to her. "I hope so." She stared at the glass doors that led to the twin rinks. "I don't ever want to go inside those rinks again, Kyle, so I hope you don't expect me to."

Kyle's eyes were green and earnest, as if making her a promise. "You don't have to do anything you don't want to do, Jessica. I'll protect you from all of that."

As opposed to Sebastien, who'd made her agree to things that she didn't want to do, just to keep their future on track.

Jessica glanced away. Her mother had never cared about Jessica doing what *she* wanted, either. Hedley Jackson had been all about the long view. "Day-to-day discipline," she'd insisted to Jessica. "Be practical in your choices." Everything her mother had achieved in her own star-studded figure-skating career had come from dedication, denial and hard work. She'd expected the same of her only child.

"I appreciate your saying that," Jessica said to Kyle. She tried to laugh, but it came out as a choke.

"I remember how hard it was for you." Kyle's face darkened. "But these are new days. I meant what I said back in the lawyer's office."

Partners, he'd said.

She nodded, swallowing. She should take her hand off his now. If Sebastien suddenly walked into the rink and saw them, it would look disloyal of her. But she knew what Kyle was doing. He wasn't trying to seduce her but to reassure her.

"Thanks," she told him. "I appreciate you helping me."

There was a cough behind them.

"Jessica," Natalie said. How long had their lawyer been watching them?

Kyle abruptly dropped his hand at the same time that Jessica stepped away from him.

"I'm giving you the key to Joe's office." Natalie pulled it off the large key ring. "You'll have the only copy, so it will be your private space."

Had Natalie noticed her discomfort? Jessica took the key, determined to get a grip. "That will be great. Thank you."

More composed now, Jessica turned to Kyle. More than ever, she needed to apologize to him for her past mistake, and she needed him to forgive her, too, but she'd wait until they were alone to discuss it. "When you come back from your walk-through, could you please stop by and see me, Kyle? I have something I need to speak to you about."

Gazing at a spot on the wall behind her, Kyle nodded once. Shortly.

That was him being strong and silent in front of the lawyer. She got that.

"Thank you," Jessica said again, quietly.

Kyle was home, healthy, doing what he was meant to do. Once she apologized for making Joe angry at him all those years ago, causing his departure, then she should be okay. At least, she hoped so.

KYLE COULD BARELY concentrate on the inspection tour ahead of him.

Natalie held a clipboard and was making notes, matching keys to locks, mainly. Besides Joe and Johnny David, Kyle was probably the only person in Wallis Point who knew all the secrets this old rink kept.

Too bad he was so fixated on Jessica. His guilt meter was through the roof. And now, not just guilt over dragging her back to face the past, but worry for her well-being, too.

Dammit. How could he ask her to come in here every day? Jessica seemed destroyed just by setting foot in this place again.

When he'd seen her face, staring at the faded spot where her picture had been, he'd been seized by the desire to take her under his wing and protect her at all costs. Which explained the touching-her-shoulder bit. That wasn't his style. Never had been.

Natalie cleared her throat, and he snapped to attention. They were in the garage bay beside the hockey rink, inspecting an aging Zamboni. He glanced at the high driver's seat, not sure if he could hoist himself up there, given his leg situation.

"Kyle," Natalie said, "I was just saying that any time you want to confer about anything, my office is open to you. That goes for Bruce, as well."

Bruce, her husband—the Navy veteran. "Are you saying this because I'm a veteran?" Kyle asked, mildly annoyed. Did she think he was emotionally damaged?

"My husband keeps in touch with a lot of your old classmates. I'm thinking maybe you'll want to catch up with some old friends as you settle back into town."

Kyle had new friends, from his time in the

service. "Thanks, but I'm okay." He turned and inspected the electric panel that controlled the rink's overhead lights.

"Of course," Natalie said. "I'm sure that you and Jessica will do just fine."

Kyle thought of the space on the wall in the lobby where her poster had been. *Jessa Hughes. World Junior Champion. The Pride of Wallis Point.* That had been the caption beneath it. "Did you ever skate here when you were a kid?" he asked Natalie.

"Yes, I did. Many Friday night open skates, back when I was in middle school."

He nodded. When Natalie was in middle school that poster of Jessica's had been front and center. Jessa Hughes's presence had brought in crowds of people to Joe's old rink. She'd been a celebrity back then.

Slowly Kyle shut the squeaking cover of the electrical box. Everybody in Wallis Point would know about her youthful disappointment. That had to be hard for her. Yet no one knew anything about his leg. No one had been told in Wallis Point. There had been no news stories. It was his secret to tell, when he was ready.

Natalie was staring at him. "I have to go now, Kyle. Will you two be okay?"

They had to be. "Yes, ma'am."

"Great. I'll check up on you next week. Remember, my office is always open."

AFTER KYLE WALKED Natalie to the front door, he knocked on Joe's door—now Jessica's door. He'd dreaded combat less than this encounter.

Bracing himself, he stepped aside as she joined him in the hallway. Through the front windows, they both watched Natalie walk down the ramp with her daughter.

"She's a great little kid," Jessica murmured. "Natalie is lucky to have her."

Kyle stuffed his hands into his jeans pockets and said nothing.

Finally, Jessica tore her attention from the scene outside and gazed up at him. She would always be pretty to him, with her liquid brown eyes and ready smile. But now she had dark circles under her eyes. Her arms were crossed, and she appeared somber.

Automatically, his neck muscles tensed.

"I got a letter from Joe." She licked her lips and gazed straight at his chest, as if embarrassed to look him in the eye. "I read it when I got home from the law office that day. I've been thinking about it ever since."

Kyle groaned inwardly. "I got a letter from him, too, but I'm not gonna read it."

Her gaze lifted to his. "That's my fault. That's what I need to apologize to you for."

"Trust me, you don't need to apologize to me about anything."

"But I do. I affected your relationship with him, and I'm sorry for that. He never should have blamed you for hurting me, Kyle."

"Sure he should have." He didn't deserve her sympathy.

"You don't understand," she said softly. "I have something I need to tell you." She stared down at her hands. Her nails were cut short. No ring on her finger today.

She glanced up, looking very serious. "You didn't hurt my knee, Kyle. You weren't responsible for that. And I'm sorry I let the charade stand."

"What charade?" She was confusing him. "I drove the Zamboni the day that you fell. You were injured because I flooded the ice. End of story."

She twisted hands. "It's not true. I know you made the ice-cut that day, and I know that Joe blamed you for flooding the ice and causing me to fall, but you didn't hurt my knee. Yes, it was true that I got a small bruise, but that was because of my own distraction, not the condition of the ice."

"But...your knee was hurt. You pulled out of

competition. You missed making the Olympic team and you never skated again."

"But not because of you." Her voice was a whisper. "You didn't hurt me. I should have told Joe that right away after the competition, but I was a stupid kid, in a lot of ways. I didn't even think how horribly he would treat you afterward or that he would send you away. I actually didn't realize until I saw Joe again a few months ago, when we first worked together in physical therapy. I told him then what I should've said years ago, that he was wrong to blame you for my knee injury."

"I'm not responsible?" His mind was reeling. He didn't even know how to process all this.

She nodded. "I'm sorry. But Joe said that he—"

"I don't give a damn what Joe said," he said coldly. "What about you? Did you even think to come back afterward to see me? That entire spring of my senior year, you never came back."

The blood drained from her face. "I was here. Just not...here at the twin rinks."

"You were in Wallis Point?" Now he really felt infuriated. "For how long?"

"I never left Wallis Point."

"Never left?"

"After I...dropped out of the competition, I came back and asked Natalie's father to help me get emancipated from my mother. We...had talks instead, and then my mother left for California. I was free from her control, but I couldn't ever contact her again. I had to support myself. So I waitressed up the coast in Portsmouth. I dyed my hair and I gained weight…and nobody recognized me."

He stared at her, feeling bug-eyed. "So while I was in my last semester of high school, being punished daily by Joe, recriminating myself with guilt, you were waitressing up the *coast*?"

She bowed her head. "I'm sorry," she whispered.

"I would've helped you, Jessa."

"I'm not Jessa," she hissed. "And back then, nobody could help me but me. And I *did it*. I saved money and put myself through physical-therapy schooling and certification. All of it."

Very impressive, he wanted to snap. *And I put myself through tours of combat. You want to see my foot?*

He was two seconds from sarcastically lifting up his pant leg and thrusting the prosthetic in her face. But the look in her eyes stopped him.

"If I could go back," she said, her voice racked with pain, "if I could have a do-over, I would have gone to see you. I would have talked to Joe. The only thing…" She wiped her eyes.

Cripes, she was crying. He balled his hands

into fists. The last thing he wanted was to see her cry.

"…the only thing I'm thankful for is that you weren't hurt in combat. If you'd been hurt, Kyle, I couldn't stand it. I never would have forgiven myself. *Never.*" Her voice cracked. She shook her head vehemently.

He stood there, the breath knocked out of him. A million emotions tore through him. He *had* been hurt, and the recovery had been hell. And in a way, now that he knew the truth, he agreed that if not for her lie, if she'd told Joe the truth, he might still be whole.

"I hope you can forgive me," she said, her head lowered. "I promise I'll keep my commitment to working thirty hours with you every week. I got my schedule shuffled at work, so I'll be here starting at six in the morning and staying until noon. But if it's okay with you, I'll keep to Joe's office. I don't want people seeing me here, and I can't answer questions about my old life on the ice. I hope you can understand that."

What could he say? *Yeah, I forgive you. No, I don't.* He honestly wasn't sure.

"I blame Joe." He never should've left this rink to both her and him. It should have gone to just him.

Jessica flinched. Yeah, he understood. She felt

guilty and bad about him and this place. And she didn't want to be reminded of the past.

"You want me to protect you," he said. "Is that it?"

Her look caught him straight in his heart. Her eyes were so big and brown and full of emotion. That soulful look that had made her such a wonder to watch, for millions of people. The lashes wet with feeling.

He would never, ever let her feel sorry for him. He would never, ever let her see his leg so she could blame herself for it.

He turned away.

"Kyle?"

"Don't worry," he said. "I'll make sure no one bothers you."

"I remember you as being happy here. Not with Joe, but with the rink. Skating on the ice was where you always seemed to want to be."

"I thought the same about you."

There was a pause. "If you come across that poster of me from the vestibule," she asked, her voice small, "could you please destroy it? It's a lie. It's not worth seeing anymore."

His hands curled and uncurled. *Damn Joe,* he thought. *Damn him to hell.*

But by the time he turned back to her, she was gone, barred inside Joe's office.

And there was nothing Kyle could do about

it, because the damage was done. For better or worse, their fates were intertwined. All he could do was bring this rink back to life and survive six months in her presence, and then she would be gone from his life.

CHAPTER FIVE

MOST OF THE anger Kyle felt dissolved the first day he unlocked the front doors of the twin rinks with his own set of keys.

He surveyed his domain, the most satisfying moment he'd had in a long time.

Maybe he couldn't fix the resentment he harbored toward Joe. Or the guilt that Jessica felt toward him. Or the apprehension his prosthetic leg gave him when he thought of the maintenance chores that lay ahead. But there was one great thing in store—and that was his love and enthusiasm for this place. Jessica had been right about that.

He remembered every detail. The parking lot that seemed huge and empty during daily sessions but never seemed to have enough spaces during weekend tournaments and competitions. The smell of "hockey" that hit him when he first walked through the double glass doors. The brush of cold air on his skin.

He'd arrived at oh-five-hundred, an hour before Jessica was due. Like her, he chose a home base: the largest corner locker room with a sink and shower inside. He needed a place to store his gear and tend to his prosthetic without being seen. He realized it was part pride, but Jessica couldn't know. After what she'd said yesterday, her finding out was something he never wanted to face as long as he lived.

So far, no one suspected. To keep it that way, he wanted to get his employees up to speed quickly and working independently as much as possible.

At oh-seven-hundred hours, in the bay where they parked the Zambonis, he met with his two maintenance employees. If there was anything the Marines had taught Kyle, it was the importance of training his people to be part of a well-ordered team.

Patrick was a young guy, thin and pale blond. Mike had been around longer; he was a retired plumber who was also a hockey nut, and wanted part-time work on nights and weekends while his wife worked. Kyle liked him on sight.

"Here's what we'll do," Kyle said, psyched to finally start turning this place around. "Patrick, your hours are going to be eight to four-thirty, Monday through Friday. You'll get a standard half hour at lunch. Mike, I'll see you at seventeen-hundred to start with, and as for Saturdays, we'll see how late we can book ice time to hockey teams."

"Sounds good, boss," Mike said.

Patrick grunted what Kyle assumed was a sign of unenthusiastic assent. Fine. But then the kid slyly glanced at his cell phone, sticking out of his front pocket.

Kyle frowned. If he'd pulled a phone out during morning formation, he would've been reamed by his CO. He barely restrained himself from confiscating it. "Stow that thing," he said.

Patrick gave him a resentful look. *I'm not in Kansas anymore,* Kyle thought. This sure wasn't the military.

"You two ever drive the Zamboni?" Kyle asked, moving on.

"I've been handling it for the high school hockey team since Joe got sick," Mike answered. "Johnny David and I did."

"Where's Johnny working now?"

"After Joe died, he found a full-time job stocking vending machines."

Patrick sneaked another look at his cell phone.

"Any chance of Johnny coming back?" Kyle asked, thinking he'd like to replace Patrick with someone who cared.

"I don't think so." Mike scratched his beard. "Johnny said the benefits are good at his new place. He's getting married and he needs that stuff now."

Kyle nodded. No way could he compete with

that. Once he got this place ramped up, though, it would be a different story.

"Fine. I'll make the ice during the day," he decided. He glanced up at the Zamboni. He would have to practice climbing into the seat. *Just another challenge to tackle.*

"What about me?" Patrick whined. "You could train me to use the Zamboni."

Not with that attitude. Not on such an expensive piece of equipment. "I've got plenty of other things for you to do," Kyle said shortly.

Patrick actually pouted.

"You want to change that up?" Kyle asked. "Driving the Zamboni is a responsibility. You'll have to prove to me you're serious here."

"I am," Patrick said stubbornly.

"Then show me evidence. Look, I don't have a lot of rules, just two that I need you to follow. One, you show up on time. Two, you need to—" Kyle leaned forward, and as he did, his left foot—his prosthetic foot—dragged and caught on the switch on the floor, the one that Joe had haphazardly installed years ago for the figure skaters. Music blared from the speakers in the adjoining figure-skating rink.

Shit. With his right foot, Kyle kicked off the switch.

He thought of Jessica. When they were teens, she used to stop by to ask him to please turn on the switch, early in the mornings. He sometimes forgot—on purpose—just to get her to come talk to him. But she'd seemed to share the in-joke with him.

Patrick and Mike were staring at him. He cleared his throat.

"Two..." Kyle continued. He'd been planning to tell them to get their work done, but that was probably self-evident. It was more important he explain Jessica's situation. "Two," he repeated, wondering how to phrase this. "I, ah, have a partner working with me. Her name's Jessica, and she'll be in the front office every morning doing paperwork."

He'd made up the paperwork part, but he didn't want anyone getting suspicious. "Please don't bother her. Don't knock on her door. Don't waylay her. Don't stop her in the parking lot."

"Yes, boss," Mike said with a straight face.

"Aye, aye," Patrick muttered.

"I'm serious. It's a fireable offense. Do not test me on this."

That had the desired effect. Patrick's eyes widened in fear.

"Hello! Is anyone out here?" called a feminine voice. "I hear voices!"

"That's Carol," Mike explained. "She runs the front office and answers the phone."

"Come on back," Kyle called. "We're having a staff meeting. Mind you don't slip on the puddle."

A woman ducked her head around the corner, smiling broadly. "Hello, I'm Carol McCarthy. And you're Kyle, Joe's stepson. I saw you at the funeral." She stuck out a pudgy hand and squeezed Kyle's for all she was worth. "I'm sorry for your loss. Joe was such a dear to all of us."

Kyle nodded, trying not to raise his brow. Carol had a monster grip. He didn't remember her from the funeral, but that wasn't surprising—he hadn't paid too much attention during much of it.

He assessed her now. His lone office employee looked to be late thirties, with dyed red hair and a lot of makeup, considering it was oh-seven-thirty at a hockey rink. He just hoped she had phone skills and that she was responsible with the till.

"We've never met, Kyle," Carol gushed, continuing to grip his hand, "but I've heard so much about you from Johnny David."

"Okay," Kyle said, attempting to withdraw his hand.

"We're getting married," Carol continued, hanging on and squeezing harder. "I need to tell you something, because being back in town, you'll probably hear the *gossip*, and I'd rather you heard it from me first."

Kyle stared at her.

"Johnny was still married when I met him,"

Carol whispered dramatically, "but only because he couldn't find his wife to serve her divorce papers. Thankfully, that is now in process. You see, she ran off with the man who used to service the Zambonis. It was *devastating* to Johnny. Joe refused to hire *that service* afterward, and I think you should do the same."

There were no words. Kyle's jaw hung open. And he'd thought Navy carrier dramas had been bad.

"...so, you can't use that service anymore," Carol insisted. "I don't want them present on these premises."

She had a furious expression on her face. Kyle realized with cold understanding that she wasn't a person to cross, under any circumstance.

Patrick made a snickering sound. Kyle whipped his head around to face him. The kid was laughing at him openly.

"Okay," Kyle said, pulling his hand from Carol's with no more nonsense. "This is what your assignment is, Carol. Go back to your office and find me the liability waivers and sign-in sheets for public-skating and open-stick-time sessions. We're going to start up operation again for next Monday morning. Then find me the phone numbers for the guy who's heading the Wallis Point youth skater teams, because I want to get their league booked into nights again. And if anyone calls about wanting to rent ice make sure you forward the calls immediately to me, and only me. Understand?"

"But—"

"No buts," Kyle said.

Patrick laughed harder, as if it was the most hilarious thing he'd ever heard.

Emboldened, Carol spoke up. "Should I say 'Yes, sir'?" she demanded. "Is that what you want me to say?"

"Look," he said, sighing, realizing he'd better be careful or he'd have an open mutiny on his hands, "you can stay in your office, and I won't bother you. Just as long as you show up and put in your hours, I'm a reasonable guy. And no, I won't hire whatever individual it is you don't want me to hire. Is that sufficient?"

Which sucked for him, seeing as he only had one operable Zamboni. But this was probably the reason for that, and Johnny David was a skilled maintenance manager. Kyle wanted to keep in his good graces.

She nodded mutely.

"Aren't you gonna tell her the part about your partner?" Patrick piped up. Kyle shot him a glance. But he had Carol's attention.

Tamping down his irritation, he said, "Patrick's right. Stay out of my partner's way. She'll be across the hall from you in Joe's old office until noon every day. Don't look at her, don't chat with her, don't knock on her door and don't even pass her a phone call."

Carol stared at him, surprise and fascination mixed on her face. "Your *partner*...?" She said it as if it was a sexual thing.

Kyle gritted his teeth. "Her name is Jessica. She's my business partner, and she's in that office doing paperwork. Don't bother her." He glanced at all three of his employees. "I'll fire anyone who disturbs her. Is that understood?"

They nodded silently.

The whole damn meeting had been a disaster. He glanced to Mike, his one seemingly sane employee. "Would you mind working with me this morning?" he asked, praying Mike would say yes. "Then we can switch you over to nights starting tomorrow. There are some plumbing issues, and we can't open for business until we get the sinks and toilets in working order."

"No problem," Mike said cheerfully. "I'll do what I can, as long as you act as my assistant."

"No problem there," Kyle said, relieved, "I'll do whatever it takes." He gave a stern look to Carol and Patrick. "The same as I expect from all of you. Whatever it takes to make our rink succeed."

THERE WERE SO many things to fix. The first day passed in a blur. As Kyle got into the swing of bringing his facility up to par, he strode back and forth between the two ice surfaces, consulting with Mike on the repairs. Mike was a skilled plumber, and Kyle was ecstatic with relief for that. The old excitement was returning—he had so many plans for this place.

First, he had dreams of expanding it. Adding another ice surface to the two that were already there, though one was in desperate need of repair. He would improve and modernize the locker/changing rooms. Add a smaller ice surface to the back, specifically for goalie training. It would be great to organize a hockey camp in the summer, and for that, four ice surfaces would be better.

If Kyle could get the figure-skating people… no, actually, he didn't think he even needed figure-skating people. That's where Joe had been wrong about this place.

By the end of the week, after concentrated effort, the bathrooms were functional, one Zamboni was in perfect operating order, and one gleaming sheet of perfectly formed ice was ready. Kyle felt as though he'd achieved nirvana. He immediately got in touch with two of his Marine buddies. TJ and Oscar both lived on the coast—TJ up in Rye, Oscar down in Amesbury, across the border into Massachusetts.

"I inherited a rink," Kyle said to TJ when he

called him. Kyle didn't go into all the details, because that wasn't the important point. Their group ice time was. "Do you want to play hockey again? I'm thinking early mornings. I want to get a group of us together."

"Holy shit," TJ said reverently. He'd been part of Kyle's initial rehabilitation group when they'd been down at Walter Reed together. He understood where Kyle was coming from.

"I know," Kyle said. "I hit the jackpot. Do you know anybody else who'd be interested?"

"I know a guy who was in our unit," TJ answered. "He played hockey as a kid, but didn't do much with it afterward. He lost his dominant arm. Do you mind a bionic-arm guy?"

"Hell, no. Bring as many of us as possible. I'm not charging for ice time because I own this place."

Or he would in six months, but he wasn't going to split hairs. He'd rather they didn't know about the arrangement with Jessica; it was easier that way.

"We'll start at oh-five-hundred," Kyle said. *An hour before Jessica arrives.* That way, she wouldn't see the prosthetics. "Spread the word to everybody, okay?"

"Can we plan for a session every morning?" TJ suggested. "Some guys might drive down once or twice a week, even if it's a hike for them. Then we could spread everybody out on a schedule."

"Great. I was thinking maybe at some point we could form teams. Or join a travel league that's already established."

"This is fantastic. You just made my day, brother."

Kyle felt pretty damn good, too. Maybe he would survive these six months, after all.

JESSICA WANTED TO help Kyle. She really, honestly did. She owed him that much.

But two weeks into the new agreement, and she wasn't feeling so hopeful.

Six hours alone, with no one to talk to, shut up in a small room by herself was far longer than she'd realized. Yes, she brought her PT paperwork with her every day, but she typically finished it within an hour. With nothing more to focus her mind on, she could hardly stand it.

Kyle never stopped by to say hello. When she'd last left him, things hadn't been great. He would probably never forgive her, and she could understand that, but at least there were no misunderstandings between them. She'd been clear about why Joe had wanted her to work with him. She'd apologized to him, and there wasn't much else she could do.

She really hadn't expected otherwise. It was

pretty horrible, what she'd done to him. Still, she felt a tad hurt, and not real happy about being dragged back into this world...

Kyle, of course, was in his glory. He arrived before she did and left at ten or eleven o'clock at night, judging by the time sheet. She didn't know how he was surviving such a rigorous schedule, but she didn't want to go through the double doors and out to the rinks to ask him. She would never go out there, and he knew that.

Then again, Kyle had said that he would make sure nobody bothered her, and thus, nobody did. Kyle was very literal minded, she was fast learning. Too bad she wasn't happy being left alone in Joe's office, as much as she wished she were.

His former space overflowed with junk Jessica would never use, none of it essential to the running of a rink. But in point of fact, *she* wasn't essential to running the rink.

Jessica just didn't know what she was supposed to *do*. Some alone time was fine, but she was used to being active, moving around, helping clients. It became clear pretty quickly that she'd better find something to keep herself occupied, because if she just sat around and did nothing, she'd only realize how lonely she was—how *unhelpful*. And unhelpful was not part of her nature.

She decided to phone Sebastien. He was on the road for the next three weeks for work. He wasn't flying home on the weekends because his company offered him more in per diem payments if he stayed where he was and saved them the expense.

"What is it, Jessica?" he asked her, sounding sleepy. "Is there an emergency there?"

She glanced at her watch. It was seven o'clock in the morning Chicago time. She sighed. "I forgot about the time difference. I'm sorry if I'm bothering you."

"You're not. Hold on, I'll be right back."

She waited until he came on the line again.

"The reception here is horrible." His voice was clearer now and he sounded wide awake. "I had to leave the hotel building and go outside. Damn, it's cold. It feels about twenty degrees below zero."

On his end, she heard cars speeding by and wind whistling. "I hope you have your coat with you."

"Yeah, I'm fine. How's it going at the rink?"

"Not as cold. But boring."

"God, I would love boring," Sebastien murmured. "Did you bring something to read?"

"I did." She'd also answered her email. Completed her time sheet for her boss at her real job. Even started plugging through her tax worksheets—that's how desperate she was. "I've got to figure something out."

"Are there many customers coming in?"

She thought of the empty parking lot she always walked through when she left the rink at noon. "No, it seems pretty dead."

"That's excellent."

She paused for a second. "Why is *that* excellent?"

"We don't want the business to be profitable, babe."

That surprised her. "Why not?"

"Because if the rink isn't profitable at the end of six months, then it'll be sold to the highest bidder and we'll get a lot more payout—and Kyle will, too."

"Okay…" she said. "I didn't realize that."

"This is why I was asking the lawyer so many questions," Sebastien said, and to Jessica his tone sounded a bit smug.

She pushed aside her irritation because he was right—she should have asked more questions. This was *her* life.

"I also read the will the lawyer gave us," Sebastien added. "It's written very clearly. If the rink is profitable, then either you or Kyle get an option to buy the other out based on an assessor's price. But if the rink isn't profitable, then it's sold on the open market and you'll split the money. I did research on the market prices, and it's clear we'll get a lot more cash if it's sold to land developers. Do you see the flaw in Joe's plan? There's no incentive for either of you to help the rink make a profit."

That he'd been thinking so deeply about this shocked her. A hesitant feeling settled in her stomach. She could ignore it, but...

"What if Kyle really does want to run the twin rinks permanently?" she asked. He was putting a lot of energy into it.

"Trust me, babe, what Kyle's doing is giving a good faith effort, because he has to. But he wants top dollar, as well. Afterward, if he still desires to work in the ice-rink business, he knows somebody will hire him because he has experience. Plus, you said he's a veteran, right? People love to hire veterans."

It did sound possible. "I suppose so," she murmured.

"Believe me, I see it every day in my line of work," Sebastien patiently explained. "Anyway, if he decides he wants to, he can build his own twin rinks with the money he'll be getting. Better rinks, more modern. He'll be much better off. You see?"

She absolutely did. In her opinion, this place was a dump. "It makes sense."

"Of course it does. I know business and finance. I know money."

She fell silent. He had a point about that.

As a child, Jessica had been brought up with money being no object. It was a hard thing to suddenly have to live fighting for existence hand-to-mouth. But now she had her physical therapy livelihood, she wasn't in debt, and she lived within her means. And she truly did try to pay attention to the larger picture when it came to finances, because finances meant security.

To begin with, accepting the deal with Kyle had been about making a life with Sebastien. Growing the tentative roots she'd put down in Wallis Point and starting something—a family—more permanent than her own.

She'd been distracted from that lately. And that she hadn't paid full attention in the lawyer's office just showed her how her emotions about the twin rinks and her guilt over separating Kyle from Joe had been getting the better of her.

Joe *had* asked her in his letter to help Kyle. Maybe the best help she could give him was to find her own tasks and let him keep busy by running this rink until such time as they made their money, and then he could build his own facility.

"Sebastien, thanks. I know what to do now."

"Glad I helped. I'll call you tonight, babe. Have a good day."

Jessica folded her hands on the cluttered desk and listened to the stillness. She had to decide which tasks she would do.

Blowing out her breath, she stood and left Joe's office, locking the door behind her and crossing the hallway to the reception vestibule.

Inside, the place looked new and bright. It also smelled of a thorough disinfecting and a fresh coat of yellow paint.

Jessica blinked, pleasantly surprised.

She didn't recognize the woman who sat behind the counter with her back to Jessica, her concentration on the magazine spread before her. But if Jessica remembered correctly, the receptionist's duty was to answer the phone, take money from skaters and, in general, deal with the public.

"Hello," she said to the startled woman. "My name is Jessica."

The woman closed her magazine and gasped. "You have to leave! I'll get in trouble if I speak to you!"

Really? This was strange. "Why?"

"Because Kyle said he'd fire me if I did."

Had he? Jessica crossed her arms. That seemed excessive.

"He doesn't want you to be bothered," the woman clarified, speaking in a rush.

"Don't worry about Kyle." Jessica walked around the counter. She pulled out a chair and sat beside the frantic woman. "What's your name?" she asked calmly.

"I'm C-Carol."

"It's nice to meet you, Carol. And don't worry, Kyle can't get angry with you because I'm half partner and I have a right to talk with you."

Carol cocked a brow, dubious.

"He can't fire you without my permission," Jessica explained, "and I won't give it to him."

But Carol was still nervous. Jessica glanced over her shoulder. The magazine she'd been reading was a bridal magazine. Carol wore a sparkly diamond on her left ring finger.

"Oh, my gosh," Jessica exclaimed. "Are you getting married? I love brides."

"We don't have a date set, but I'm hoping for June." Carol beamed despite her worries. "Guess who my fiancé is." She leaned closer and whispered, "Johnny David. You remember him, don't you?"

Jessica did. But what most concerned her was the feeling that Carol knew exactly who she was. *Jessa Hughes.*

She swallowed. She could get up and leave, go back into Joe's office and no one would ever question her about it. But would she never get over how awkward and shameful it felt? She was lucky that in her line of work she mainly dealt with kids who were born after she had her massive collapse and embarrassment in the limelight.

Maybe she was tired of feeling ashamed and

embarrassed. Maybe she *wanted* to talk to Carol about weddings.

"Yes, I do remember your fiancé," Jessica said.

Carol looked at her expectantly, so Jessica continued. "He isn't much older than me. He...drove the Zamboni when I was a teen. I remember he sometimes sneaked me cold bottled waters from the vending machine whenever the guy who restocked it came in."

"That sounds exactly like my Johnny. He's such a caring man." Carol sighed and stared into space. Jessica hoped she would feel the same way when it was her turn with Sebastien.

She glanced at the bridal magazine open on Carol's desk. But then a woman and two kids appeared in the hallway, beyond the glass doors.

Jessica swiveled in her chair and bent over as if tying her sneaker. The trio came into the office. Jessica continued to stay low as the woman paid for the two kids to go skating on the public ice. She also asked for two chits to rent skates for them.

Once the woman and children were gone, Jessica raised her head. "Sorry about that," she said sheepishly to Carol.

"I completely understand," Carol confided. "Lord knows, I'm no stranger to notoriety myself."

"Really?" Jessica couldn't help asking.

"Johnny was a *married man*—" Carol whispered the words "—until just two weeks ago when he tracked down his ex-wife in Vegas. He's filed for a quickie divorce and we've put a notice about it in the paper, but that still doesn't stop *some people* from whispering behind my back."

"That's hard," Jessica agreed.

Carol nodded. "I knew you'd understand." She cocked her head at Jessica. "Though, with your hair long like that, frankly, I didn't recognize you at first. I don't think anyone who doesn't know you already could possibly recognize you. And don't worry—none of us here will ever say a word." Carol made the sign of an X over her closed lips.

Jessica felt touched by Carol's concern. "Ah, who else is working here besides you?"

"Just Patrick and Mike, but I don't see Mike much because he works nights and weekends. Patrick is around during the days." Carol pointed to the freshly painted wall. "In fact, he did this for me because I asked him to."

"That's great. It looks so much better." Jessica glanced at Carol. "What if I were to paint my—Joe's old office? Who here would I go to for supplies?"

"Patrick said he used up all the paint that was on hand. You'll have to ask Kyle if you want to buy more."

No, Jessica wouldn't do that. Kyle was obviously avoiding her. Besides, she was half owner.

"There must be a storeroom somewhere," Jessica murmured aloud. She was foggy on this maintenance stuff. In the old days, she used to show up, stretch, do her off-ice jumps, and then focus on her skating sessions. Back then, she'd had a personal ballet teacher and all kinds of coaches and choreographers. She'd known little about the behind-the-scenes infrastructure of this place.

"Joe had an account with Pete's Paints," Carol offered.

Jessica knew Pete's Paints, near the Kimball Family Law offices.

"I think they'll even deliver, too," Carol said.

It couldn't hurt to call them. And there was no need to alert Kyle. Jessica picked up her phone and dialed Pete's. A clerk answered.

"Hi. This is Jessica, I'm calling from the twin rinks. I need to order some paint. Carol said you guys will deliver it for us?"

"Yeah, hold on a second," the clerk said.

While Jessica was on hold, she imagined what colors she wanted. A mint green for the main walls and a yellow for the alcove. She would clear out all Joe's old stuff and re-cover the desk chair in a new, cute fabric. She would bring in her sewing machine. Make some pillows and some curtains. She'd lived on the cheap for so many years. Jessica knew how to stretch a dollar.

The clerk returned to the line. "That account's still open. What do you need, miss?"

"I need paint."

"Number of cans, color, texture? Do you need any brushes?"

Hmm. This would be more fun than she'd thought. But she couldn't leave, though, and go over to the store to look at samples.

"There's a color wheel on the manufacturer's web site," the clerk said. "Maybe you could check that out."

"Okay. I'll call you back."

Jessica spent a pleasant afternoon with Carol playing interior-decorator style maven. Jessica chose her wall colors. She even measured the room and calculated how many cans of paint she needed using the handy chart on the website. Then she figured out what she needed for a roller and paint brushes, since Carol said that Patrick had tossed out the rink's old, used supplies. Carol found her a stepstool from the corner of her office, too. Neither of them mentioned telling Kyle what Jessica was up to.

The next day was even busier.

Jessica gutted the place. Hauled everything out—or rather, Carol corralled the maintenance worker, Patrick. Jessica found him cheerful and willing, if a bit shy with her.

"Where do you live, Patrick?"

"Wallis Point. Do you know where the firehouse is?"

"I do."

She discovered that Patrick's father was a firefighter, and that's what Patrick wanted to be, too, but he had to wait a few more months to take the entrance exam again. Jessica wished him luck.

A week passed, quite happily. Patrick carted some of the boxes from Joe's room to the local Salvation Army store—the junk he heaved into the trash receptacle in the back of the parking lot. Jessica was happy. It beat doing nothing. She spent another day scrubbing and shining Joe's floors. Then she painted. A rich, minty green and a cheerful pale yellow. She left the couch alone for now, but thoroughly cleared out the desk and polished its wooden top. Found a new carpet at a half-price sale. She cleaned the windows, high up in the office, by standing on a rickety ladder.

The old leather couch was in decent condition. She ordered some leather cleaner from the hardware store and spruced it up. It smelled good when she was finished. Jessica was handy with a sewing machine—she'd gone through a period of sewing her own skating costumes, and had taken design tips from some of the best seamstresses in the world. So she made new pillow covers for pillows that Carol donated to the cause.

She brought in a radio. At work, in her physical therapy practice, she was used to working with a television on all the time. She'd forgotten how used to background noise she was.

Coming in from six to noon was no longer so lonely. She had Carol to talk with. And Carol's office had an espresso maker, so they met each day for midmorning coffee.

"Why did Joe leave the rink to you?" Carol asked, one rainy Wednesday after they'd been working together for nearly two weeks. "Kyle I can understand, but why you?"

"Crazy, isn't it?" Jessica replied. She well knew why Joe had done it—he'd said in his letter that he'd wanted her to help Kyle.

As if Kyle would even let me help him, she thought, sipping her cappuccino. But she looked at Carol and smiled. "Maybe because Joe knew me from being a physical therapy client."

"Amazing what a young pretty girl can do with an old coot."

Jessica laughed so hard, she snorted coffee. Old Joe, thinking of her that way? *Right.*

"I knew Kyle growing up," Jessica said, by way of an explanation.

Carol's expression turned sour. "He doesn't say much, does he, outside of barking orders?"

"Umm…" Jessica wasn't going to gossip or betray Kyle—not for anything.

"Did you know that Patrick doesn't like him?" Carol confided, leaning closer. "He says Kyle treats him like he's in the Marines."

"Kyle is a Marine," Jessica said, nibbling on one of Carol's homemade cookies. "He's not active duty, true, but I'm told it never leaves your blood. Besides, I'm working on Patrick—I asked him to be patient with Kyle."

"Nothing's working right in this rink," Carol said nonchalantly, now that it was established Jessica wasn't going to gossip with her. "I think it's frustrating Kyle."

Interesting. Jessica stopped chewing.

"Did you know he's skating in the morning?" Carol asked. "Five o'clock with some injured soldiers. Patrick thinks that Kyle wants to expand that to take over the figure-skating rink. He thinks that's all Kyle cares about."

Jessica's jaw fell open. "I didn't know that," she let slip out.

Carol nodded. "Patrick told me. I'm not in early enough to see them all, but…"

Carol suddenly looked up, and her eyes widened. "Speak of the devil," she whispered.

It was Kyle. Jessica turned, shocked to finally see him. He looked damn good, too. He wore a green plaid shirt that perfectly matched his eyes.

She'd missed him, with his neat but bushy beard with the interesting copper highlights.

He glared at Carol. *What had he heard?* Jessica automatically thought.

"We're ending public skate an hour early today," Kyle announced. "Mechanical trouble."

He stood stiffly, with an angry expression. He didn't even look at Jessica.

"Hello, Kyle," she said.

He nodded shortly to her.

"Did you put out the liability forms today?" he asked Carol. "I don't see them here on the counter."

Carol glanced at Jessica. "Isn't she part-owner, too?" she asked boldly.

Jessica tried not to wince.

"Did you put out the liability forms today?" Kyle repeated to Carol.

"Of course I did." Carol leaned over and pulled them from beneath a stack of colorful brochures. She waved them in her hand. "I've worked here six years. With *Joe*," she emphasized.

Kyle's face turned red.

"Um, I'll assist Carol with the desk duties today," Jessica said gently. "We'll be fine."

"You don't have to do that," Kyle said.

Carol glanced at Jessica, a brow raised. Jessica just smiled at her.

"I've decided I do want to work around here, Kyle," Jessica said. "Can I help you in any way?"

"Sure," he snapped. "If you know how to re-build burned-out engines on the cheap, I could use the assistance."

He was frustrated with the rink. She knew it wasn't about her or Carol. Still, he didn't need to be harsh. Jessica shook her head at him.

Kyle ground his teeth and turned back to Carol. "Just send Patrick to me if he turns up again," he said quietly.

After he left, Carol sighed. "He can be so rude to everybody."

That wasn't the Kyle she'd known. Something was wrong. Jessica put down her coffee mug and went out to the hallway after him. But before she could call his name, he was already beyond the double doors that led to the twin arenas.

She stood still, not willing to go that far for him.

"How long do you think you'll last here?" Carol asked.

Jessica turned. Carol had followed her.

"Six months," Jessica answered her. "That's how long."

"Okay," Carol replied, nodding. "Patrick and I were both going to quit next week to work part time at Johnny's company, but if you want us to stay while you're here, we will."

Jessica blinked, horrified. "Of course I want you both to stay." She stared at Carol. "Honestly? You were going to leave?"

"Patrick's sick of Kyle barking orders at him. And you saw how he treats me. He's angry all the time."

Like Joe. Kyle is acting like Joe did.

Jessica put her hand to her head, stunned. She was sure Kyle had no idea he was doing that. The last person he'd want to behave like would be his stepfather.

KYLE STOMPED INTO the rink where he'd been directing Patrick how to use the edger machine to maintain the ice—at least, he had been until the kid had disappeared on him. Kyle was filled with frustration. He'd wanted to get out there and do it himself, as he had a hundred times in the past. But the job involved walking, in street shoes, onto the ice and working around the edge with a motorized cutting machine. He couldn't risk it with the prosthetic foot, because even though the technology had gotten pretty close, the sole of his prosthetic foot didn't flex like a human foot, and it was prone to slippage.

If he didn't have to worry about Carol or Patrick walking in on him, he might attempt the chore. But they were already gossiping about him, and he refused to give them more grist for the mill.

Of course he hadn't told Patrick about his prosthetic leg because it wasn't Patrick's business. The kid was infuriating—he took numerous cigarette breaks and constantly stopped to yap with Carol in the office instead of doing his work.

This was a head-scratcher to Kyle—how had Joe put up with the two of them? They weren't the most dedicated workers. Kyle missed the crew he remembered—Johnny David, for one, came to mind as their best leader. Joe used to have a real crack team.

Kyle had been feeling sentimental about missing morning formation on his military base, truth be told. Receiving—and giving—the day's orders, and actually having his subordinates carrying out what he said with a "Yes, sir," and no back talk. Even at the Department of Defense, he'd become used to structure and order. Weekly meetings. Time sheets. Goals. Repercussions.

Not at this rink.

Apparently a lot of things had fallen apart with Joe in the past few years. The rink had never been in such disgraceful shape.

Jessica had known Joe of late. Kyle itched to ask her what had been going on with him. But

Kyle didn't want to talk to her about his failed relationship with his stepfather.

He'd only realized how sick Joe must have been when he dug into the inner workings of the twin rinks. This place used to be Joe's pride and joy, and now it had all gone to crap.

Kyle pushed his hand over his head, took off his cap, then put it back on again. Nearly a month they'd been here, and he felt as though he was squandering time. Natalie had phoned him; she'd received the bank statements and she wanted to see him about his receipts. She'd quizzed him about revenue—what could he do to bring in more? How could he cut his expenses? He kept putting her questions off, distracted by the broken machinery, but he couldn't do that much longer.

It killed him, but he needed advice with bringing in money and managing his employees. And he knew exactly what Natalie would say.

Ask Jessica to help.

That could never happen. He was keeping the existence of his prosthetic leg from her. He was protecting her from having to do anything with him or this place, and that was that...

But then he drove into the parking lot the next morning at his usual time...and was shocked to see Jessica's orange Volkswagen idling in her regular spot, with pale gray exhaust curling upward in the early spring air. What was she doing here?

"Hi, Kyle!" Jessica leaned out the window. She was actually smiling at him. "I brought you some breakfast."

CHAPTER SIX

"WILL YOU JOIN ME?" Jessica asked Kyle.

She had to look up at him because his truck was so much higher than her small car. She'd parked in her usual spot and had left his spot open, but he'd chosen to take the space on the left side of her car, perhaps being thoughtful, because that made it easier for her to speak with him.

He leaned over his passenger seat and gazed down at her through his open window. "Is everything okay?" he asked softly.

Maybe he wasn't as angry with her as she'd thought. "Yes. I made you some muffins," she said, encouraged. "And brought coffee, like when we were teens." She held up the thermos. "I noticed from the sign-in sheets that you like to come in early, so…"

He looked at her a long moment, his eyes visibly softened. "Thanks. I'll come to you," he murmured.

Within moments, Kyle stood beside her driver's side window. He leaned down to peer in at her.

He'd trimmed his beard so that it was cropped

close to his face. She saw more clearly the contours of his strong jaw, the cheekbones she'd remembered so well. Something was happening to her heart, as if it was opening up to him, because she was suddenly happy—agenda or not—that she'd driven over so early to see him.

"You want me to get inside?" he asked.

She blushed, suddenly shy. She'd come with the intent to talk with him about Patrick and Carol. It seemed that priority had flown out the window.

"Yes, please," she said, patting the passenger seat beside her. She'd pushed the seat as far back as it would go, to accommodate his long legs. "I noticed that you're always eating fast food, so I made you a real breakfast. My specialty— English muffins, eggs, bacon and cheese, all in a sandwich. Do you like egg sandwiches?" she asked hopefully.

He smiled. She could actually see his lips now, with the beard being trimmed. He was quite handsome, more than she'd realized.

"It smells great," he said. "Thanks."

As he walked around the back of her car, she watched him in the rearview mirror, fascinated by him. When he reached the passenger door, she leaned over and pushed it open for him. Sometimes the lock stuck.

Awkwardly, he lowered himself and swung his

legs inside. He was just so large, and her car so tiny. She wasn't prepared for the way he filled her interior with his presence.

The door shut with a *clap*. They were alone, entirely enclosed together. Sharing the same air. She gulped. It wasn't yet daybreak so she'd left her interior light on, illuminating the two travel mugs that she'd arranged on the middle console. The spotlights from the rink shone brightly over-head, more on her face than on his. She felt Kyle's presence better than she could see him.

She turned to him, suddenly nervous. "I hope you like it. Usually, I only cook for myself. I made up the recipe when I was in college and had to drive to early classes."

She couldn't afford fast food then, and so had needed to be inventive, but she kept that part to herself.

She passed him the container from her back-seat, and he chose one of the sandwiches. She waited as he took a big bite.

He leaned forward, just enough into the light that she could see the pleasure break out on his face. "This is delicious. How'd you keep it hot?"

He noticed. She blushed again. It had been no mean feat to time her operation this morning just so. She'd had to wrap up everything and race from tiny kitchen to car to rink, hoping he arrived in the parking lot when she expected him to.

"It's my secret," she said, winking at him, and then took a sandwich herself. "I brought us hot coffee, too. There's a mug for you in the console."

"I keep forgetting to buy coffee for Joe's coffeemaker at home. I've been stopping at a drive-through place in the morning but today the line was long and I gave up. Thanks for this." He held up the mug.

She smiled at him. It was great to feel useful and appreciated. "Maybe we could do this once a week or something."

The words had slipped out. She hadn't planned to say that.

He nodded at her, his eyes seeking hers. He seemed to not have any ulterior motives other than the pleasure of her company.

As when they were teens, she felt like she could breathe with him.

They both ate their breakfast, the toasted muffins crunching as they chewed. After a time, Kyle wiped his mouth with his napkin. "I'm sorry I was sharp with you yesterday," he said.

"I know," she said simply. "I know that's not who you are."

He tilted his head at her. "How do you know that?"

She shrugged. "I think it's just the stress of everything. Joe talked like that. That's him saying those things, not you. You and Joe were both strong people, but you're thoughtful. You care about people."

Kyle had gone silent. His hands were cupped around the mug of coffee.

"I appreciate you protecting me, so much," she said quietly. "But...I think I'm ready to poke out my head a little. I'm okay with Patrick and Carol. I like their company."

He frowned, so she turned to him, putting her hand on his arm. "I'm okay with you, too." *Very okay.* More than she'd imagined.

"You know," he murmured, shifting in the seat, "you shouldn't have to be here at the rink at all. You're a damn good physical therapist, Jessica. That's what I've been hearing from people."

"You have?" she asked, surprised by him. "How have you heard?"

He shrugged. "I've asked around."

She laughed at him. "Flattery?" she teased. "I didn't expect that from you, of all people."

With his mouth full, he held up a muffin from the basket. "These are good."

"Thanks. You're good, too."

He scoffed. "Why do you say that?"

"I don't know. Maybe it's just fun to be here so early like this, when the rest of the world is still sleeping."

He nodded.

She could tell that he felt the same way. It filled her with a glow of happiness.

But when the glare of headlights flashed through the car, they both turned. Their moment was interrupted as two trucks headed into the lot.

"Those are my friends TJ and Oscar," Kyle said.

"The wounded-warrior skaters?"

"You know about that?"

"Carol told me. Were they in your unit?"

He was still for a moment, then nodded.

"That's cool. I wish I could watch you skate with them."

He looked down. Then his gaze flicked to hers. He seemed like he wanted to say something, so she waited.

"Well, I should be going." He reached for the door handle.

"Wait." She touched his arm. "Will you please trust me that I can be useful to the rink? On my terms, with what I'm good at?"

He stared at her. "Of course. Jess…yeah. I've always believed in you."

Once they had been friends of a sort, however awkward or unspoken.

She smiled sadly. "Thanks, I need that. I guess we're both learning how to be partners." She handed him the container of muffins. "Here. Go skate. These are for you to keep."

KYLE WAS STILL rattled by Jess's showing up to see him so early. Yet he'd gone from feeling uptight and worried about money and business and the rink to being more relaxed. Even jazzed. As when he'd been a kid, and there had always been something magical and inspiring to him about Jessica's presence.

He skated his pick-up game with his friends, then took his shower and dressed, as normal. But he was preoccupied with thinking about her.

She'd shown up to see him, for seemingly no reason other than to let him know she wanted to contribute. He really respected that. He found himself grinning like a fool.

On his way to the maintenance garage, he took a couple of the muffins she'd made to Patrick. "Here," Kyle said. "These are for you. Jessica made them. Thought you might be hungry."

"Yeah." Patrick's eyes lit up. "Thanks, Kyle."

"No problem."

Then Kyle headed to the front office. "Good morning," he said to Carol as she settled in behind her desk.

Carol stared at him bug-eyed. Come to think of it, Jessica was right. He didn't like that reaction—in no way was he like Joe. He didn't want his employees thinking that he was a jerk and rode them too hard. Just the thought turned his stomach.

"You're doing a good job," he said to Carol. "I appreciate you working for me."

She gave him a suspicious look. "Are you looking for Jessica?"

"No. But now that you mention it, is she around?"

"If her door is closed, then she's studying. She signed up for an online class last week. Something to do with biology or psychology or something like that."

"Thanks," he said, curious about what Jess was doing.

He swung out to Jessica's office, and sure enough, her door was closed. He placed his palm on the door, reluctant to leave just yet. She'd asked him to let her be useful. That meant she wanted to work with him.

"Kyle!"

Patrick came running through the glass doors, breathless. "There's a kid bleeding on the public ice!"

Holy hell. Kyle ran after Patrick as fast as he could on his walking leg. As he rounded the corner to the hockey rink, he saw a young girl sitting by the boards, holding her hand and wailing. A trail of blood across the ice confirmed the story.

A frantic woman Kyle guessed was the girl's frightened mom hovered over the girl, and beside them, with his small head buried in the woman's parka, was a boy who looked like a frightened little brother.

"Justin skated on my hand," the girl wailed. Kyle was thankful he hadn't sharpened the rental skates enough to really do damage, or the accident could've been worse.

"Let me see the wound," he said to the girl. Standing with her on the rubber matting, he gave her cut and bloody palm a cursory glance. He'd had enough basic first-aid training in the Marines to know that she didn't need stitches, but until it was bandaged, it would be messy.

He curled her hand into a fist and told her to hold it still in order to stanch the bleeding. Now he needed disinfectant and clean bandages.

"There's a first-aid kit in the front office," Kyle said to the woman. "I'd like you all to follow me."

"Aren't you going to call an EMT for my daughter?" the woman asked shrilly.

Inwardly, he cringed. The cut seemed like a minor childhood scrape. He hoped the lady didn't make a mountain out of a molehill, because as a small business owner, being sued was one of his prime worries. He also hoped Natalie had taken care of his liability insurance.

"Let's get your daughter cleaned up a bit first, all right?" He thought fast—Jessica was a credentialed medical professional. Should he bring her into this?

Will you please trust me?

"We have a skilled medical professional in the front office," Kyle said. "I'll bring your daughter to see her."

"But what if my daughter bleeds to death before we can get her help?"

"I assure you, ma'am, that won't happen." Not for the first time, Kyle wished he had a beeper or other method to easily get Carol's attention. But he bundled up the kid and helped her as best he could, praying he didn't stumble on his prosthetic foot.

Inside Carol's office, he paused beside the girl, who had stopped crying. Her mother was close behind, asking nonstop questions.

"I'm going to get Jessica," Kyle quietly informed Carol. "Will you please stay with this family until I come back?"

"Of course!" Carol rushed around the desk, and Kyle headed across the hall.

Jessica, I need you...

On the first knock, she opened her office door. Her face brightened at first, then turned quizzical. "What's wrong, Kyle?"

"There's a little girl hurt."

"I'm coming!" Jessica hurried into the front office with him. With one glance, she capably took in what had happened. "I'm a licensed physical therapist," she informed the woman. "I specialize in working with children. Is this your daughter?"

Kyle could have kissed her.

"Yes," the woman said eagerly.

"Wonderful, with your permission, it will only take a few minutes to get her fixed up. Honey, will you let me see your hand?" Jessica asked, switching her attention to the girl. "What's your name?"

"K-Kimmie."

"Kimmie, I bet you're about nine. Am I right?"

Kimmie nodded, her expression perking up.

"Okay, Kimmie, we're going to step into this room where there's a clean sink that has warm water. That way, I can clean your cut and put on a bandage. Then your mom is going to take off your skates and put on your sneakers for you so you'll be comfortable. Does that sound okay?"

Jessica glanced from both Kimmie to her mother.

"W-will it sting?" Kimmie asked.

"Oh, no," Jessica replied. "I only use nonstinging ointment." She whispered to the girl in a conspiratorial tone, "I'm a baby about stings myself."

Kimmie smiled at her, putty in Jessica's hands.

Nice to see I'm not the only one, he thought.

Even the mom had shrunk into the background, letting Jessica take charge.

Kyle followed them and stayed back in the

corner, out of their way. He probably could leave—he was no longer needed and he had tons to do, but he was fascinated watching Jessica in action.

Nothing fragile or lost about her, not when she was in her element. She had a way with people, a knack of getting them—especially kids—to trust her.

And then Jessica leaned over. She was bending over to retrieve some supplies from the lower first-aid shelf, and Kyle had to inhale. Beneath the baggy PT clothes she wore, Jessica had a great butt. He couldn't help staring, suddenly and massively attracted to her.

Wow. Where had that come from? This was neither the time nor place.

Not to mention, she was his business partner and was dating somebody else.

JESSICA TRIED TO ignore Kyle watching her from the corner, his eyes hooded. Ever since this morning, she'd been feeling an electricity when he was around her, and even a medical emergency with a little girl didn't disperse it.

Swallowing, determined to concentrate, she leaned over the sink and studied Kimmie's small palm under the bright lighting.

"It's a shallow cut," Jessica said. "I don't think it's serious, but it does need a bandage."

"What's your name?" asked the woman.

Jessica glanced up, stiffening. "Um, Jessica."

"Well, Jessica, Kimmie has been watching the figure skaters on TV this weekend, and she wants to try what they're doing. Could you please tell her to knock that off before she kills herself?"

Jessica's hand stilled on the bacterial ointment. It was late March and the world championships were always scheduled at about this time. She hadn't watched them in years, though.

Kyle's eyes locked with hers briefly, and she felt like she could read his mind. He was worried about her.

She inhaled. It was nice to know that somebody noticed and cared, so she gave him a quick smile.

She glanced back at Kimmie's palm, focusing on spreading ointment on the cleaned skin. The girl deserved her concentration. She expertly opened the bandage and dressed the wound.

"There, you're all set." She contemplated telling the girl to mind her mother, but Jessica wasn't that much of a hypocrite.

While she helped the girl up from the chair, Kyle gestured discreetly to her by tilting his head. In his deep voice, he asked, "Could I talk to you for a minute, Jess?"

She nodded, following him a few steps away from Kimmie and her mom. Kyle was so tall, she had to look up at him. He stood close to her, she could smell the soap he'd showered with, presumably after his skating session this morning.

"Thanks," he murmured to Jessica. "You did a good job with our emergency."

She hadn't expected that from him at all.

"Are you okay?" he murmured. "Your face is pale."

She decided to make a joke of it. "I wasn't sure if our insurance was paid up."

He cocked his head. "You know about that?"

"I'm in the healthcare business," she said breezily.

She flicked a glance at Kimmie's mom, leaning over her daughter. Judging from the body language, she seemed to be berating her daughter quietly.

"I'll finish up here," Jessica murmured to Kyle. "You don't need to stay."

"That's fine." But Kyle made no movement to leave.

Jessica went back to Kimmie, who was wiping tears from her cheeks. Kimmie's mother hissed at her in low tones. It reminded Jessica of her own mom.

"What were you trying to do, sweetie?" Jessica casually asked Kimmie as she wiped down the sink and washed her own hands.

"I wanted to jump," Kimmie said stubbornly. "But then I fell. That's when Justin crashed into me."

"The people you see on television have had lots of practice," Jessica said gently to Kimmie. "Many, many hours dedicated to this one sport." *With coaches and choreographers and off-ice training,* she added silently.

"Can you skate?" Kimmie asked. "Could you show me what to do?"

"No, I don't think so," Jessica murmured.

KYLE HATED TO admit it, but he felt bad for Jessica. She'd visibly stiffened at the mom's reaction to her daughter.

Kyle didn't always pick up on these kinds of things, but with Jessica, the more he got to know her, the more he was learning what to look for.

He leaned in closer, eavesdropping.

"I wanted to sign her up for learn-to-skate," the mom said to Jessica, "but there isn't a program yet this winter."

"I'm sure it will be coming," Jessica murmured. She finished washing her hands and tossed out the paper towels.

"The rink was closed for s-o-o-o long," Kimmie said. "I've been waiting all winter to practice."

"The only other rink is too far of a drive for us," her mother told her.

"I wanted to do one of those twirly jumps in the air," Kimmie insisted.

"She's fearless," her mother told Jessica. "And reckless."

Jessica's mouth worked. Finally she said, "Okay. I think you should start with trying to glide first, Kimmie."

"That's easy. I can already do that."

Jessica was silent a moment. "Did you try gliding on one foot first, and then the other foot?" She demonstrated in her street shoes.

Kimmie watched intently. "How did you do that?"

Jessica paused. To Kyle, she looked pale again. Blinking fast, she took a breath.

"Are you a coach?" the mother asked. "I haven't seen you here before."

Jessica shook her head. Kyle wondered if he should step in.

"Do you know how to skate?" Kimmie repeated.

"I used to," Jessica answered. "But I can't anymore. I'm really sorry, honey."

To Kyle, skating was like riding a bike. If a person learned as a kid, then they never forgot how. Even with one leg, Kyle still remembered how. There was a guy in his unit who'd never skated as a kid, and Kyle had taught him, too, so even adults could learn. It was fun. There was nothing like the wind in your face, especially when you didn't have to do it perfectly. When you could just do it like a kid and have fun...

Jessica can't have fun with it.

He paused, sad for her. She used to have such love for the sport. She protested against it now, but Kyle couldn't be wrong. He'd seen it in her back then.

She'd been so happy at one time—his dream girl. Everybody's dream girl. Once, a camera crew had come to the rink because Jessica was going to be featured in a television commercial for the upcoming national championships. They were all in awe of her. She had handled it just as naturally as she had just put a bandage on a young girl's palm. Jessica was that special. And here she was, unable to give some simple answers that he knew she could spout off in her sleep?

But the not-so-kind mother turned to Jessica, and again Jessica turned away. He saw now that her negative body language had to do with the mom, not with the curious girl who wanted to skate.

Kyle had always known Jessica's mother was pushy. Nasty at times, especially to him, but never to Joe—she knew where her bread was buttered, as the expression went. Joe had given her a deal on private ice time. He let Jessica's mother have the run of the place. He'd even renovated a room especially for her daughter's morning warm-up sessions.

Kyle used to sneak-watch Jessica sometimes. Her mother was always present, always hovering. She let the coach have control of the lessons, but who knew what was being said at home. He should have thought of all this when she'd been telling him about emancipating herself from her mother. He'd been distracted by his anger that day, though. By learning that he'd never really hurt her.

Kyle left the group and went back to the maintenance garage. He should just be happy that Jessica had handled a sticky situation for him. There would likely be no lawsuits. Nothing that would cost him money or hurt his profitability. He had to stop thinking about this woman, because the thoughts he was having about her wouldn't do either of them any good.

"BUT I WOBBLE too much when I do that," Kimmie said to Jessica.

The girl had dragged her back into the hallway. Kimmie's mother had left, walking outside to take a phone call, and she'd dragged Kimmie's brother with her.

Jessica had wanted to go back inside her private office, had wanted to forget about helping Kimmie, but Kimmie had dogged her until Jessica had shown her again how to glide.

"Okay, just this one little hint," Jessica relented.

She balanced on one foot. Bent her knee, showing Kimmie how to distribute her weight without cocking her hip out to the side. Kimmie mimicked her perfectly.

"See, you can do it. That's what you need to do when you're on the ice," Jessica said.

"I know," Kimmie said excitedly. "I watched some videos on YouTube. But when I tried to do it on the skates, my feet flopped over."

"Show me the skates you're using."

Kimmie went back to the front desk where her mom had left her skates and brought them to Jessica.

Jessica stared at them, appalled. She hadn't noticed their condition in the excitement surrounding Kimmie's cut hand. Nobody could skate in equipment like this. The hand-me-down skates were well past their prime. The ankles flopped and no longer provided any support. No wonder the girl couldn't stand upright.

I outgrew and gave away skates a hundred times better than these, Jessica thought.

"Let me find you another pair from our rental shop," Jessica told the girl. They had to have a pair in better shape than this. "Come with me."

Jessica took Kimmie's hand and resolved to have a talk with Kyle. Whoever was fitting the rental skates needed some professional help.

They headed down the hallway. When they faced the glass double doors and the bare—now painted-over—spot on the wall where her poster once hung, Jessica paused. With a last *should I or shouldn't I?* moment, she finally squared her shoulders and pushed through the doors, heading toward the junction between the twin ice surfaces. The colder air, closer to the ice, hit her all at once, but Jessica gritted her teeth and kept striding.

The skate-rental stand was halfway along the corridor between the front office and the big hockey rink. Jessica had never actually been inside the rental stand—she'd had no reason for it. She'd always owned her own skates, custom-purchased for her foot's measurement, ordered from an experienced boot fitter down near Boston.

With Jessica's skates, the blades were sold separately and special-ordered from England. Her blades wore down faster than the boots; she only got a couple of dozen sharpenings from them, at most, and they never lasted more than a few months at a time. She couldn't imagine skating in such a broken-down pair of ice skates as Kimmie had shown her.

Jessica stood before the skate-rental stand, not sure how to get inside. The door was locked.

"There you are!" Kimmie's mom joined them, breathing faster from the exertion of the walk. Her young son was firmly in tow, hand clasped in hers.

"I'm finding Kimmie a better-fitting pair of rental skates," Jessica explained. "What size shoe is your daughter?"

"She's a four."

That meant Kimmie was a size two in skates.

"The boot should fit her like a glove," Jessica said. "Next time, put your daughter in tights, if possible. Since she's interested in taking figure-skating lessons, I'll find her a pair with laces. I'll show her how to tie them tightly to give her good ankle support."

"But there are no figure-skating lessons available here."

"Well, I'll talk to Kyle about adding a learn-to-skate program."

"Who's Kyle?"

"He's my part—" Jessica paused. He really was her partner. She felt it. She wasn't alone. A warm glow inside her chest, she glanced up and down the corridor for Kyle.

He rounded the corner, just when he was needed. Relieved, she paused, one hand on the doorknob. She couldn't help staring.

He wore what she was beginning to see was his work uniform: blue jeans, worn and snug in interesting places. A heavy navy hooded sweatshirt. A baseball cap with the Marines logo. Work boots.

When he saw her on this side of the double doors, his taciturn expression changed to one of surprise. "Jess?"

"I need the key to the rental-skate room." She couldn't tear her gaze from his. In this lighting, his eyes were pale green, like spring grass.

He cocked his head. "Are you sure?"

"I need to fit Kimmie's skates for her."

He glanced at Kimmie and her mother. "They asked for a size four."

"I know." Taking the key from him, she unlocked the door and walked inside without hesitation.

The smell of old leather and dust was strong. Feeling along the wall, she found the light switch. Row upon row of shelves full of skates of all kinds greeted her eyes. She walked along the metal racks, searching for any indicator of size. At the end of the aisle, she put out her finger and collected a streak of dust. "It's dirty in here," she said.

"I know," he answered in a low voice, "I've been going through the facility, room by room, making progress, but I haven't gotten here yet."

She nodded, sorry she hadn't helped him with this task earlier.

"There are the size-four skates." Kyle pointed to a shelf.

"Where are the twos?"

Kyle pointed to another rack. A label was marked "Size 2" in faded, stenciled black paint. Scanning the shelf, she saw that there was a mishmash of styles. Lace-up, Velcro, hockey, figure skates. Boys' black styles were mixed up with girls' colors, white and pink.

"Joe used to collect lots of different types of skates for people to choose from," Kyle said. "When it got crowded in the rink, you could get twenty kids all needing the same size skate."

"That makes sense." She picked up a white, lace-up figure-skating pair with toe picks on the blades, thinking they'd work for what Kimmie needed, but when she loosened the laces, she noticed a patch of white mold inside the leather.

Jessica shuddered and dropped them. "When I think of all the perfectly good skates that I tossed out…"

Kyle picked up the pair that she'd dropped. "Why, are these bad?"

"They're not hygienic. I doubt any of them are. Kyle, we need to buy all new skates. If we're going to have public skate, if we're going to let kids rent skates—"

"That's why I'm not charging for the rentals," Kyle explained. "There's no income generated here. This is just a service I have for kids who don't own their own skates. Not every kid is wealthy, you know."

Was that a dig against her? Jessica's mother had spared no expense when it came to her training.

"I know I was privileged," she said quietly. "This isn't news to me."

He took a breath. "Jess, I'm not talking about you."

"Aren't you?"

KYLE DIDN'T KNOW what to do. Sooner or later, it seemed, he always made a mistake with her. Even their teen "friendship" had been awkward at best. And it wasn't just on her end, it was his. He didn't always converse well with people. He felt stiff and uncomfortable most of the time. With Jessica he was getting better, but this was an emotionally charged subject for her.

He took the pair of skates from her. He found a clean cloth and a can of antiseptic spray, and he cleaned the leather as best he could. Then he took a dry rag and ran it along the dusty blades. And since they were as dull as old butter knives, he brought the skates over to the sharpening machine, set them up quickly and gave them a couple of passes on the electric grinding wheel. He'd done this a thousand times as a kid.

Jessica watched him. He didn't remember her ever watching him sharpen skates before. As a rule, the figure skaters in the club didn't let him touch their blades. They drove down to Massachusetts to get their skates sharpened by a figure-skating specialist.

Carefully, Kyle pivoted. Held out the girl's skates to her.

"Thank you," Jessica said quietly.

"You're welcome."

She took the skates out to Kimmie. Went down on her knees, loosened the laces, took off one of the girl's layers of heavy socks, put her foot inside. Spoke in low tones and showed her how to lace up the boots as tightly as possible. She asked the girl to stand. Tested her toes.

"The toes should be touching the end of the boot," she explained to Kimmie's mother. "Because it's a sport of balance, it's important that her feet have good control over the blade."

Then she showed Kimmie how to stand, to hold herself on the ice. How to bend her knees so they went over her toes, and not roll to the inside. She showed her how to keep her back straight and her chin up. Her arms out to the sides.

"Are you sure you're not available to teach lessons?" the mother asked again.

"No," was all Jessica said.

"It's a shame. You're the first person I've seen here who knows what she's doing."

Jessica turned to Kyle. "Do we have somebody who can give basic lessons?"

Kyle shook his head. "The figure-skating ice isn't ready yet." *The compressor is broken.*

"I know, but can't we have a program during the public-skate time?"

"I'd like to," he admitted, "but I don't know anybody."

She shook her head. "I'm sorry," she said to the girl. "I need to get back to the office now."

"Thank you for the bandage," Kimmie said. "And the skates. These feel better."

"Then you can keep them." Jessica glanced at Kyle, as if asking him not to tell her she couldn't do that.

He didn't. But if she gifted skates to every kid who came along looking for help, she'd empty out his stock.

Crossing her arms, Jessica headed back to her office.

He glanced over to the ice surface. Kimmie was stepping back out there, determined. Three other adult skaters were on the ice. A retired gentleman was doing laps on hockey skates, listening to a book on tape, as he'd told Kyle. A woman was practicing old-time figure eights in the corner. And another woman stood at the boards near the door, busy strapping on wrist guards. Alert, she smiled when she saw Kyle gazing at her through the glass.

He approached her and carefully leaned into the doorway to speak. "Would you, uh, mind keeping an eye out for that little girl? Give me a signal if you think she needs any help?"

"Where'd her mom go?" the woman asked.

"I think she's running around after her other kid."

The woman nodded. As a rink owner's son, Kyle had well known about some parents who would drop their kids off and leave them unsupervised. The practice was frowned upon, but what could he do?

Jessica would be the perfect person to teach a class of kids, he thought. She'd been great with Kimmie. It killed him that her past experiences had caused her such pain that she didn't even want to go out and instruct Kimmie for a few minutes.

Help her, Natalie had suggested.

But short of writing her the weekly check so Jessica could please her damn boyfriend, Kyle didn't see what else he could do.

He headed back to the skate-rental room to lock up, feeling impotent and jealous and hating it. Today, he'd single-handedly fixed a Zamboni, a broken air-conditioning duct and two stopped-up sinks, but he couldn't figure out how to deal with his feelings for Jessica.

"May I talk to you?"

He nearly jumped. Jessica again. She'd waylaid him inside the doorway. Her arms were crossed, her glossy hair up in a ponytail, and she wore that pink sweater that looked soft to the touch.

"Kyle, I know we originally agreed that you would handle the decision making. But when kids are affected, I feel I must give you my strong opinion." She set her chin. "We really need to order new rental skates for the kids."

"I'd like to help you," he said patiently. "But I don't see how."

"I do. I'll ask Carol for the phone number of the supply company Joe used. I'll call them and have the skates delivered."

"No," he said flustered. "That's not what I meant."

"Could you explain it to me?" She uncrossed her arms.

He let out a breath. He couldn't expect her to understand about their finances, because he hadn't shared the numbers with her yet. "Well, we can't order skates because we don't have money in the budget."

"But aren't the kids more important than that? I mean, I appreciate that you gave Kimmie a stop-gap solution, but the rest of those skates are old, they're unhygienic and, in my opinion, unfit for use by children." She set her chin again.

"It would cost a fortune to replace them all," he said, flabbergasted. "Even if I wanted to, which I do, we can't afford it."

"It's a hazard," Jessica pressed. With a gleam in her eyes, she said, "Didn't the lawyer caution you about watching for liability issues?"

"Well, yeah." That wasn't fair. "How about if we don't offer any rental skates at all? Then we won't have that problem."

"And what happens if a kid gets invited to a birthday party, for example, and doesn't have a pair that fits?"

Birthday parties—this was why he needed Jessica! He hadn't even thought of offering those. He'd been thinking strictly in terms of hockey as far as his revenue-stream went.

"Do you think we could do birthday parties?" he asked aloud.

Her jaw clamped. He'd pushed her too far. But after a moment, she said softly, "Kids would love birthday parties."

"It's a great idea, Jessica. We should do it."

She looked at him, surprised, and...dare he think it? *Pleased.*

"Kids are important to me," she said hesitatingly, confiding in him. A wistful look passed across her face. "I wish I could give every kid a great childhood."

"Because yours wasn't?"

"I was actually very lucky in many ways," she murmured. "I had the best of everything."

"Where's your mom now?" he asked.

"Kyle, can we please order those skates?" She shifted on her feet. "Safety is important to me. I don't want anyone hurt."

He didn't take offense to her ignoring his question. He knew her mother was a sore spot with her. But she shut down so easily.

Maybe he did, too.

"How many sizes do you want me to order?" he asked quietly.

"Um." She looked surprised that he'd yielded. "Sizes twelve through seven at least, please. And half sizes, too."

"Fifteen pairs," he reckoned.

"No, we'll need multiple pairs per size."

"Look, Jess, I can give you two pairs per size. That's thirty pairs, at about fifty dollars each, I'm guessing, that's fifteen hundred dollars." *The cost of a generator.* Dammit, he'd be in the hole now.

He didn't want to be in the hole. It made Natalie frown at him, and he suspected it might make the bank think he'd be a bad business bet. Then he'd have trouble getting loan money to buy Jessica out at the end of August.

"Thank you, Kyle," Jessica said, smiling at him with shining eyes.

His resolve just crumpled. He had the fear he'd give her anything she wanted just to earn a smile like that again.

Still smiling, she turned to leave, but then changed her mind and turned around again. "I'll help you when the skates come in. I'll clean out the rental room and organize the pairs on the shelves."

"You don't have to do that," he said softly.

"I know, but I want to."

"Okay." He paused. "I'd...like that."

She met his gaze, a long look that was private between him and her. Her liquid brown eyes searched his.

Once in a while, she gazed at him like that, and when it happened it was like Cupid's arrow piercing his heart. He could probably go weeks on a smile like that.

Shaking it off, he headed back to the main office. Automatically, he glanced at the sign-in sheet. Two kids and three adults had paid their fees this past hour. Barely enough money to cover the electricity cost of the lights shining overhead.

"We need more revenue during the school-day hours," he muttered, then went into the file cabinet behind Carol's workstation and riffled through the old papers.

"Need help finding something?" Carol asked, uncharacteristically. Maybe because he'd said "good morning" to her. *Hunh.*

"Thanks, but I got it," he answered. And he pulled out the folder for the skate supply company.

Walking slowly, he retreated to his corner locker room. He took out his cell phone, plus his personal credit card, and prepared to go into debt for the sake of a woman who cared about children's safety. But before he could make the call, a slip of paper fell out of the folder and fluttered to the floor.

With difficulty, he stooped and picked it up. It was a receipt for a pair of skate boots and a pair of blades. "Jessa Hughes," read the neat printing. The receipt was dated the last year she'd skated, before she'd been hurt, before she'd cried on national television.

He closed his eyes. He still remembered every detail. He would never forget.

Joe was always so angry and harsh toward him, but on that day it had hurt even more. Kyle's hockey team had been on a winning streak, gunning for the state finals, they'd lost in a heartbreaker that afternoon and Kyle had been crushed. He'd returned home from a long weekend trip away, needing sympathy, and instead received a harsh order to report back to the rink.

"Resurface the ice in the figure-skating rink," Joe had said. That was where Jessica was preparing for the national championships. It was a big competition for her, it was an Olympic year, and everybody on that side of the twin rinks was on edge. Jessa Hughes was reigning World Junior Champion. There was pressure, endorsements, sponsors. Everyone expected her to make the Olympic team. There was no reason she shouldn't.

And stupid Kyle, stupid seventeen-year-old Kyle, maybe disappointed with his own losses, with his own team's failure, with Joe's attitude of not caring—he hadn't even cared enough to show up for their important game—had, in a flash of a second, done one stupid thing. He'd flooded the ice with water, deliberately, just to make a mess and get back at Joe.

A petty thing. Kyle was no hero. A minor villain, not even a successful one, because he'd secretly nursed a heavy crush on Jessa, as had mostly every other boy in town.

She'd stepped out on the ice. And almost immediately, he'd heard her go down. Skidding across that puddle of water with a cry. When he'd dared to look, his heart sinking, he saw her soaked tights first. He could still see the water stains on both her knees.

When she stood up, she'd cried. She'd really

been hurt, even if now she claimed she hadn't been. Why else would she have pulled herself from Olympic contention?

Two weeks later were the national championships, the final round. Jessica led after her short program. She was a shoo-in for the Olympic team. But she couldn't put weight on her knee. Her slight, thin body had just given out on her.

The whole town had been watching her on a cable feed that night. Wallis Point had one movie theater, in a restored antique building, and they'd sold special tickets to watch the local skater who trained at their twin rinks. Jessa Hughes had put their little town of Wallis Point on the national map.

He could still remember the sound of silence in that theater. The close-up on the big movie screen had been on Jessica's face, pained, as tears rolled down her cheeks. As she pointed to her knee. Her legendary figure-skating mother, distraught, had stood and left the arena, waving the cameras away. Her coach had spoken for Jessica. "Years of dedicated training...the loss of a dream..."

Unlike her mother, Kyle had stayed and listened to the commentary afterward. He'd forced himself to stay until the bitter end, until all the competitors had skated and the winners were declared. The Olympic team assembled, and Jessa Hughes's name was not on the list.

She'd dropped out of sight. He knew now where she'd been, but back then, he'd searched for her. The cottage on the beach that Jessica and her mother had rented was vacated. Jessica never went to school. It was February of his senior year in high school.

"You did this to her," Joe said to him, soon after it happened, and Kyle didn't argue. Though he did protest when Joe informed him that there was no longer a place for him at his rink.

In late May, Kyle graduated high school. Tired of fighting with Joe, two weeks later, he was in Parris Island, training to be a Marine.

Kyle sat on the bench. He'd been standing on his prosthetic leg for so many hours now his leg was sore. But he forced himself to look at that slip of paper in his hand, that old receipt for a pair of ladies' figure skates.

Jessa Hughes.

Kyle phoned the supply company and ordered the kids' skates, just as he'd promised her. And while he was on the phone, he ordered her a pair, too. The same brand, same size, same color, same blade as she'd been used to. Her professional pair cost him as much as all the kids' rental skates put together.

Dumb of him, maybe. He didn't know why or what for. He only knew that at some point, within these remaining months, he wanted to get her back on the ice.

He needed to do it, because she was wounded—every bit as much as he was. Except while his wound was physical, hers was surely emotional.

There was something healing about skating purely for fun. In the privacy of the morning hours there was that peace, that pure pleasure. The exhilaration of the muscles being used, a sense of health and well-being. It made him walk a bit taller, breathe a bit deeper, exhale more calmly.

If he could help her feel that, then maybe it would help him, too. He was fast seeing how important that was to him.

CHAPTER SEVEN

TWO WEEKS LATER, when Jessica had an hour free between her rink time and her physical therapy jobs, she took a long walk on the beach to clear her head. It was mid-April, and there was still some snow, but spring was on its way.

She wrapped her arms around her winter coat and pulled the collar up higher, then tugged her soft woolen scarf around her face.

The waves rolled in from the sea. Though cold—typical New England spring weather—it was a sunny afternoon, and in the distance she could see the offshore islands.

It was a confusing time for her. Jessica had spent six weeks at the twin rinks and her life was turning upside down.

The place was growing on her. Kyle, too.

Seeing him in the early mornings had become a brightening point in her life. She'd brought him breakfast five more times, and he'd brought her donuts once. They were fantastic donuts, freshly made from Donuts on the Beach.

As a girl, she'd never been allowed to eat at

the famous Wallis Point donut shop. Too bad, because they were delicious—gooey and hot and sweet with sticky melted sugar—and she'd licked her fingers to get every last taste. She'd laughed a long time with Kyle that morning. But it helped her get through the days. As always, she avoided going near the ice surfaces.

Jessica took out her phone and glanced at it again. Sebastien had sent her a text message this morning: Coming home on Thursday night.

She put her phone away, not sure how she felt about it.

Without Sebastien's pushing her into this partnership with Kyle, she wouldn't even be at the twin rinks. Honestly, she'd been furious with Sebastien about that at first, but now...it had only done her good.

On impulse, she took out her phone and called Sebastien. His number rang, but he didn't pick up. Maybe he was on a sales call. Or in training again. He worked such long hours—working for their future, as he often reminded her.

She stopped in front of his rented cottage. Curious, she walked round to the front, but his car wasn't there. Of course it wasn't—she knew it wouldn't be. So why was she checking?

Next door, Sebastien's neighbor, Ed, was locking the front door and heading down to his car. His wife, Edie, was with him. Jessica waved to the retired couple with the similar names, aptly paired, considering they did everything together.

"Hi, Jessa," Edie called.

Edie was one of the only people that Jessica never corrected about her name. The woman was in her nineties. Jessica didn't feel it would be respectful, and besides, she liked the older woman. Edie was polite—never asked Jessica about her past. Never spoke of skating.

Jessica liked people like Edie. People with "company manners." She was never comfortable with those who spilled their guts to anyone, indiscriminately. And, unfortunately, in Jessica's line of work, while she was in the midst of massaging a back or a knee or a wrist, people often felt compelled to tell her not only their life stories, but their deepest, innermost secrets.

"It's nice to see you," Jessica replied to Edie, waving back. On impulse, she headed over for a longer chat. She just wanted to watch them together. It was like viewing a master class in how to manage a long-term relationship.

"Is there anything we can help you with, dear?" Edie asked.

"No. I'm just on a break, taking a walk."

"Perfect day for it," Ed remarked. "Did you find any driftwood on the beach?"

Ed had noticed that Jessica liked to pick up shells, smooth rocks, interestingly shaped driftwood washed in by the tides. "Not today." She'd been thinking too much.

"Sebastien mentioned that you're working at the twin rinks," Ed said.

Jessica went still. "He told you that?"

"Yes. Sebastien said the rink will be open for a few more months but will be sold by the end of summer. Is that true? I told him it was a shame."

"It is," Jessica murmured.

"Ah, well, it's difficult to run a business in the current climate."

That sounded like something Sebastien would say. Jessica kept the smile on her face for Ed's sake.

"I think it's nice you're back at the rink, helping out the community," Edie chimed in. "Our boys loved skating there when they lived at home." She shared a smile with her husband. "That was before your time, though." She directed the last comment to Jessica.

Jessica nodded, but she couldn't stop thinking about what Sebastien had said to them. Why was he talking about her working at the rink? He knew she wanted to keep these six months as contained as possible.

She waited until the couple's car pulled out, then stood and gazed between Sebastien's beautiful house and the homey cottage next door where Ed and Edie lived.

She wanted so badly to have what Ed and Edie had. But Jessica was a daughter of a broken home with a celebrity mom, always on the fly. A dad her mom had been divorced from before he died young. Jessica had always felt alone at heart, and she was tired of it.

She thought of Kimmie—the girl at the rink who'd wanted Jessica's help. Jessica had wanted to help her, too, had done the best she could, but deep down, she knew it wasn't enough. Jessica thought about Kyle, the one person left who brought together her past and her present. She looked forward to seeing him in the morning and lingered before she left at noon. His attitude had been improving so much—trying to help and be kind to all the staff in his gruff way.

Maybe Maureen had said it best—Kyle was shy. Maybe even socially awkward. At heart, Jessica wasn't. She'd just been traumatized for so long by her past experience in "breaking up" with her mother that she'd closed herself off to relationships that demanded too much from her. She'd always felt scared that, if she wasn't careful, she would get steamrolled by someone else's agenda again. That she would fall apart, lose herself.

Wow. Was *that* why Sebastien complained about her holding herself back from him?

Jessica very much doubted that Edie held back anything important from Ed. They worked in such harmony together.

Maybe it was time she got over her fear.

Kyle was back in town, getting over his anger at Joe, wasn't he?

Sighing, she headed back to her car. Until now, she'd been helping Kyle because it was making her happy and giving her something constructive to do, even though it did go against what Sebastien had suggested.

Sebastien wanted Kyle to build a new rink. Jessica was pretty sure Kyle wanted to keep his old rink. She didn't understand why—surely he had bad memories of the place, too, even more than she did. But if bringing the twin rinks to their former glory was what he wanted, then she would respect that. When Sebastien came home, she would have an honest talk with him about it, first thing.

WHEN KYLE CAME in the next morning, he automatically looked for Jessica's orange Volkswagen. But, of course, it was Wednesday, and Jessica never came for breakfast on Wednesday because Tuesday evenings she worked late at Wallis Point Physical Therapy.

Disappointment engulfed him. He'd gotten to rely on her company, and he knew that wasn't good.

He glanced at his watch.

Oh-five-hundred. Kyle's time with Oscar and TJ.

Stepping carefully down from the cab, he reached into the bed of his truck and grabbed his hockey gear, including a new stick he'd bought. Maybe he'd try and get a pro shop up and running at their rink. Not an offshoot from a national chain, but a little guy, local and independent.

Pausing, Kyle took out a notepad and made a note to talk to Natalie about that. He had a meeting with her at ten-hundred-hours. He had a bunch of stuff to talk to her about; namely, she'd promised to coach him on how to keep the books.

He unlocked the back door of the rink and headed in. They had an hour to skate before the ice was leased to an early-morning men's pickup league that he'd signed. That sale had made him proud—made him think that maybe he could make the rinks profitable without Jessica's help on the figure-skating side.

He went into his locker room—his private office—and changed into his hockey gear. He used a different prosthetic foot for the hockey skate than he did with his street shoes. He kept that prosthesis in his locker. Each switch involved changing socks, changing the gel covering. It took extra time, but he was used to it.

Still, he paused. He always paused at the sight of his injury. He'd been told by guys who'd lived with this a lot longer than he had that in time he would get used to it. But Kyle couldn't imagine that day. His stomach still clenched at the sight.

He was usually so stoic. He hadn't cried, not when it had happened, not when he sat there in the ruined Humvee, seeing the torn-off door, knowing that something was wrong. A part of his brain had just shut off. He'd done what he needed to do, always had. Just methodically take one small action at a time. *Don't think. Just do.*

He stood and faced the mirror in the attached bathroom. He was all kitted up. He looked like any hockey player. No one would know he was missing part of a limb.

He grabbed his new stick, taped it up and headed out to the ice. TJ and Oscar were already there. Kyle had cleared the ice last night before he'd closed the place, so the surface condition wasn't great—a consequence of letting it sit over-night—but it was decent enough to play on. Kyle flipped the switch for just one overhead light, a concession to saving electricity.

TJ had brought three other guys; two had driven up from Massachusetts and one down from Maine. TJ was more social and knew more people than Kyle did.

They had a great pick-up game. Kyle caught sight of himself in the reflection of the glass a few times, and he looked okay, like a normal skater, although maybe his glide was jerkier and slower than it should have been. He couldn't feel the ice with his prosthetic foot. It was like skating on stilts on one side. But he was damned grateful he could skate at all. He knew he was lucky. Some guys—and gals—had lost more than one leg, and that was much tougher to get around with. TJ had lost his leg above the knee, making his journey more challenging than Kyle's and Oscar's. He'd needed a lot more rehab and training to use his "bionic leg" as TJ called it.

This was high-tech stuff—real expensive and needed to be adjusted every so often with the computer. They were military people, so at least they had much of their bills covered.

Kyle snagged a pass and slapped the puck toward the open net. TJ reacted for the block, but went down hard as Oscar playfully checked him instead.

TJ's knee twisted sideways, and if a person didn't know he wore a prosthesis, they would think he had suffered a gruesome injury.

TJ got up laughing, and with help from Oscar, adjusted his leg. Kyle shuddered. He did everything possible to remain upright, always. No friggin' way was he falling down and risking that happening. "Hey, you want to try out for a traveling league?" Oscar asked him.

"Not possible," Kyle said. "I gotta stay here, I can't go on the road." He spent every waking moment at these rinks. He wanted to make the business profitable. He wanted that loan from the bank to buy Jessica out in August.

He glanced at the clock—Jessica would be in soon. She'd never come out to the ice surface, had never watched him play, but he wasn't taking any chances.

Quickly, he headed to his locker room, took a much-needed shower. Wiped down his hockey skates, his equipment. Put everything into the locker, locked it. Went through the steps of putting on his prosthetic—first the lotion on his skin, then the neoprene gel sock, the second sock, the prosthetic and the adjustment of the sock over the leg.

He had to be so damn careful. Early on, he'd had a staph-infection scare. He didn't want to go through that again.

Before he left the locker room, he dressed in something appropriate to meet with the lawyer— a button-down shirt with a pullover sweater. He spent two hours preparing the paperwork for Natalie that she'd requested. Then, on the way out, he headed over to the front office to let Carol know he'd be gone for an hour.

He went by Jessica's closed door, figuring she was inside, as usual. He was shocked when he rounded the corner and saw her at the entrance, standing above him, close to the top of a six-foot ladder.

Oh, hell. He stopped short, staring at her stupidly. He couldn't climb a ladder, but she didn't know that.

She smiled at him. "Hi, Kyle."

Her glossy brown hair in a ponytail, she'd bundled up in a heavy sweater—because the rink was cold and he was conserving heat. She looked as if she was attempting to wash the windows.

It was an item on his never-ending tick-list that needed to be handled. He stood before her, staring upward and feeling bleak, not knowing what to say.

Her cheeks were two bright pink spots. "Would you mind bringing that bucket up the ladder for me? It'll save me a trip."

He wished he could. God, he wished he could. "Uh…I'll get Patrick to help you."

She gave him a confused look. "That's okay, if you just—"

"I need to go to the lawyer's now," he interrupted, hating himself.

She hesitated before speaking. "To see Natalie?"

"Yeah." Maybe he should ask her to go, too? They were partners.

He wanted to shift feet, but with his leg, he couldn't do that. He gritted his teeth and fought to stand still.

"Why?" she asked him. "Is there something going on I should know about?"

"No." He felt bad that he wasn't being truthful with her, but he didn't know what to say.

If he asked her to go with him, then they would be sharing a ride, specifically in his truck, where he'd made adjustments with his pedals. Riding in the cab with him, she'd definitely become suspicious.

He held out his laptop case. "Natalie's husband is going to show me how to use accounting software that's specific to the rink business."

"Oh." Jessica backed down the ladder, then picked up the bucket of cleaning fluid, and with effort, trudged back up the ladder. "Okay. I guess you don't need me then."

I always need you. He clenched his jaw. This was torture, not being able to help her or to tell her why.

"I'll, uh, go find Patrick," he said again.

"No, I told Patrick he could take a break."

"Jess, that kid is always on break—"

But just then, the glass doors opened and a gray-haired couple entered. "Do you have walk-on sessions for ice dancers?" the woman asked them.

Jessica turned her face to the wall, so Kyle answered for them both. "Not yet, but we hope to soon. Try calling in another week or two. For now, we just have public ice."

"Can we dance on public ice?"

"Yes. Just no personal iPods, sticks, pucks, jumping and moves or spins with blades in the air."

"Sounds fine. Thank you." The couple headed toward the office.

When they were alone again, Jessica turned back to him, looking sheepish. "Sorry about that."

"No problem." They each had something to hide, but he was hiding from her, while she'd already been honest with him about her fears. He stared out at the parking lot.

"You should get going or the lawyer might charge you extra," she said lightly.

"Yeah," he mumbled. He knew she felt hurt.

It killed him, but there was nothing he could do about that. He headed out the door, where a gust of wind caught him on the landing, nearly knocking him off balance and off his leg. But he caught himself and headed down the walkway to his truck.

He passed Patrick, leaning on his shovel and taking a cigarette break.

"Help Jessica with the window cleaning in the front lobby," Kyle said by rote.

"She told me she wants to do it herself," Patrick returned sullenly.

"And I'm telling you to help her anyway." Kyle glanced back and saw Jessica, watching him from inside.

Ah, hell. "*Please*," Kyle said, turning back to Patrick. "*Please* help Jessica with her window washing as a favor to me. I didn't mean to snap at you, all right? I'm sorry."

"Okay, dude," Patrick said, nodding at him.

Miracle of miracles, Patrick picked up his shovel and headed toward Jessica.

TEN MINUTES LATER Kyle walked into Natalie's law firm with his laptop in hand. Her husband, Bruce, met him at the door.

"Come on back," Bruce said. "I've got an hour for lunch. I'd like to get you started."

Bruce led Kyle into the small conference room, the one in the back where Jessica and Sebastien had sat on the afternoon of the will reading.

"How complicated is this system you're gonna

be showing me?" Kyle asked, setting his laptop down on the conference table.

"Have you worked much with accounting packages before?" Bruce asked.

"On a large scale, but not for my own business." Carefully Kyle sat, pulling his chair in close to the table. "I'm proficient enough at the basics, though."

"You'll be fine, then." Bruce pulled up a chair beside him and held out a thumb drive. "Do you mind me installing the package on your laptop? The features are specialized for the rink business. We can start the setup today, then work some more with it next week. I can meet you during my lunch hours."

"Uh, Natalie told you I can't afford—?"

"It's gratis," Bruce said shortly. "This is me helping a veteran. I appreciate you guys. I was never in combat, so…"

"You're ex-military," Kyle said.

"Navy. By way of the Naval Academy."

Kyle nodded. He remembered that from Joe's funeral service. "What unit were you in?"

"Deployed on submarine service, and it was top secret. I'd have to kill you if I told you about it."

Kyle smirked and pushed the laptop toward him. "Go ahead. You do the driving."

But he looked sideways at Bruce as he inserted

the thumb drive and waited for the processor to bring up a menu.

"Were you in when they had women in the submarines?" Kyle asked.

"No," Bruce said, "though it would have been a lot more interesting." He typed some commands into the laptop. "Truthfully, I'm more suited to civilian life. Though I'm grateful for my time in the Navy. It was all I ever wanted as a kid. My gramps was in the Navy. South Pacific, World War II."

Kyle nodded. "Joe, my stepfather, was regular Army. Vietnam. Drafted."

Bruce nodded as he whizzed through a bunch of menus in the new accounting package on Kyle's machine. Took command of the keyboard, hit a bunch of keys.

"How are things going for you, back in civilian life?" Bruce asked casually.

"Fine. Good."

Bruce gave a wry smile. "Yeah, I used to say the same thing."

"It's ah...different." Kyle debated whether to share more, but he figured he'd risk it. "It's not like being on a combat team where everybody looks out for each other and has the same goals."

Bruce glanced up at him. "I'm getting together with some people tomorrow night. Want to join us?"

If someone who hadn't served had asked him that, Kyle would have given him a flat *no*.

"Maybe another time. This Friday night I'm working until ten," Kyle said. "The high school JV is having a late practice."

"We'll probably still be there at ten. Moroney's Pub on the beach. My friend owns it. You remember John Kennedy from Wallis Point High?"

He was a couple years older than Kyle. "Yeah, I do. Thanks, I'll keep it in mind."

There was a knock on the door behind them. Natalie stood on the threshold, a serious expression on her face, holding a pile of folders.

Bruce stopped typing and stood. "Why don't you come by for lunch tomorrow," he said to Kyle, "and again every other day for the next couple of weeks? We'll do a half hour per session. It takes a while to get used to a new system."

"I'd like that. There's more to running a small business than I'd realized."

"There is." Natalie smiled, spreading her arms. "I've been running this place for the past few years. It's a lot of work, but it's also rewarding serving a small community. I can do things for people that I couldn't do when I worked for a boss."

"You're right," Kyle said, gathering his laptop and thinking of that order he'd put in for new kids' skates. He gave Bruce a nod.

"Will Jessica be coming today?" Natalie asked, as he headed down the hallway with her.

"Not today," Kyle said.

"Okay. Well, you can let her know what my concerns are, then."

"Concerns?"

Natalie smiled tightly, then led him into her smaller, personal office and sat down behind her desk. "Please take a seat." She spread a stack of bills before Kyle. "I'm getting Joe's mail delivered to me, since technically his estate is still in probate."

Uneasily, Kyle glanced at the notices. Electricity, taxes and water bills for the twin rinks. He should have expected this, but the numbers had more zeroes on the end than he'd expected. He winced. He needed to run the numbers to see how bad the damage was.

"This all goes into the accounting program Bruce loaded?" Kyle asked.

"Kyle, you could hire a bookkeeper, but frankly…"

"Yes, I know. I don't have the money." Kyle cleared his throat. "I appreciate your giving me the receipts. I'll straighten it out. Thanks for your time today." He stood, in a rush to get out of there, gathering the papers. But as he turned… his prosthetic foot got wedged in between the chair and the desk.

Dammit. Without looking at Natalie, he put everything down and bent to adjust himself, as discreetly as he could. When he rose again, Natalie was staring at him with kind eyes.

She'd seen. His stomach clenched.

"I already knew," Natalie said softly.

His pulse kicked up, and sweat broke out on his forehead. "How?" he asked in a low voice.

Natalie swallowed. "Before Joe died, he told me and Bruce what had happened to you."

Kyle was so stunned he couldn't think.

"Joe was in with me preparing his will, and... well, he said you hadn't officially told him. He said he understood why. He was a veteran, too, and—"

"How'd he know?" Kyle asked roughly.

Natalie shook her head. "I don't know. Did he mention anything to you in his letter?"

Kyle still hadn't read it.

He groaned, sitting again, his head in his hands. Did Joe think him a cripple? Is *that* why he'd included Jessica in the partnership?

"Did he tell Jessica in her letter?" he asked.

"Not that I'm aware of."

He ground his teeth, thinking back to their recent exchanges. Was it possible that she knew?

If she had, she probably wouldn't have asked him to climb up a ladder with a window-washing pail. He was probably safe, but he wasn't sure.

One thing he could be sure of was that if Joe knew, other people might know, too.

Dammit, he thought. This was all leading to one thing. He had to be the one to tell her. If he didn't, eventually somebody else would.

"This is really gonna suck," he muttered.

With a start, he realized that Natalie was gazing at him with kind eyes.

He owed her an explanation. She and Bruce had been pretty decent to him so far. "I didn't tell Jessica because she already feels responsible for me leaving town and joining the Marines. It'll devastate her."

"I'm sorry," Natalie murmured.

"She said she was grateful that nothing happened to me while I was deployed. That it was her biggest fear."

"That's hard."

He rubbed his hand over his face. "Yeah." Maybe because Natalie's husband had been a good guy to him, he wasn't leaving the seat yet. "The truth is, I started out not wanting her to know because I was pissed off about it. Then, I didn't want her to feel bad. Now, I just hope she can accept it. I don't want any sympathy."

"I think it's brave, what you're doing."

Brave? He hadn't done anything yet. Lowering his head, he gathered up the papers again.

"Kyle," Natalie said gently. "It's probably unprofessional admitting this as I am, but I'm going to do it anyway."

Out of curiosity, he paused.

"I've been through it, too." She tapped her ear lobe. "I went a long time—too long—before I admitted to people that I'd lost my hearing. I was able to cover for it because I'm a pretty decent lip reader. But eventually…" She tapped her ears again. Kyle had already seen the small hearing aids. She wore her long blond hair curled behind her ears, not even attempting to hide them. "The longer I went without saying anything, the more I found that it was an obstacle. It's just made my life easier to come clean about it."

"My military friends know," Kyle said. "Prosthetic legs aren't as rare in the Marines as they are in the civilian world."

"Well, whenever you're ready to make it public, Bruce and I will support you."

Kyle scrubbed his hands over his eyes. He felt better talking to Natalie, and her husband was a nice guy, too. "Thanks. And thank Bruce for me. I'll load these expenses into the computer system."

"That will help. And do try to trim them, because remember, your end goal is to be profitable. If you're not, then you know what happens." She smiled uncomfortably.

He gave her a quizzical look. "I'm not sure what you mean?"

"Well, your revenues have to outweigh your expenses, or there's nothing I can do."

He must have given her a blank look, because she continued. "If your expenses outweigh your earnings at the end of six months, I have no choice but to take the highest bid, and then you and Jessica will split the payment from whoever else buys the rink."

"What?" he asked flatly.

She peered at him. "You were aware of that, aren't you, Kyle?"

"No, I wasn't until now."

"I'm sorry if you didn't understand, I thought I explained it all," she said. "It's clearly specified in the will. Jessica and her friend asked many detailed, pointed questions that day."

"So...you're saying that Jessica is fully aware that if the rink isn't profitable in six months, then I stand no chance of running it?" Despite himself, his voice was rising. "Of the twin rinks surviving at all?"

"We had an extensive discussion on these points, yes."

"*Sebastien* did, you mean," Kyle spit. "*He's* the one who asked the questions."

Natalie said nothing.

Kyle blew out a breath. He couldn't help thinking of the kids' rental skates he'd purchased at

Jessica's insistence. She hadn't been purposely increasing his expenses, had she?

He spread the bills Natalie had given him across her desk.

Pete's Paints. A number of purchase items made over several dates. Jessica's name was printed on the receipts. *Paints. Brushes. Tape.*

While Kyle had been unable to pay to have the compressor fixed in the second rink, she had been spending money that they didn't have on nonessentials. Had she done it knowing that it would hurt his chances for profitability, and thus put more money in her and Sebastien's pockets once the rink sold to land developers?

Furious, he jerked to his feet.

"Kyle?" Natalie asked.

"I need to go," he said curtly.

He stalked outside to his truck and climbed in, tossing his laptop onto the seat beside him. He felt stabbed in the back.

All these weeks, when he'd thought that he and Jessica been getting closer, had he been wrong? Had she been playing him for a fool while working against him?

Ordering stuff. Conspiring with Carol to accept deliveries. Probably laughing with Sebastien over it, too.

Kyle started the engine. He needed to confront her before it got any worse.

CHAPTER EIGHT

ON THURSDAY MORNING, Jessica kept busy by using a hammer and nails to tack down the rubber matting that curled on the edges. At least the rink's vestibule wasn't so dirty and dilapidated now.

She sat back, admiring her work. But then the door opened, a blast of cool air rushing in. She shivered in her thin sweatshirt.

Kimmie strode inside, and Jessica waved cheerfully. The girl carried the rental skates Jessica had let her keep. She greeted Jessica then headed toward the hockey rink for her public skating time, while her mother drove off in her car.

Jessica was gathering her tools, preparing to head back to her office, when the door opened once more. This time, it was Kyle.

"You weren't at breakfast," she said casually. He looked cute today, quite sexy. She was getting used to the beard. She liked the hints of copper that wound through it and the way his Adam's apple showed through. He didn't have his ball cap on this morning, either—he had really great hair.

But he was looking at her strangely.

"What?" she asked him, laughing.

He didn't even crack a smile. "The lawyer showed me a few things yesterday."

"Oh?" She stood, brushing off her palms, a sense of foreboding threatening her heart. "Is... something wrong?"

He glanced at the hammer in her hand, then at the matting. "What are you doing?"

But before she could answer, the door opened, and another skater walked in with a skate bag over her shoulder. Jessica stepped aside to make room. As she did, she accidentally brushed Kyle's arm.

His face hardened, and he didn't meet her eyes.

She felt the chill spread over her body. Something was very wrong.

KYLE DIDN'T UNDERSTAND. Sometimes Jessica acted as though she cared about this place—and about him. So was she sabotaging him or not? He needed to know.

Turning red in the face, Jessica abruptly left the glassed-in lobby and headed for the main office where Carol was on the phone.

"Wait," Kyle said, following her inside.

Behind the desk, Carol spoke in hushed tones, with laughter in her voice. It sounded like a personal call.

He did his best to tamp down his irritation. He didn't have Call Waiting on the phone service, so a customer attempting to call would encounter a busy signal.

With one eye on Jessica, Kyle gave Carol a look. But she kept talking. Giving her a dark look, he drew a line across his throat. Carol turned around and outright ignored him.

It wasn't easy being a boss in civilian life. In the military world, orders were answered, the hierarchy was clear. Insubordination, and you were written up. That didn't work here.

He looked to Jessica. She'd crossed her arms and sat in the empty chair near Carol.

"We need to talk in private," he said to Jessica.

Without a word, she stood, crossed the hall and opened her office door for him. Belatedly, he realized he hadn't been inside this room since he was eighteen, raging at Joe and bearing the brunt of his ire. That night, Joe had hit him. Closed his fist and punched Kyle straight in the face. That's when Kyle had gone home, packed a duffel bag and left Wallis Point for good.

Kyle walked inside and stopped dead in his tracks. Gone was the dank and cluttered man cave. In its place was a sanctuary that anybody would love to hang out in.

Jessica had transformed the place. Joe's old office was bright and airy. Fresh paint was on the walls and there was a cleared space on the floor. Curtains and pillows were spread across a couch, with everything done up in a beach theme. A bowl of shells sat on a glass table, weathered gray driftwood beside it. And on a side table, a microwave, small fridge and radio perched.

This was where his money had gone.

Kyle felt his jaw tightening anew. "Tell me the truth. Are you sabotaging me?"

"What?" she asked, surprised.

"Are you sabotaging me? I saw a list of expenses from a bunch of places in town." He swept his arm over the place. "Did you know, Jessica, that if the business—our business—isn't showing a profit by the end of August, then Natalie will be forced to sell it to the highest bidder?"

"Well…yes."

"You knew that?" he repeated.

She placed her hand on Joe's desk. "Didn't you?"

"I do now," he sputtered.

She gave him a pleading look. "Kyle, I know you love this place, but with all the money you'll get from the sale, you could build a new, more modern twin rinks for Wallis Point. The machinery would work properly, and everything would be great. You wouldn't be so stressed all the time."

"Where in God's name did you get that idea?" he roared.

She stared at him with those wide brown eyes. "You don't like it?"

"Jessica, it's a fairy tale. It can't happen." He shook his head. "Don't you think I know the rink business? There's no way I'd get enough money to build a new rink even if I wanted to, which frankly, I don't. I want *these* rinks," he said, pointing at the walls. "I want to fix this facility."

"I…didn't know it wouldn't be enough money." Her face fell. "I really didn't."

He sighed at her. "Jess, if your plan was for this place to fail, then why are you out there doing things to improve it? Why the window washing? The floor repairs? The cleaning up the kids' skates? Why do you bother if you just want it torn down?"

"I…don't want it torn down. That's not my aim."

"So you're not sabotaging me?" He tried to be patient. "Then what do you want?"

"The money," she said simply. "And also, to help you find a rink that you can manage if this one doesn't make it."

"Jessa," he spoke as clearly as he knew how, "if I lose this property, then I have nowhere else to work, to go."

"But any rink would hire you," she protested. "You're a great manager!"

No, he wasn't. If he was, then he wouldn't be having these money and personnel problems.

"And you're a Marine, Kyle. A veteran." Her eyes were so bright. "Any rink owner would love to hire you."

Oh, cripes, she had no idea. He couldn't even climb a ladder. It was all he could do to hoist himself aboard the Zamboni.

She stared at him, clearly not understanding why he was pacing and combing his hands through his hair. But he couldn't expect her to understand. He hadn't been honest with her. He'd hidden himself.

As she hid herself.

Yes, they'd been making progress, but it wasn't enough. It wouldn't be enough, until he told her the truth. Until then, they were as unlike a team as possible.

He paused, considering Joe's old desk, newly transformed. If he didn't get Jessica on his side, then he would never find his place in Wallis Point. That was the bottom line. That was the reality that Joe had set up.

"Can I sit?" he asked, hating that his voice sounded shaky. But there was only one thing left to do.

CHAPTER NINE

JESSICA'S HEART FLUTTERED RAPIDLY. She'd tried to clear this office of Joe's influence, but for Kyle, maybe it was still too much of a reminder, just as the figure-skating rink was a reminder for her.

Jessa. He'd called her *Jessa.* And instead of upsetting her, it felt…intimate.

She licked her lips. "You don't have to ask me permission, Kyle. Of course you can sit."

"Thanks," he said in his deep, gruff voice. His eyes sought hers, and she swallowed. She twisted her hands together as he felt for the couch behind him, and then lowered himself, never taking his gaze from hers.

She inhaled. There was so much tension in the room. He wore a button-down shirt with the top two buttons undone. She could see the smooth skin on his neck. The muscles and the Adam's apple. He was so male…

"Jessa, I don't know how to tell you this," he said in a low voice. Her heart hammered. He dipped his head and held it in his hands. Large hands. His hair was brown and thick with strands of copper throughout.

"Kyle?" she whispered.

He sucked in his breath. Finally, he looked up. Those green, pained eyes that were broken. Like she felt broken sometimes. Like a fundamental piece of her was missing that other people had. Did Kyle feel like that, too?

"I'm not who you think I am," he said. "You remember those guys I skate with in the morning… TJ… Oscar?"

"Your friends from your military unit? Yes, of course I remember."

"Well…I wasn't exactly upfront with you about them." He sighed. "TJ and Oscar weren't in my unit. I met them down in Walter Reed Medical Center. Oscar was having a pretty rough time." He cocked his head. "Do you know what PTSD is?"

"Post-traumatic stress disorder," she said. "Right?"

He hesitated. Had he gone through PTSD? She wouldn't think any less of him if he had.

"Kyle," she said gently, "I don't know about the emotional aspects of being in a war, but I have worked with pediatric amputees, so at least where Oscar and TJ are concerned, I'm aware of what's involved with the loss of a limb. I can imagine the emotional pain they've been through."

Kyle stiffened.

"You work with amputees?" he said.

"Yes," she repeated. "Sometimes I help with OT treatments—that's occupational therapy, as opposed to physical therapy. At the moment, I have one client, Benjamin is his name. He's five. He was born without feet, and I've been working with him to adjust to a new set of prosthetics. He recently had surgery to remove some bone spurs on his stump and he…"

The blood drained from Kyle's face. She understood. Not many people could stand to think about what five-year-old Benjamin was going through. Even big strong Marines who thought they'd seen everything could get squeamish.

"I know that it's hard," she said.

Without a word, Kyle got up and left her office.

Alone, her hand went to her mouth. She didn't understand him sometimes. Benjamin was facing a physical challenge similar to that of Kyle's friends, so why was Kyle reacting this way?

Then again, Sebastien didn't always understand her job, either. He didn't talk about it with her except in a surface way. She assumed he looked at her time spent performing physical therapy as just something she did in order to earn money. Jessica looked at it as a vitally important calling. Her job meant something to her because it helped other people heal, mostly young, physically injured children, many of whom felt frightened and alone, just as she had as a child.

Her gaze flicked to the wall, to an old photo that Joe had hung of Kyle's hockey team when Kyle was about eight or nine years old. It was the only personal item of Joe's that she'd left in the office. She enjoyed looking at young Kyle in his uniform and holding his stick, a proud smile on his face.

Working at this rink, being around people who healed from skating, was *Kyle's* calling. She should have understood that before this conversation with him.

When Jessica had been a young skater, a broadcaster in a television booth had once opined that her great strength was her "ability to connect with an audience." That was so ironic to her now. Back then, *Jessa Hughes* could take a piece of music, a piece of choreography, and translate it so that people could feel the emotion along with her. Using her body to communicate. It was what she did.

But, when her skating career had ended, she'd felt herself lose a lot of that ability to connect. Children seemed to be the one exception. She'd always felt it was why she liked working with kids. A simple smile was enough for them. The gentle touch of the prescribed massage.

Working at this rink, with Kyle, had been

building her confidence again. And he was a big part of her progress.

She stood and opened the door, intent on finding him.

He was in the foyer just outside her door, head down and staring at his feet.

"What am I doing wrong?" she asked him softly. "I mean, I know you're upset about the rink, but why have you been angry with me for the past couple days? Like yesterday on the ladder."

Kyle looked up at her, his face bleak. "I just… had no idea you worked with amputees."

"Benjamin is okay emotionally. You don't have to feel sorry for him, or for me."

Kyle nodded. Grimly, he motioned her back inside her office and then shut the door behind them. This time they stayed standing, where they were.

"Benjamin can join the wounded warriors on the ice if he'd like," Kyle said. "I'd like to open up a program for amputees who want to skate. Kids, especially."

"That's…great! I'll tell Benjamin and his parents. I'm sure they'll be pleased."

"But, Jessica…" He gazed at her intently, with such raw pain that it took her breath away. "That is one reason we need to keep the rink open beyond the end of summer. We can't let a land developer take it away."

"But where did the wounded warriors skate before?" she murmured, feeling worried for him. "There's a rink thirty minutes north. Another one thirty minutes west. You could set up something there."

"No, Jessica, I couldn't," he said flatly.

"Are you just being stubborn?"

"I wish that's all it was. Trust me." Kyle's voice had gone hoarse. "If I could go back and not volunteer for that last tour…but I did. I had nowhere else to go. Just like now, I have nowhere else to go. I can't work in an office again, and I can't…"

His voice trailed off. Kyle hadn't said so many words to her in days. She was almost there again. She was almost connecting with him.

"Kyle, please, tell me what's wrong."

She waited for him. And waited. But it was to no avail. Maybe he thought she couldn't give him what he needed.

She gazed into his eyes…

He lifted his head and looked at her, breathing deeply, his chest rising and falling. There was a thin sheen of sweat on his forehead.

"Kyle…?" she whispered.

With a great sigh, he reached down and lifted up his pants leg. Attached to his sneaker, she saw the familiar metal rod of a prosthetic leg.

Involuntarily, a gasp came out of her. She'd seen them before, dozens of times, but on Kyle? Her Kyle? Big, strong, hockey-playing Kyle?

Oh, God. She began to gasp in and out, the beginnings of hyperventilation. How had she not seen this?

She couldn't meet his eyes. Her own eyes were filling with tears, her vision blurry. She wanted to get up and run. To cry. She'd had no idea. None. *None.*

"Don't be sorry for me," he said harshly.

"I'm…" *I'm not,* she wanted to say. But her voice was lost. Her throat hurt. And her hands were shaking.

Why didn't I put two and two together?

He was so cagey about keeping her from his truck. About not climbing ladders in front of her. About hiding out in his locker room. He'd been hiding a lot of things from her. It must have taken a huge effort to maintain his deception.

She reached out and smacked him on the chest. "*How* could you do this? Hiding this from me like you didn't care? How could you, of all people, be such a jerk—?"

He rose and pulled her to him. Lowered his head and kissed her on the lips.

She was so stunned that for a split second, she froze. The tips of her breasts were pressed to his chest, his strong hands gripped her upper arms.

And then a current went through her. A rush of desire. Her nerve endings felt alive. With a soft noise coming from her throat, she melted into him and kissed him back. Opened her mouth and let her tongue find his.

His kiss turned surprisingly gentle. Cupping her head, he sifted his fingers through her hair. She felt the soft tickle of his beard against her cheek, the brush of his warm breath on her skin.

She clung to him, her back against the wooden door, her hips pressed close to his. She felt sexy and alive in a way she never had before, and never with anyone besides him.

KNOCK, KNOCK, KNOCK.

The sound of knuckles rapping on the door behind Jessica snapped Kyle to his senses, and he drew back, separating from her.

What had he just done?

She backed away, too, a hand to her lips. Her eyes were hooded and she looked dazed.

They stared at each other, breathing heavily.

Knock, knock, knock. Someone was on the other side of the door.

"Ignore it," Jessica whispered. She reached for him and kissed him again. A soft brush against his lips. A kiss that a woman gave a man when she was giving him acceptance.

She didn't mind about his leg. She'd minded that he'd lied to her. That's what she was telling him.

"Jessica!" It was Carol's voice. She'd been the person knocking on the door. "Jessica, open up. Sebastien is on the phone and he wants to talk to you. Jessica?"

Kyle watched as Jessica's eyes widened. She glanced away from him, as if jolted back to reality, and his heart sank.

"Tell him I'll phone him back later," Jessica called.

"He said he tried to call you but you weren't picking up," Carol spoke loudly.

"I *said*, I'll call him back. Please tell him that."

Jessica glanced back to Kyle, but he'd already stepped away from her.

The writing was on the wall. He felt for this woman, but he couldn't have her. He wasn't meant to have her.

"This was a mistake," he said quietly. "I'm sorry." He didn't know what had possessed him. "I guess it was hard for me to tell you and I got swept away."

But her face had already solidified into a mask. Her eyes darted from side to side as if thinking, and not really listening to him at the moment. Then, with quiet conviction, her gaze locked on his.

"Kyle...I am going to help you get this rink.

I don't care if it means less money for me, I'm going to help you be profitable. I owe you that much. I won't betray your trust with your leg, but I want us to be in partnership. That means that I support you, and you support me. We'll be open. We'll have trust and respect for each other." Her head tilted in a pleading gesture. "Can you do that?"

He stared at her, horrified. She wasn't even addressing the kiss—she was alleviating her guilt over his leg and making it up to him by talking about a *business* partnership.

He stared at her, heart sinking. It was the best thing, what he'd wanted when he'd originally come into the room, but…it bothered him now. A lot.

CHAPTER TEN

WHEN JESSICA SAW the secluded table for two at Chez Louis, the same seaside restaurant where she and Sebastien had spent their first date, she knew right away she'd made a mistake.

She clutched her abalone pendant so hard she feared she might break it.

She wasn't ready to sit down with Sebastien just yet. After she'd left the rink this afternoon, still in shock from everything that had happened with Kyle, her schedule had been packed with physical therapy clients. She'd barely had time to collect herself, never mind to think.

The last thing she'd expected was for Kyle to kiss her. Or for her body to react the way it had when he'd touched her…

"This is Jessica," Sebastien said to the hostess, as the woman held Jessica's chair and helped her get settled at the table with the romantic red rose and two champagne glasses already set out.

Jessica's nerves were a jittery mess. She did her best to smooth her skirt and smile at them both.

"I was *such* a big fan of yours growing up,"

the woman gushed, handing her a menu. "I can't believe I'm finally meeting you."

Jessica's smile froze. She glanced at Sebastien, but he didn't flinch.

"Thanks, Bethany," he murmured, and gave her a subtle tilt of his head.

"Oh, right. I'll get that champagne right away." But Bethany lingered, staring at Jessica with an awestruck look on her face.

Jessica kept her eyes glued on the red rose.

When the hostess finally departed, Jessica faced Sebastien. "Did you talk to her about me?"

"She's on your side," Sebastien said. "You know we all are."

"But she doesn't even know me!"

"Jess," he said patiently, "when people watch you on TV like that, caught in a dramatic moment, they pretty much feel like they do know you. Can't you cut her some slack?"

Can't you cut me *some slack?* That's what he was really saying.

He didn't want to hear about her problems. During the drive over, he'd spoken about his exhausting plane trip. About his long week and how happy he was to be home and not have to travel again for a while.

It was as if he wanted to believe that everything had gone smoothly at home for her while he'd been gone, even though it hadn't. Her life was not smooth. It was complicated.

Her muscles tensed so tightly she trembled. But it wasn't all his fault; she'd been lying to him, too.

I want us to be in partnership.

She'd talked to Kyle about trust and respect and telling the truth when, in fact, she was the one not telling the truth. To anybody.

Reaching for her water glass, she took a long gulp, the ice tinkling. She wanted a partnership with Sebastien, too—a life partnership. More than anything, she wanted him to understand and respect her. And yet she'd never communicated to him the heart of her problem. Kyle had come clean with his secret to her, so should she to Sebastien.

"Sebastien, I have something to tell you." Jessica placed her palms firmly on the crisp white tablecloth and leaned forward to face him. "I lied."

Sebastien lowered the menu he'd been glancing at and met her gaze over the top.

"About what?" he asked cautiously.

"About…" *Everything.* She swallowed and met his gaze. "I've never told anyone this before."

"Okay-y-y." He drew the word out.

"I wasn't injured," she said quickly, before she could change her mind. "Nobody should have cried along with me that day on television or ever, because I made it all up. That's why I'm so sensitive about it."

He titled his head quizzically. "What are you talking about?"

"What you just said to me, with Bethany. When everyone was rooting for me at the skating championships, I didn't want to do it anymore. I couldn't do it anymore. So I lied about being injured, to everybody."

His eyes widened.

Her words came out in a rush. "I went out on the ice that day and I cried to the referee and pointed to my knee and shook my head. But there was nothing wrong with my knee. Nothing. I used it as an excuse because I thought it was the only way to make my pain stop. I was so unhappy and trapped in my life. And it's my biggest regret...my biggest..."

She stopped because she was realizing anew all that her lie had done to Kyle. Her actions had hurt him. He wouldn't have been wounded if not for her. She put her head in her hands. She felt like weeping.

"Wow," Sebastien said. "That's..."

Horrible, she answered silently.

"You know, you should write a book," Sebastien mused. "People are interested in you, Jessica. They'd be interested in what you have to say about that time in your life."

"What?" She could only stare at him.

"A lot of people remember you, especially women. The fact that your dream didn't come true is what makes you so lovable. Anybody can relate to that. It's a gift."

She kept staring at him. He didn't get it. He didn't understand that her desire wasn't to relate to strangers.

She only cared about fixing her past mistakes with the people who'd been close to her that she'd hurt. Like Kyle.

"I don't want to write a book," she said.

"Why not? I bet you'd make some decent money. You must have so many cool stories about the celebrities you rubbed shoulders with. I saw something on YouTube about you…you were being interviewed by the people on that morning show…the one out of New York. And you even did national television commercials. You weren't small potatoes, Jessica. You had wide appeal."

That was what impressed him? The outward prestige of her past life?

She took a deep breath, trying to remain patient. If she wasn't honest with Sebastien now, then how could she expect him to understand what was important to her and what she was trying to do?

She took a fortifying drink from her water glass. "I told you about my mother, right? I promised her I wouldn't give her any bad publicity. She makes her living as a figure skating commentator. She simply doesn't talk about me anymore—" Her voice broke unexpectedly. Jessica put her hand to her mouth.

"Hey, hey…" Sebastien took her other hand. "This is supposed to be a good night for us. A great night. We don't have to talk about any of that stuff now, not here."

She bit her lip.

"It's a beautiful place," he said. "Look at the moon, Jess. And the ocean…" He grinned at her, gave her that old lovable Sebastien smile that she'd fallen for after she'd helped him heal his knee at her physical therapy practice. She'd fallen for him even harder after he was no longer her patient and he'd brought her to dinner at this romantic restaurant under a full moon on Valentine's Day. That was when he'd begun his campaign to sweep her off her feet. And she had gladly fallen.

He'd been so easy to fall for back then.

"Jess, I asked you here for a reason." He squeezed her hand, and she realized that he was hot and flushed. Sweating, and Sebastien never perspired.

Bethany returned with the wine steward, who opened an expensive bottle of champagne and poured it into the two fancy flutes without asking. Jessica was starting to realize that Sebastien had called ahead and arranged all this. A small plate of oysters, their shells arranged prettily over ice, also appeared on the table.

"I, uh, wanted this to go well." His voice sounded nervous. "Wow," he said, laughing. He was usually so smooth. So polished and urbane. He looked out over the railing, at the water and exhaled loudly.

Is this the moment I've been waiting for? she thought to herself, as his fingers drummed on the table. *It's happening now?*

"Okay, let's do it," he muttered.

Her fingers curled around the edges of her seat. And all she could think of was Kyle. That kiss with Kyle…

Sebastien withdrew something from inside his jacket pocket and slid it across the crisp white tablecloth to her.

A pale blue box, a Tiffany jeweler's box. She heard herself gasp. This was even more spectacular than she'd imagined. More than she'd ever dared expect.

"Will you marry me, Jessica?"

THE DAWN WAS brightening and the birds were starting to sing when Kyle drove into the twin rinks' parking lot the next morning, hoping he'd see Jessica's little orange Volkswagen parked in her customary space.

Her space was empty. All the spaces were empty. She wasn't there.

He parked in his spot but left the engine idling. There was an uneasiness inside him, and only Jessica's presence would make it better.

He closed his eyes and waited. Maybe she would drive up in a moment or two. She always came in early on Fridays. For an entire month they'd had breakfast together on Fridays—he'd brought the food. Today he had donuts for them. He breathed evenly, letting the comforting, doughy smell of Donuts on the Beach soothe his brain.

He needed to see her. Needed to talk to her.

They'd kissed, and there had been something real there.

The sound of a vehicle approaching knocked him from his thoughts, and for a split second he jerked his head up, happy, until he saw that it wasn't her.

Oscar hopped down from the cab of his pickup, a hockey bag and stick slung over his good shoulder. He strode across the pavement toward Kyle, his boots making a gravelly noise as he walked.

"You coming inside?" he asked Kyle, leaning in his truck's window.

"Give me ten minutes," Kyle muttered. If Jessica showed up and he wasn't present in the parking lot, then she might chicken out, go into her front office and hide from him again.

He wasn't having that anymore.

"Kyle, you're the one with the key," Oscar pointed out. "Unless you want to hand it over to me, I'm stuck out here."

Kyle sighed. "Okay, I'm coming." He opened the truck door.

Oscar grinned. "Excellent," he said, sniffing the air. "You brought donuts."

Kyle reached into the cab, handed Oscar the bag and said nothing about Jessica.

JESSICA CLOSED HER EYES, breathing in the cool air of the ice rink.

She heard the unmistakable sounds of her childhood: a hockey stick connecting with a rubber puck in a resounding slap shot. The whacks of more sticks hitting ice. The skid of blades scraping to stop, and the laughter and shouts of men as they skated.

Kyle's voice. She opened her eyes because she wanted to see him. Was dying to see him skate.

Even all these years later, he was easy to pick out of the crowd. Strong and commanding, he stood out, his distinctive red-gold beard contrasted against his white helmet. He wore a full hockey-player uniform: skates, pants, shoulder pads, a jersey with NORTHRUP and his number—19—written across the back. With all that padding, and with the smooth, sure, explosive way he stroked across the ice, who could even tell he was a wounded warrior?

I'm a professional. I should have known.

She'd lain awake all last night thinking about him. There had been signs, of course. His slightly flatfooted gait. His way of walking carefully.

But she'd been filled with such blinding resolve to hide her own problems that she'd missed it. She'd wanted so much to keep a tightly controlled lid on what was going on with her. And look what had happened as a result! She'd been ignorant about what had really been going on with him.

She tried to remember Kyle's teen years. He'd had a longer stride then, more energy. He'd swaggered, that was the word. Proud of being selected captain of Wallis Point High School's varsity hockey team.

How difficult such an injury must be for someone used to being so active. She knew from her training how long it took to rehabilitate. His was a traumatic injury she assumed—she'd purposely not asked him how it had happened. She wanted to know—badly—but that story was for him to tell when he felt like it. He would have likely faced multiple difficult surgeries and an emotional readjustment to his new physical limitations, as well.

But Kyle drove a truck. He played hockey. He ran an ice rink.

Jessica climbed the wooden stands until she reached a middle row in the bleachers, high enough for a bird's-eye view of the whole ice surface where he skated.

Curling her knees beneath her chin and clasping her arms round her calves, she watched him. None of the players noticed her. They were too deep into their game.

From the shouts and laughter coming from the men, she could tell they took genuine pleasure in it. Kyle and his friends teased each other with guys' easy, cheerful trash talk. They zipped around the rink, passing the puck back and forth and stealing it from each other, playfully knocking their opponents into the boards.

Their vibe was easy. Fun. She sensed that Kyle was happy during these early morning times. She liked that he was happy—it was important to her. Yet she'd never expected to feel that way about him, and she needed to stop. She couldn't be physically attracted to him anymore.

Enough. While Kyle skated to the net in the far end, Jessica quietly stepped down. The decision was already made—she was marrying Sebastien. She'd accepted his ring last night. She'd invested so much in their relationship already—and they wanted the same things for their future.

The only thing—the most important thing— she could do for Kyle was to be more proactive in helping him make his rink profitable so he could keep it. That would be her parting gift to him.

Taking a shaky breath, she headed for the ballet room beside the wooden stands. The door was locked, as it always had been in her youth, but weeks ago she'd found the key inside the clutter of Joe's old office. Now she maneuvered the cranky mechanism easily, remembering how to do it as if she'd never taken a hiatus from the six o'clock morning stretch sessions she'd enjoyed as a teen.

Once inside the old ballet studio, Jessica switched on the overhead lights and observed the familiar walls covered in mirrors. Gym mats were spread over the middle of the hardwood floor. A free-standing ballet barre was aligned against the longest wall. And in the corner she recognized a sound system that had been state-of-the-art when she'd last seen it.

The room was fairly clean and usable. Excellent, because she planned on suggesting to Kyle that he negotiate a deal with a group of ice dancers who sometimes came in for the public skate. This could provide some much-needed revenue for him. She recalled them mentioning once that they were looking for access to a warm-up area, and this old room would fit the bill.

She turned to leave, the key in her hand, but hesitated. Like Kyle on the ice with his friends playing early-morning hockey, she'd once been happiest during these quiet early morning alone times. Her mother used to drop her off so Jessica could warm up before the day began. Then her mother went to pick up coffee for herself and Jessica's coach.

In the forty-five minutes it typically took her mother to return from that errand, Jessica would slip inside the ballet room, put whatever music she wanted on the sound system, stretch and dance. Daydream. Do whatever she felt like doing without the customary supervision and pressure that had seemed to always hang over her head.

Jessica rubbed her hands over her eyes. Without knowing why she was doing it, she stripped out of her bulky long sweater-coat. Took off her sneakers and stepped onto the mats, which smelled clean, as if they'd been washed and sprinkled with freshener. Jessica had worn yoga pants and a comfortable scoop-neck T-shirt, so she settled into a seated hamstring stretch, her legs in front of her, toes pointed.

She could stand to take better care of herself. For so long she'd been adamant about not dieting. About eating whatever she felt like. About refusing to enter into any kind of regular fitness regimen. Rebellion, she supposed, against her mother's control-freak system.

But who had Jessica hurt by shutting herself off from her old pleasurable routines?

Only herself.

She went over to the music system and figured out which cable to use to attach the speakers to her phone. She scrolled through her music until she found something upbeat, with no association to her ice princess years. Doing her stretches, she let herself get lost in the joy of the movement.

KYLE HAD STOPPED to tilt his water bottle toward his mouth when he saw Patrick, hands cupped around his eyes and his nose pressed to the glass of the ballet room. Light was shining from inside the window.

Kyle paused, staring. He'd cleaned that room just recently with the hopes that maybe Jessica might use it as she had years ago. That it was occupied now seemed too much of a coincidence. Kyle put down his water bottle.

"Hey," he called to Patrick, pounding on the spectator glass above the rink boards. "What's going on in there?"

Patrick turned.

Kyle clearly saw that it *was* Jessica inside her old ballet room. And she wore a sexy, black,

body-hugging outfit that looked like a catsuit.
He could see her standing in profile against the
barre, holding her leg up in a position that immediately made him choke on his water bottle
because all he could suddenly think of was *sex*.

With Jessica. Wearing that hot outfit.

Patrick grinned at him.

Oh, hell, no. Furious, Kyle skated toward the
door, intent on throttling Patrick. Over Kyle's
dead body would anyone leer at Jessica, except
maybe him.

He skated as hard as he could, ready to get his
hands around Patrick's neck. Breathing heavily,
timing the door coming up to him, Kyle turned
his ankles sideways to execute his regular hockey
stop, intent on hitting the mats running.

But his blade must have hit a rut wrong because the next thing Kyle knew, he was flat on
his back, the wind knocked out of him.

Oh, shit. What's my leg doing?

He sat up on his elbows in time to see his left
skate bent at a crazy angle. If a civilian saw it,
they would think his leg had been broken and
twisted backward. In reality, Kyle just felt a dull
throbbing because he'd been stressing his residual
leg with all this skating of late, anyway.

TJ skated over, holding out his hand to pull
Kyle up, but one of the other guys bumped into TJ
and they fell into a pile, like the Three Stooges.

TJ thought it was hilarious. He couldn't stop laughing. "We finally took you out," he said to Kyle.

"Yeah, yeah. Very funny."

Their guffaws turned to silence when they saw Jessica, gasping, rushing out onto the ice in her stocking feet and wearing that hot black catsuit.

"Whoa," TJ murmured. Then he sprawled out like a dead man on the ice.

"Will you help me, Jessica?" TJ wailed piteously. "I've fallen and I can't get up. I need mouth-to-mouth resuscitation."

"Maybe you can get one of your friends to do that for you," Jessica said cheerfully.

There was a round of good-natured snickering. Jessica gave as good as she got with them, too, but Kyle didn't feel like laughing. On the contrary, he wanted to punch something.

He untangled himself and sat up, but the blood drained from his head and he felt dizzy.

Jessica knelt beside Kyle. "Let me see your—"

"No," he said between his teeth. He reached his foot to twist it the right way around at the same time she placed her hand on his prosthetic leg.

"I said *don't*!" He swatted her hand.

She blinked, looking hurt.

"You're not my doctor," he said quietly as he stood.

There was silence.

"I am a professional, Kyle."

"Yeah? Well, I want to do it myself. Give me that dignity," he snapped.

This was why he hadn't wanted to tell her about his leg in the first place. He was damned if he'd look weak or helpless to her. He wanted her to be interested in him for himself, not for his injury.

He picked up his fallen hockey stick. TJ, Oscar and the three other guys were staring at him.

Kyle shook it off and glided over to the boards. Jessica had dropped a sweater in the doorway. He picked that up and glanced back at her. She was still kneeling on the ice, her arms wrapped around her chest, saying nothing.

His friends were still standing there, too, looking at her.

He skated back with the sweater. Draped it over her shoulders. She pulled it tightly around herself. She looked so damn vulnerable. So upset. And he was sorry. He knew he was being an ass. But no way, no how, was she ever touching him there. He didn't care if she was a professional; the point was, she wasn't *his* professional.

He didn't want that kind of relationship with her. He was a man, and he wanted her to look at him as a man, not as a patient.

She stood, shivering, taking a step toward the door. Luckily, the ice was pretty ground up from their hockey game. She could walk without slipping or falling if she was careful.

But what he would give to be able to pick her up and carry her. If he didn't have the prosthetic leg, he would do it in a heartbeat, with ease, but that was no longer his reality.

He turned and headed to his locker room, not saying a word to anyone.

"KYLE?" JESSICA POUNDED on the locker room door he'd disappeared behind. "Kyle, open up! I don't want you to go away being mad at me. Please, Kyle."

She paused, but he wasn't answering. Obviously, he was sensitive about his injury and he didn't want her to touch it. Message received. But they still had to work together. That's why she was here. This was what it was all about.

"Will you talk with me about some ideas I have?" she called through the door. "For revenue. That's why I was in the ballet room today, I was checking out the facility to see if we could rent it. Plus, I have a lead on a birthday party. If you want to make the call… Kyle? Please open up."

More silence. He was definitely avoiding her, and that wasn't right. It was no way to solve their problems.

She pounded on the door once more. "I'm not

going back to Joe's office without having a conversation about this."

The door jerked open and Kyle stuck his head out. "Can't you let me take a shower in peace, woman?"

She stared at him. He'd taken off his helmet and jersey and shoulder pads. His chest was bare, hard and muscled, with a smattering of light brown hair.

He crossed his arms, and Jessica sucked in a ragged breath. Seeing him naked from the waist up wasn't what she'd been expecting. He looked good. *Really* good. And he was taller with his skates on, which she noted that he hadn't taken off yet. He wasn't risking her seeing his prosthetic foot—that was for sure.

She put a hand on her hip, suddenly angry again. "No, I'm not letting you off the hook just yet. *Talk* to me. You can take your shower when we're done."

He glared at her, and she held her breath. She'd never put her foot down with him before, and it felt good.

Grudgingly, he opened the door wider. "Fine," he growled. "But don't tell me I didn't warn you."

"About what?"

"You're in a men's locker room. With me."

CHAPTER ELEVEN

HE MAY NOT have realized, but Jessica didn't mind that at all. She crossed the threshold of his locker room—as far as he let her go before blocking her—and glanced at as much of the inner sanctum of his private space as she could see, gawking.

Kyle's sweatshirt and jeans were on the bench, folded. A locker was open with a towel and flip-flops inside. To the right was a doorway that she knew led to a separate room with a shower.

But this was nicer than a regular rink locker room, because it was Kyle's and that made it intimate to her. It was also cleaner and smelled nice, like sandalwood soap.

"If you don't mind, Jessica," Kyle said tightly. "I need to take my shower."

She noticed that he stood awkwardly, as if he was blocking something from her, behind the open door.

She peered around his shoulder. "What are you hiding?"

When he didn't answer, she walked around him to the back corner of the room.

Leaning against the wall was the missing poster of her, performing on the ice in her skating costume from the World Junior Championship.

"Why…?" she asked him.

"…didn't I throw it out?" he finished dully.

She nodded. "Yes. I asked you to."

He shrugged. "It's a good picture. Maybe I wanted to decorate my locker room."

"I don't get it, Kyle."

"How can you not get it, Jessa?"

"It's an embarrassing picture. I was a stupid girl who did everything wrong back then—"

"Like hell you did." He uncrossed his arms and ran a hand through his hair. He wasn't looking at her. "I had a crush on you." In a lower voice, he added, "Maybe I still do."

She clutched her throat. "You do?"

"You think that kiss was by accident?" he shot at her.

She focused on his chest. His beautiful, muscular chest that she'd laid her cheek against less than a day ago. A small noise came from her throat. She didn't want it to be so, but she'd enjoyed that kiss more than the one her boyfriend—fiancé—had given her after he'd proposed to her with his grandmother's antique Tiffany ring.

Her cheeks were flaming. She pressed her palms to them, not able to tear her gaze from

Kyle, from his intense, deep-green eyes. "But…
you said it was a mistake."

He snorted. "It was. It is. You and I are business partners and that's it." He took down the
framed portrait of her and thrust it into her hands.
It was heavy. So heavy. She didn't want it. She'd
said she hadn't wanted it, and she still didn't.

She held out the portrait and let it drop to the
floor.

Crack! The shatter of glass reverberated
through the concrete walls. Kyle's mouth opened
in shock.

"I told you I don't want it," she said. "And you
shouldn't have admired me back then, either. Not
only did you *not* cause my injured knee, but I lied
about even having an injury, Kyle. Physically I
was fine, but I was in so much emotional pain
that I just went to the referee during the championship and lied to him. It was easier to lie to
the world than to tell the truth to myself. I just…
snapped. And it was wrong, not least of which
because it hurt you. It hurt a lot of people. I let a
lot of people down, and I wish there was something I could do. I wish, but it's too late."

Exhaling, Kyle lowered himself to the bench.
Leaning his forearms on his knees, he ran a hand
through his hair.

She held her breath. She had likely killed any
admiration he had for her. Maybe that was good,

though. He'd left home as a result of her lie, and then he'd lost his leg. There was no denying that.

He lifted his head to her. "Do you have any more bombshells, or is this the last one?"

"I…"

He shook his head. "It doesn't matter, Jess. Just leave."

She blinked at him. "What?"

"Get out of my locker room."

JESSICA'S EYES TEARED UP. Whatever admiration he'd had left for her, she'd just killed. He looked furious and hurt, and she couldn't blame him.

She stooped and picked up the ruined picture. There was one long, jagged break across the glass. Feeling sad, she carried the poster out of his locker room so he'd never have to look at it again.

Outside his locker room, the rink air cooled her flushed face. She strode toward her office. Patrick sidled up to her. "We have a youth hockey group coming in later," he said.

"Okay," she answered absently.

"It's a day off from school. Kyle signed them as a special event."

At the mention of Kyle, she felt terrible all over again. But, really, if she was as sorry as she'd said, there was only one thing to do to make it up to him.

"Are you going to your office?" Patrick asked.

"Yes. You might want to let Kyle alone for a while. If you need help for any reason, come get me. Will you do that?"

Patrick nodded. At the junction where the hallways met, he left her.

She lowered her head and continued to her office. All she wanted was to show him how sorry she really was.

Inside her office, she placed her framed, broken portrait against the wall and then sat at her desk, nudging open her purse where she'd left it earlier. She pulled out the antique ring box that Sebastien had given her and flipped open the lid. The diamond solitaire sparkled.

The only reason she hadn't put the ring on her finger already was that the band was too small and she needed it resized.

She set the box on her desk blotter as a reminder of who she was and what she really wanted. This—marrying Sebastien—was the right thing to do. She was doing the right thing.

Jessica fished out her cell phone and pressed the call button for her work number. Dawn, their morning receptionist, answered. "Wallis Point Physical Therapy."

"Dawn, this is Jessica. I noticed that Gwen has an early appointment tomorrow." Jessica had massaged Gwen's hip once, helping her with a bursitis treatment while Gwen's main therapist was on vacation. "Could you please ask her to call me when she has a chance? You can give her my cell number."

"Sure, Jess," Dawn said. "Are you coming in this afternoon?"

"No, I'm off today."

"Have fun. I'll let Gwen know you're looking for her."

"Thank you." Jessica clicked off her phone and put her head on her desk. She had to be insane. As a result of this call with Gwen, she would be deliberately outing herself in her workplace as the former Jessa Hughes.

Five minutes later, her cell phone rang. Jessica squeezed her eyes shut. But she knew she had no choice if she wanted to help Kyle *and* if she wanted to live with herself again.

She picked up the phone. "This is Jessica."

"Hi, Jessica, this is Gwen. Dawn gave me your number."

"Thanks for calling." Jessica swallowed. "Um, I'm not sure if you're aware, but I also work mornings at the Wallis Point Twin Rinks. I've seen you skating on the public ice here."

"I wasn't aware that you worked—" Gwen paused. "Are you *Jessa* Hughes?"

Jessica pressed her hand to her temple. This

was exactly what she'd expected. "Well, I'm *Jessica* Hughes now."

"Of course. Goodness, I didn't even realize!" Gwen laughed. "And there I was going on and on about my skating hobby to you! You should have said something," she chided.

"Honestly, I was enjoying listening to your enthusiasm. And you made me think. That's…why I'm calling." Jessica licked her dry lips. She was actually shaking. She was a horrible saleswoman, had never really done anything like this, but she was trying her best. "I…noticed from the sign-in sheets that you and your skating friends have been stopping by the public ice fairly frequently. I know it can get crowded on that ice, and sometimes it's hard to find rinks with open dance sessions, so I wanted to call and personally offer some space to you."

"Oh. Well, what did you have in mind?"

"On weekday mornings between eight and noon we have ice available for rent at reasonable rates, and you could control who skates on it—any number up to twenty people. You'd have the dedicated sound system—not the overhead radio—so you could play whatever dance music you'd like. In addition, I'd include the private dance studio with mirrors and mats, which you could use as a warm-up and meeting space. I thought of you first, Gwen, before offering this to any other skating groups. If you'd like I can email you our rate sheet and terms." Jessica paused, breathless from her pitch.

"That's…interesting," Gwen said.

"When you were telling me how hard it was to find practice ice, I really was listening."

Gwen paused. "The place up the coast used to provide a coffee machine."

"We can do that." Jessica thought of the machine in Carol's office. "Um, what's your email address? I'll send the term sheet to you so you can review it."

With the phone against her ear, Jessica pulled a pen from the container on her desk and sorted through her purse for a notepad. As Gwen spelled out her address, Jessica copied it down.

"Great," Jessica said, clicking shut her pen. "I'll send you that file now."

"I'm not promising anything," Gwen said. "But I'll pass it along and see if there's any interest."

"That's all I'm asking."

"Good-bye, then. I'll look for you the next time I'm at the twin rinks. I'd love to see you skate again. We were all such fans!"

"Yes, good-bye, Gwen." Jessica fought the urge to knock her forehead on her desk and instead ran over to Carol's office. Carol had just gotten in. She was yawning and loading up her espresso machine with fresh coffee beans.

"Carol, I need to use the computer now. Can you please bring up Kyle's file with the rink rental rates and terms? It's an emergency."

"A rink-rental emergency. That's a new one." Carol laughed. "Can't we wait until we have coffee?"

"I wish we could, but I really need to pursue this sale."

Carol gave her a strange look. But with a shrug she shuffled over and sat at the rolling desk chair before the rink's huge, slightly outdated office computer.

"Kyle keeps the files on his laptop," Carol admitted. "I don't know if this is the most recent version."

"Take a look at the date stamp on it."

Carol squinted. "It's from last week."

"Great. Pull up email. Attach the file. I need to send it to someone."

Carol did as Jessica asked. Jessica held out the scrap paper she'd jotted Gwen's email address on, and Carol keyed it in. Then she ceded her chair, and Jessica slipped in, quickly typing out a cheery greeting to Gwen.

She pressed the send button and then steepled her hands. "Please, Gwen," she murmured. "Accept the offer…"

Carol fired up her espresso machine. The

whine of coffee beans being pulverized overrode all conversation.

Jessica sniffed the air. "I love the smell of coffee!" she shouted.

Carol shut off the bean grinder. "Have you had any yet?"

"No. It's been…an eventful morning."

Kyle had fallen on the ice, pushed her away, shown her that he'd saved her rink poster from being destroyed, and then had thrown her out of his locker room after she'd confessed to him her darkest secret. "Give me a double shot, please," she said to Carol.

Carol programmed the machine, put two mugs in place and then sat facing her. "Why are you selling ice time for Kyle?"

Because I owe him. Because I want to see him succeed. Because I'm terrified that I'm a horrible person.

"Jessica?" Carol slid a tin in front of her and pried off the cover. Homemade blueberry muffins, six of them.

"Oh, you're bribing me, I see." Jessica smiled at her and took the smallest muffin. "Well," she said, tearing back the wax-paper muffin cup, "don't you think that someone needs to help Kyle? If this place goes under, consider the people who'll be without jobs and the kids in town who won't have a local place to skate."

Carol nodded. "I think you'd be a much better salesperson than he is."

"You think so? I mean," she corrected herself quickly, "this isn't a knock on Kyle or anything, but I have to say, nobody has ever before implied that I could be a good salesperson."

Jessica's cell phone rang.

She and Carol glanced at one another. "Pick it up," Carol said.

Jessica grabbed for it. The screen showed a phone number with a Wallis Point exchange. *Gwen?*

"Answer it!" Carol said.

Jessica pressed the touchscreen. "Hello?"

"Jessica, it's Gwen. Your rates are not inexpensive."

Jessica's heart sank. "Hello, Gwen."

"But perhaps if you skated with us in the mornings…"

"I no longer own a pair of skates. Sorry."

"That's a shame."

Jessica said nothing. She would not be bribed to skate, for anyone. That was nonnegotiable. If Gwen turned down the offer, then…then Jessica would fail.

Carol put a mug of steaming coffee down on the desk in front of Jess. "What did she say?" she mouthed.

Jessica licked her lips. She'd watched her

mother negotiate with rink owners many times. Silence could be a potent method...

The seconds ticked. Jessica kept her mouth clamped shut. Finally, Gwen sighed. "We'll take Tuesday and Thursday mornings, eight to ten. Mind you, it will be a trial basis, just through the summer."

That's all Kyle needed for his profitability goal. "Excellent," Jessica said. And then she felt bold. "If you know of any other groups you could refer to us, please spread the word, okay?"

"Of course. Can I count on you to work with me on my hip appointments from now on?"

"My hours are cut way back, and I'm focusing almost exclusively on children. But for you, I'll make an exception."

"Wonderful. I'll look at the appointment book with Dawn and see what I can do."

"And I will see your group next week, Tuesday, at eight o'clock."

Carol jumped up and broke into her version of a happy dance.

Jessica hung up. And immediately joined Carol in happy dancing. She laughed, out of breath and still shaking. "I can't believe it! My first sale!"

"When will you tell Kyle?" Carol asked.

"After I make a call to sell a birthday party."

"A birthday party?"

Jessica felt giddy. "A mom whose boy I work

on mentioned that she's looking for an idea for her daughter's birthday party. I thought I'd call her, too."

Carol went over to the computer again. "Kyle had me make up a brochure for birthday parties."

"Did he?"

"Last week. He hasn't sent it out, though."

"Please print me a copy."

"Here it is." Carol pulled the sheet off the printer and handed it to Jessica.

Jessica read it while she finished her blueberry muffin. Then she took her coffee mug and the birthday-party brochure and headed back into Joe's office.

An hour later, she had one birthday party booked and two more under consideration. Pleased with herself, she sat back in her desk chair. She'd done it. She'd really done it.

There was a knock on her door.

Kyle? She reached for her notes. Hopefully, it would show him her commitment to righting her mistake with him. Hopefully, he would see how serious she was and find it in his heart to forgive her so they could at least be friends again.

Drawing a shaky breath, she gathered the papers where she'd transcribed the details on the bookings. "Come in!" she called.

But it wasn't Kyle who'd come to see her, it

was Patrick. He stuck his head in the door and scratched his head while he glanced all around.

"Um," he said, finally looking directly at her, "I searched for Kyle but I couldn't find him anywhere. He's not in the rink and his truck is gone."

Her heart sank. "Well…maybe he's out doing an errand."

"Nope." Patrick shook his head. "He's been gone since his warrior friends left. Now that youth group is out there, and the organizers were looking for him."

"I wish you'd told me!" she scolded him as she stood.

He lifted his chin. "I handled them," he said with pride. "I answered all their questions."

She smiled at Patrick. Jessica couldn't be angry with him because she knew exactly how he felt. She'd just spent the last two hours handling an agenda list that she'd never tackled before, either. And it had felt good.

"Do you need anything from me, then?" she asked.

"Yeah," Patrick said. "The key for the skate-rental stand. I don't have it, and an adult with the group wants to rent a pair of skates."

"I'll go with you." Jessica tucked the paper with the ice-booking information into her pocket in case Kyle came back and she bumped into him. Closing the door behind her, she hustled with

Patrick toward the rental-skate stand, amazed at how noisy the rink had gotten in the short time since she'd retreated to her office. A group of boy skaters and their parents had descended upon the open space in front of the hockey area. Mainly dads were present, but there were a few moms, too, gathered in small groups by the stands.

"This is the youth hockey league, I presume?" she asked Patrick, stopping as a little guy hauling an oversized gear bag nearly ran them down.

"Yeah. The Wallis Point schools are off today for teacher training. The league booked a special morning session to get ready for summer camp sign-ups. It's like an open house for them."

"Okay," Jessica said, dodging the end of a carelessly wielded hockey stick. "Let's get these folks set up, then." She unlocked the skate-rental shop, her key ring jangling in her hand, and headed toward the storage closet.

As she switched on the overhead light, she gasped. The shelves of new skates were sparkling clean and organized. She hadn't even been aware that they'd been delivered.

"I did it," Patrick said proudly again.

"It looks so great!" She inspected the new kids' skates that Kyle had ordered. They were sturdy, well made, and state-of-the-art. He'd made the investment for her, and that just showed how much he'd appreciated her opinion.

"These will work great," she said, opening the tongue of a boot and inspecting inside. "We'll charge a fee for them, definitely."

"Too bad we don't have new ones in adult sizes. Oh, wait. There was one pair." Patrick ambled from the closet over to the counter, and Jessica followed him.

He crouched down and pulled a box from a cubbyhole. A very familiar box. "Kyle told me not to touch these, but I don't see why we can't—"

"Can I see that box?" Her voice wobbled. "Who ordered these?"

"Kyle did. I don't know why. I was just gonna check the size. The lady out there wanted a seven and—"

"These aren't sevens." Jessica's throat choked up. She knelt beside Patrick and opened the cardboard box, the same cardboard box that had been delivered to her year after year.

Inside were her skating boots. The same old style, but the model updated with new stitching and a slightly different tongue. She ran her fingers over the shiny white sheen, smelled the distinctive scent of fresh new leather.

Feeling excited, she flipped the boots over. The blades were already mounted to the soles, and they were sharpened. They weren't shipped this way, so Kyle must have done it. Her brand of

English blades, in the length that had been most comfortable for her.

Holding them by the soles, she tucked the boots close to her chest. Kyle had even threaded her preferred type of heavy white laces through all the little eyelet holes.

Oh, Kyle, Kyle, Kyle.

He'd done this for her. Why?

"Um, Jessica?"

"Yes?" She saw the scene from Patrick's eyes, her kneeling on the cement floor with skates cradled in her lap. Quickly, she stood. Put the skates back in the box and shoved it in the cubbyhole.

"You don't think we should use them?" Patrick asked.

"No. Kyle's right. Respect his wishes."

"Okay." Patrick shrugged. "I'm just trying to make you guys some money. Kyle's always harping about that, so..."

She smiled at him. She really loved that Patrick was so sweet in his unique way. They were all forming their own little team, including Patrick. He seemed to have no appreciation or frame of reference for who she was, and that was fine with her. Carol had surely told him, and that was fine with Jessica, too. She didn't need to worry or fret or hide or change anything. Not with them. Maybe not even with Gwen or her workmates. Her morning calls and the success with making her sales had actually helped to make her feel better.

"Are you okay?" Patrick asked.

"I think I am," she said giddily. "Come on, let's go wait on our customers." She stood and stuck her head out over the counter. "Did someone here want to rent skates?" she called.

A petite lady trying to corral two little hockey guys taking turns whacking each other with their plastic helmets raised her tired hand. "That would be me!"

Jessica went over to her. Patrick followed. "Would you like to rent figure skates or hockey skates?" Jessica asked the lady.

She scrunched up her face. "What's the difference? Does it matter, I mean?"

"Oh, yes. The figure skates have a toe pick."

"In case you want to do a triple axel," Patrick added.

"I'll take the hockey skates," the lady quickly said.

Patrick nodded. "Good choice."

Jessica smiled at him, giving Patrick the thumbs up and extricating herself so he could take over. She went back to the counter, enjoying herself as she watched him wait solicitously on his customer.

WHEN KYLE TURNED into the rink driveway fifteen minutes later, he was shocked to find the lot jammed with cars and milling with people. The place looked like it had been overrun by an army of munchkins and their parents.

He slapped his hand to his head. He'd completely forgotten about the youth league open house he'd booked weeks ago.

Cursing himself, he climbed down from his truck and headed straight for the hockey rink. After he'd told Jessica to leave him alone, he'd taken a short, angry shower followed by a long drive up the coast with the windows down. He'd hoped the sea air would clear the cobwebs from his head.

It hadn't. He still had no idea what to do about his feelings for her.

Taking off for three hours hadn't solved a thing. He'd even made it worse because, by storming off the way he had, he'd unwittingly shirked his job.

Inside the rink he immediately picked Jessica out. She walked with a clipboard—pale, but present. Her long sweater covered her hips and she still wore her black yoga pants and sneakers. Her hair was in the high ponytail she favored, and she wore no makeup or jewelry.

When she saw him, she stilled. He wasn't sure if he was imagining it, but her expression seemed to freeze. Was she afraid of him?

Biting her lip, she tucked the clipboard under her arm and wove her way through the crowd to him. They stood in a private corner, gazing at each other.

"Hi, Kyle." She smiled at him. Not the fake golden-girl grin she'd given strangers when they were kids, or the hesitant, beaten look she sometimes gave when it came to rink matters. This smile showed a quiet calm. "I'm glad you're back."

Was she? He'd been embarrassed when she'd seen his screwed-up leg. And the picture of her in his locker room. And there was the booking he'd forgotten about. Worst of all, he cringed for the anger he'd shown her when he'd tossed her out of his locker room.

He *couldn't* toss her out. They were running a business together. He crossed his arms. "I'm sorry I'm late. I didn't mean to be. Is everything going okay here?"

"Y-yes." She smiled—a genuinely happy smile—and it rocked him back on his heels. "Patrick has been handling everything really well. He only came and got me when he needed a key to the skate-rental room. I've been helping him. It's…sort of fun."

Wow. She couldn't have shocked him any more if she'd tried.

Smiling, her pink lips glossy, she reached into her sweater pocket and unfolded a slip of paper.

"I want to show you some ice time I've booked for us."

He stared at the sheet, then at her. "*You* booked ice time?"

She nodded and leaned closer to him. She smelled like shampoo or skin cream that was lightly scented with something good enough to eat. He'd noticed that earlier on the ice with her, too.

"You know Gwen?" she was saying. "The lady who ice dances with her retired husband during public ice at noon? Well, it turns out she's a client at Wallis Point PT. I called her this morning and she agreed to organize an ice-dancers' morning coffee club at our rink. Isn't that good news?"

"I don't believe it." It came out harsher than he'd wanted.

She looked deflated. "Look, Kyle, I'm sorry I smashed the picture on your floor. And I'm sorry about our fight. I don't want to be at odds with you, ever."

"That wasn't a fight, and I'm not at odds with you."

Absently she stared at her chewed-down thumbnail. "The past is screwed up between us. I never wanted to address it because I thought we could ignore it and just focus on the future." She curled a piece of hair around her ear and gazed up at him, pleading. "But it doesn't work like that, does it? You can't just ignore things and hope they go away."

"No," he said softly. *No, you can't.*

"So...maybe it wasn't a fight we had, but all the cobwebs *are* coming to light, and..." Funny she'd used that word *cobwebs* "...and getting cleared out, and maybe it's just hard for us to deal with."

"It's not hard for me, Jessica," he said firmly. "I've forgiven you for the past."

Her face brightened. "You have?"

"Yes," he said gently. Because forgiving her wasn't his real problem.

"Whew!" She gave him a relieved smile. "I've been so worried about that."

"Don't be. I asked you to leave my locker room because I wanted to think."

"And?" She drew her toe in a small circle on the floor. "What did you decide?"

That you can show a woman how you feel about her, but you can't make her love you the way that you want her to.

And he wasn't going to change things by walking around being angry all the time. Like Joe.

He took the folded paper from her. "Why don't you show me what you did, partner?"

"Oh!" She grinned. "Well, I booked business for us."

"Uh-huh," he said, not really sure he believed it. "When, where and what time?"

"Well, since we only have the one usable ice surface and we're basically only earning income from high school hockey and kids' nights-and-weekends leagues, we really need to do everything possible to fill the ice during the off-peak times during the day when the kids are in school. Right?"

That, in a nutshell, was the problem he'd been dealing with. When had she gotten so smart about the business? "Yes, that's right."

"And that got me thinking..."

He nodded. He was listening.

"Gwen agreed to pay our full rate to reserve the ice in the main rink on Tuesday and Thursday mornings from eight until ten until at least the end of the summer. We're including use of the ballet room so they can set up some tables and have coffee, plus have a private spot to stretch and play music. We'll only have to clear the ice once for the start of the session. And, she's willing to spread the word so we can sign on other groups like hers."

"That's..." Pretty great.

"And, talking to Gwen gave me another idea. Kyle, a lot of retirees live on the beach year-round. Sebastien's neighbors Ed and Edie, for example. I'm thinking we could organize an adult-only skate from one to two in the afternoon, after public ice and before the kids get out of school. If you'll set up the sound system, then we can put on music. Maybe move Carol's coffee machine out here. You know, make it special and festive. Now that I'm thinking aloud, we could advertise and make it a regular event. A mid-day coffee and socializing break, with exercise and instruction."

"Can we do this?" he asked.

"Many other rinks do, Kyle."

"I didn't know."

"And another thing that's unique to us in Wallis Point is that once the summer starts, we'll have vacationing families. Skating at public ice is a great rainy-day activity for kids. We should advertise in the local hotels and tourist literature!"

"Okay. Yes. You're right. Those are good ideas."

"I'm relieved you think so." She smiled and started to say something else, but there was a sudden shriek of noise. There were a lot of kids running around and it was loud.

Then a kid came crashing toward them, sobbing his eyes out.

"Whoa, hey." Kyle caught the kid before he ran into Jessica. "What's going on, buddy? Why aren't you in your skates?"

"I don't wanna do it!"

A frazzled lady came running over. She was holding a pair of shiny new hockey skates. "Honey, if you'll just try—"

"I don't wanna try!"

Kyle kept a loose grip on the boy's arm. The lady looked familiar. "Hi," he said, holding out his right hand. "I'm Kyle Northrup. This is Jessica." He turned, and Jessica made a small wave to the lady. "Sorry," Kyle said, turning back, "I'm not placing your name."

"Oh, Kyle! I didn't know you were in town. It's Sandy Dublin. I'm married to Steve Poisson."

Steve had been one of Kyle's defensemen for all four years of high school. "Hi, Sandy." Kyle ruffled the hair on her son's head. "What's going on?"

"I can't get him to go out on the ice," she whispered. "Steve signed him up and he's not going to be happy. He would've been here, but he works the early shift and he's a supervisor, so…"

Kyle would have knelt to the kid's height, but that was awkward with his leg, so he settled for leaning over. "What's your name?" he asked the boy.

"Stephen."

"Hi, Stephen. I'm Kyle. I used to play hockey with your dad."

Stephen looked unimpressed. Sandy gave him a distressed look.

Kyle directed his words to the boy. "Nobody's going to force you to skate, Stephen," he said quietly. "Hockey's a great sport, but you have to want to do it. Maybe you could watch the kids for a while and see what you think."

He straightened as Stephen gazed up at him, eyes wide.

"Steve isn't gonna be happy," Sandy muttered to him.

"Tell him to call me when he gets out of work, okay?" Kyle took a notepad and pen out of his back pocket and wrote down his cell number. Tearing the slip of paper from the pad, he held it out to her.

She took it, grateful. "Thanks."

Kyle wouldn't say so in front of the boy, but he thought the boy's reluctance might be because of his young age. He didn't look older than three or maybe four. In any event, Kyle would do what he could for them. Steve had been a friend. Actually, the boy was the spit of his father. Maybe that was part of the problem, too.

"See you around," Kyle said to Sandy. "Make sure Steve calls."

"I will," she said. "We'll just...go sit on the bleachers for now."

"Sounds good."

When Kyle turned around, Jessica was watching him with a smile.

"What?" he asked.

"I like what you just did," she said softly. "I like it a lot."

Well, he liked her, too. He liked the way her black yoga pants hugged all her curves, and how her glossy ponytail swung past her long neck with that sliver of bare skin right at the nape.

She caught him looking at her and gave him a secret, pleased smile.

He could go all day on a look like that. He let himself sink deep into the beauty of her warm brown eyes. He could stare at her forever.

Another kid ran by, too close, and Jessica steadied herself by lightly clasping Kyle's bicep. In return, he lightly touched her waist.

She leaned a bit closer, her eyes never leaving his. To Kyle, the air felt so much hotter.

"Jessica!" Carol came barreling down the hallway toward them with arms outstretched, waving in excitement, a long necklace bouncing against her ample breasts as she ran. "I have such good news!" When she came to them, she swept Jessica into a hug and lifted her off her sneakers.

"What is it?" Jessica asked, laughing.

"I'm engaged!" Carol shrieked.

I thought she already was...

Jessica went pale, maybe from force of that

bear hug. "But I thought you already were engaged." *Great minds think alike.*

"I know, *technically*, yes, I was." Carol laughed joyously. "But it's official now—Johnny's divorce is finalized!" She turned to Kyle, still beaming. "We're having a June wedding and I want everyone here to come!"

"June, that's...great," Jessica said, licking her lips and glancing from Carol to Kyle. Talking to him, she'd forgotten about her own engagement. At least, until Carol had reminded her.

"Everybody, save the date," Carol said. "It will be either the third or fourth Friday in June—my sister works at the Grand Beachfront Hotel, and she's looking into it for me. She thinks that both Fridays are open, but she's not sure."

"Great," Jessica said, not daring to look at Kyle. She would have a problem if she wasn't careful.

"And you," Carol said, gripping Jessica by the shoulders, "are going to be my bridesmaid. Please," she pleaded. "My sister is matron of honor but I would be honored if you stood for me, too."

"Of course," Jessica said, touched.

She glanced at Kyle again, but someone had pulled him away—a father or a coach. Kyle waved at her discreetly when he saw her looking at him. She waved back.

What was she doing?

"Sebastien told me that you got engaged as well," Carol said.

Jessica snapped her head back toward her. "What?"

"He showed me your ring." Carol *tsked* her. "Why didn't you tell me?"

"Because…the ring hasn't been sized yet and I wanted to wait until I could wear it. Carol, is Sebastien here now?"

"He came walking in from the parking lot with Johnny. They're both in your office as we speak."

"In *my* office?" Oh, why hadn't she locked it? Without looking back at Kyle, she jogged through the rink, down the hallway and through the double doors.

Sebastien was sitting in her desk chair, smiling at Johnny, who was perched on the edge of her desk.

Jessica froze. She felt invaded.

"Hey, babe." Sebastien stood and kissed her. He was wearing his navy blue suit and he swung his car keys in the hand that also held his cell phone. "I came to take you out to lunch." He smiled shyly at her. "Would you like to meet my sister? I called her early this morning to tell her our news and she, uh, surprised me by driving up from New York."

Jessica could only stare at him.

"She's out in the car. So...you want to get going?"

"I… Yes, of course." She'd wanted to meet Sebastien's family for some time now.

Everything was moving so quickly.

She glanced down at her clothes. Sebastien had expensive tastes in restaurants. "I need to change," she mumbled.

"No problem." He glanced behind Jessica to someone in her doorway. "Oh, hey."

Cringing to herself, she turned. Kyle had walked in, followed by Patrick and Carol.

Just great.

She flashed them all a wide smile. "I wasn't going to say anything until my ring got sized, but…" She looked at Sebastien, hoping her face wasn't as red as it felt. "Sebastien and I got engaged last night."

"Dude." Patrick ambled over to Sebastien and shook his hand. "Congratulations."

"When's the date?" Carol asked.

"We...haven't discussed that yet."

"As soon as possible," Sebastien piped in.

From the corner of her eye, Jessica saw Kyle flinch.

She was flinching, too, on the inside. And that wasn't good.

"So, let's get going." Jessica swept up her

purse, checked that Sebastien had put her ring
box inside—he had—and then gave a quick nod
to Johnny, still sitting on the edge of her desk.

"Great. See you all later." Sebastien bent to the
couch and scooped up the old picture of her with
its shattered glass. Jessa Hughes, World Junior
Champion, the Pride of Wallis Point.

"No," Jessica blurted. Sebastien looked up at
her. "Don't take it. Please."

"Why not? I thought we'd fix the glass and
hang it in the house."

After last night's confession, he really, honestly
thought she'd want that?

She didn't know what to say.

"It belongs here," Kyle said, his deep voice
booming. "Leave it."

Everyone was silent. This was the first Kyle
had spoken. Jessica hardly dared to look at him,
but she did.

He was somber. His green eyes bored a hole
through Sebastien's forehead.

"It…could stay here, yes," Jessica agreed. "I
suppose it is rink property."

Sebastien laughed it off. "Okay," he said, smiling at Jessica. But he turned to Kyle. "It doesn't
matter anyway. I've got the real thing right here."

CHAPTER TWELVE

ONCE THEY WERE outside on the cement walkway, Jessica put her hand to her head, reeling. She felt blindsided—by her crazy attraction to Kyle, by his forgiveness, by his kindness.

But it wasn't right for her to be behaving in a disloyal manner to Sebastien. She'd said yes to him. Just because he was a little clueless and thickheaded about her sensitivity regarding her past life wasn't a reason to cancel an engagement. She needed to be practical. Sebastien was the right choice for her—for what she needed, for what was good for the future.

"Hold on a second." Sebastien stopped short at the bottom of the stairs, glancing at his cell phone. "I have to answer this text message."

"Sure. I'll go meet your sister."

"Thanks." He gave her a grateful smile. "I'll be right there."

Jessica knew from experience that it might be a while before he finished his work call, but she nodded and kept walking. Sebastien's car was parked close by. The sunroof was open, and music drifted from the window. A woman sat in the passenger seat. Jessica assumed she was Caroline, Sebastien's twin sister.

Jessica headed for the passenger window, then smiled. "Caroline? I'm Jessica. It's so nice to finally meet you."

Caroline's lips smiled, but it was hard to see what the rest of her face was doing. She wore a pair of oversized black sunglasses that hid her expression but magnified a distorted image of Jessica's expression back at her.

"Hello," she said, her manicured fingernail sweeping a strand of errant hair from her forehead and tucking it behind her ear. Her fine, straight hair was twisted into a perfect bun. She wore a formfitting sleeveless shirt that showcased toned and tanned arms, and a linen pencil skirt that displayed how thin and elegant she was.

Jessica's smile wavered. She tried not to mind that she was still in her sneakers and a cable-knit sweater with a hole in the elbow. It was also likely that her yoga pants were dirty on the bum, due to Jessica's sitting on rubber matting and tying little kids' skates for a good part of the morning.

"Um, I understand that you're a lawyer," Jessica said, trying desperately to make conversation. She managed a quick sideways glance in her peripheral vision, only to see that Sebastien was transfixed by his phone, furiously typing something with one finger.

"I'm an *attorney*, yes. For a securities firm on Wall Street." Caroline tilted her head to get a better look at the front entrance of the Wallis Point Twin Rinks. The corners of her lips edged down. "Sebastien told me about the unusual will you're involved with. How unfortunate you have to spend time here."

"It's not that bad," Jessica murmured. Honestly, she felt a lot better about it after this morning.

"May I see my grandmother's ring?" Caroline asked. "How does it look on you?"

"Your...?" Oh, great. Jessica bunched her hands into a fist inside her sweater pockets. "Um, the ring needs to be resized, so I can't wear it just yet." She pulled her hands from her pockets and reached inside the purse over her shoulder for the antique Tiffany box.

"Your hands are quite large," Caroline remarked. "My grandmother had petite bone structure."

Jessica sucked in a breath, but kept smiling. She removed the Tiffany box and handed it over.

"Beautiful." Caroline took the box from Jessica, opened it and slid the elegant diamond solitaire onto her left ring finger. Jessica couldn't get the ring past the second knuckle on her pinky finger. But it fit Sebastien's sister like Cinderella's shoe.

Caroline held her hand forward and let the half-carat, nearly flawless stone catch the light. Rainbows sparkled across the front dashboard of Sebastien's black Nissan.

"There were two antique pieces that my grandmother left us," Caroline said. "This diamond anniversary ring, and the diamond-cluster earrings my grandfather presented her with when my father was born. I was given my choice before Sebastien and I chose the earrings, of course."

Jessica got the distinct feeling that Caroline would have preferred to own the matching ring, as well. Caroline kept the ring on her finger, admiring it as she spoke.

"Are those the diamond earrings?" Jessica asked politely, referring to the pretty pair that Caroline wore. Though they were colored, she'd heard that diamonds came in other shades besides clear. Canary yellow, for one.

"Goodness, no. These are citrine. Rather inexpensive."

Jessica doubted that. Caroline looked as if she had good taste, and the settings were surely solid gold.

Caroline sighed. "The last I saw the pieces together was at Christmas when my mother passed them to Sebastien and me. I wondered what Sebastien would do with his choice."

She pulled off the ring and returned it to the box, and the box to Jessica, without comment.

No ally here, Jessica thought. She stood awkwardly for a moment, wondering what to do. Finally, she walked over and waited beside Sebastien.

He glanced up at her, then back to his phone. "My deal's falling apart," he muttered. "Sorry."

"Maybe we should reschedule lunch?"

He gave her a wry smile. "You're really great, do you know that?"

She swallowed. She wasn't great. She'd been spending more time and having more intimate conversations with Kyle lately than she'd ever had with Sebastien. Secrets, all around. Except with Kyle, of course.

Sebastien stuck his phone in his pocket. "Never mind, I'll deal with it Monday. I have something I really want to show you now."

"What?" she asked.

Sebastien's gaze flicked up and down the length of her. "You want to get changed first, right?"

Yes, she said that she had. "Where are we having lunch?"

"Ogunquit. The lobster place on the water."

"That sounds good." She kept her chin down

and her gaze from the rink as Sebastien curled his arm around her and strolled with her back to his car.

"We'll leave your car here," Sebastien said.

"Fine. I'll zip home and change, and then meet you back here."

"No, what I want to show you is on the way past your house."

Jessica groaned inwardly. After Caroline's grilling, she wasn't looking forward to the woman getting a look at the dive apartment that Jessica called home these days.

But there was no help for it. Sebastien swung into the driver's seat. Caroline didn't appear to be budging, so Jessica took the backseat.

Sebastien turned in the seat toward the two women in his life, his easy smile and handsome face smoothing over all their awkwardness. "Did you ladies say hello? Jess, you met my sister? Cookie, you met Jess?"

"We did," Caroline reported without looking at Jessica. "Are we meeting Jess's family, too?" Here, she turned to face Jessica, and this time she took off her sunglasses. "My parents are flying out from Ohio next month. They want to meet Sebastien's fiancée and talk about the wedding plans with you and your parents."

Jessica swallowed again. "There's just me," she said softly.

Sebastien had his arm curled around the seat, concentrating on backing the Nissan safely out of the parking space.

Caroline stared at Jessica, her silence demanding an explanation.

"There's really nothing to plan from my end." Jessica's throat felt dry. Short of a few colleagues from her physical therapy clinic, Edie and Ed, and her new friends at the twin rinks, Jessica didn't have anyone she particularly wanted to invite.

Kyle? No way. The thought of Kyle being present while she married Sebastien made her queasy.

She closed her eyes and leaned her head back on the seat. She had a sinking feeling, as if she was making a huge mistake. But that couldn't be right.

Sebastien cheerfully drove across town and turned down the side street across the busy highway from the beach where she'd been renting month-to-month this winter. Jessica couldn't help imagining the place through Caroline's eyes. A dump, she would think it. A low, squat cottage with peeling white paint and the broken carcass of an old gas grill blocking the front walkway. Her landlord was feverishly getting ready for the start of summer season only two weeks away.

To Jessica, though, it was hers. She'd fought

hard to be independent. To live life on her own terms, beholden to no one else's agenda.

Jessica shut her car door and headed to the side porch. Sebastien ambled inside the cottage, too, and Caroline followed him.

The tiny living area and kitchenette were stacked with moving boxes. Her bedroom was an obstacle course. Jessica changed her clothes inside the bathroom in world-record time. She pulled a favorite dress over her head and slipped her feet into summery sandals. There was no fixing the fact that she badly needed a pedicure and a haircut, but she had so little time these days. So she ran a comb through her tangled hair, secured it with a clip, swiped on lipstick and found a clutch to carry rather than her usual mountain-sized purse.

In the kitchen, Sebastien grabbed a water bottle from her fridge, and Caroline looked horrified as she squinted at the age and condition of the rental-unit appliances.

"So," Jessica said cheerfully, "we're on our way to Ogunquit?"

"God, you look great." Sebastien gathered her close and gave her a wet kiss on the lips as they went out to the car.

Nothing. It wasn't working right now, she thought with a sinking heart. Hopefully, her romantic feelings for him would bounce back soon.

Out on the main drag, along the beach high-way, Sebastien popped open the sunroof and turned up the radio. They zipped along with traffic, heading north. Caroline was draped in the front seat like an empress, her head back, eyes closed and sunglasses in place.

"Here we are," Sebastien said.

They pulled into Ed and Edie's driveway next to Sebastien's rental house. Jessica looked at him, confused.

Caroline got out of the car and stretched her legs. She looked infinitely happier and more comfortable in this wealthier part of Wallis Point's beach community.

Jessica stepped out of the car and took off her sandals. Soft, warm beach sand caressed the soles of her feet, and at Sebastien's invitation of an out-stretched hand, she followed him down the path that led to a more remote outcropping closer to the surf.

Once they were out of earshot of Caroline, Jessica whispered to him, "What are we doing here?"

"I want to show you where you and I are going to live," Sebastien said. "And there it is." He pointed to the most beautiful home on this stretch of beach. In her wildest dreams she could never afford to live here. She snorted.

Sebastien smiled at her skeptical look. "I already talked with Maureen Cole. The property will be going on the market at the end of summer and you and I have the inside track."

"But…how can that be?"

"Forget about that for now." Sebastien took her hand. "Let's imagine the possibilities instead." He led her around to the back where a small garden with beach roses and grass plantings lined a polished stone walkway. The home belonged in an architectural magazine. It was more stunning than even the beach cottage that Sebastien currently rented.

"Do you see those second-story windows there?" Sebastien pointed up. "Those are three small bedrooms, one for each kid." He pointed to the other end of the house, at a private wrought iron balcony that reminded her of a romantic Romeo and Juliet scene. "That's the master bedroom," Sebastien said, smiling. "Our room." He took her hand and moved her along farther into the garden. "Downstairs, there's the biggest open kitchen you've ever seen, and once Maureen gets us inside for a walk-through, you'll see how your whole cottage could fit inside the great room."

It was tempting for certain. Children, kitchens, master suites. But why was he torturing her with stories of what could never be? "Sebastien, neither of us has this kind of money."

A sea breeze blew through his hair, ruffling it,

and Sebastien pushed it back. "I ran the numbers with Maureen," he insisted. "She said it's doable. She'll work with us to put in the first bid when it goes on the market."

"How?" Jessica pushed.

"Can't you just trust me? I'm good with managing money. I know how to make numbers work. If you'll believe in me, then you're looking at your next home right now. Do you believe in me?"

She put her hand to her mouth. He was serious.

The best part that he'd shown her today had been the bedrooms—enough for three kids. She really wanted a family. She wanted a home, too, and, yes, she could envision herself here. Before her mom had gotten divorced when Jessica was little, they'd used to live in beautiful homes like this one.

"But you have to do your part," Sebastien said, reading her face.

"My part?" she asked.

"The rink can't be profitable, Jess. You understand that, right?"

She felt the horror rise within her. "Are you asking me to sabotage the rink operations?"

"No!" Sebastien laughed indulgently. He caught her cheeks with his palms and smiled into her eyes. He had such a sweet, charming smile. Except at this moment, she didn't *feel* charmed.

"You're a good person, Jess. You could never do that, and I wouldn't expect you to. I'm just asking you not to help it along as much as you have been."

Did he have spies in the building? She'd made all those calls today to drum up revenue. Covered for Kyle with his absence, and she'd fitted kids' skates, too.

Sebastien tilted his head to her. "I know I've been on the road for work these last few weeks. But I thought you were going to stay in your office and do your PT paperwork? What happened with that?"

"I do my paperwork in my office, yes."

"Carol said you were helping out in the rink today. I thought you didn't like to go near the ice?"

"The rink is my inheritance," she said calmly. "And I will treat it as I see fit." She had to make this clear to him, because he was confusing her. "Look, I appreciate you looked out for me in the lawyer's office that first day when I wasn't being forceful enough to ask good questions. But I'm on my feet now, and I'm capable of handling my own finances. I've been doing it for a long time by myself, actually."

"You have. But we're getting married now, and then it will be joint." Sebastien licked his lips. Maybe he was nervous.

She had to be clear with him, though. The last time she hadn't been upfront about what she needed, she'd blown up a competition—she'd ruined her reputation and ultimately lost her mother.

Not to mention, Kyle lost his leg.

She took a breath. "Sebastien, please trust me that I know what I need to do."

"Are you telling me you don't want this?" He indicated the beach house.

That was the hard part, because she really did want it. Sebastien was the right person for her. "I want to settle down with you," she said firmly. "But if you're asking me to avoid helping the rink business, then that's just wrong. It's wrong for me. I'm not comfortable with it. Joe left half of his rink to me for a reason, and I intend to honor that."

"You can't always have it both ways, Jess. You have to be prepared to choose."

"Well, I think I *can* have it both ways. Who's to stop me?"

Sebastien stared at her for a long time, and she stared back. She was serious and he needed to see that.

"Okay," he said. "Do what you feel you have to. I'll find the money some other way."

"Thank you for understanding," she said quietly.

He nodded. Caroline was heading their way, so Sebastien turned to meet her.

"I definitely approve of this place," Jessica heard Caroline say, even from the distance she was at. Sebastien's reply was unintelligible, lost in the wind.

Jessica shivered, rubbing her hands against the bare skin on her arms. Maybe she had won a small victory in standing her sandy ground with Sebastien but she felt uneasy, as if there was something more to lose. Something that she suspected but wasn't ready to admit just yet.

ON SATURDAY MORNING Kyle opened the tailgate of his pickup truck. He stood aside as the assistant at Pete's Paints loaded the box containing the sheet of glass that Kyle had just purchased.

Kyle had measured Jessica's poster. This new glass should fit the frame so he could repair it and leave it in Jessica's office, as she'd asked. He was still surprised over the discovery that she and Sebastien were engaged, but the way Sebastien had treated her told Kyle he still had a chance. By fixing the glass he was sending her a message. He hadn't given up.

Whatever she decided to do with it after that was up to her, but he hoped that she could see her way to feeling good about the poster someday.

"Thanks," Kyle said to the assistant, and shut the tailgate. He was just about to head back to the twin rinks when Johnny David called to him from across the parking lot.

"Kyle!"

Kyle waited while Joe's former maintenance manager strolled over from an outdoor stand where he'd been checking out twenty-pound bags of potting soil.

"What are you up to?" Johnny asked.

"Nothing much." Kyle crossed his arms and leaned against the cab. "You doing some gardening?"

"Carol has her heart set on tomato plants. I told her they'd have to be in pots on the porch, because my back isn't up to cutting out lawn to make vegetable gardens these days."

"I didn't know you had a bad back," Kyle remarked.

"A-yup. It's why I stopped working at the rinks. Too much up and down ladders, heavy lifting, that kind of thing. No offense to you."

"None taken," Kyle said.

Johnny scratched his neck. "Truth is, I miss it." He glanced to Kyle. "Now that my soon-to-be wife is working there permanently, I'd love to get back."

"Honestly, I wish I could afford you." Kyle eyed Johnny. "A lot of it depends if I can get the figure-skating rink up and running."

"I guessed that would be a problem."

"That you know how to fix?" Kyle added.

Johnny grinned at him, a twinkle in his eye. "I can fix anything…"

For a price, he insinuated. Kyle remembered that Johnny always had his price.

Kyle sighed. Still, an ice surface with unsold ice wasn't doing him any good. "How much?" he asked quietly.

"I've been thinking." Johnny shifted his feet. A grimace crossed his face and he reached for his back.

Kyle knew what muscle pain felt like. He'd been dealing with it in his phantom leg of late. "You want to sit?" Kyle asked.

"Yup, let's." Johnny glanced at Kyle. "On second thought, grab a beer with me tonight. How about ten o'clock at Moroney's?"

Kyle should be finished closing up the twin rinks by that time. He nodded, frowning to himself. He wasn't big on social places like Moroney's Pub, but he needed that ice surface up and running.

AT TEN O'CLOCK Kyle nursed a beer, sitting at a bar stool with his back to the wall and a view of the front door. He could barely keep his eyes open. He'd been working overtime to get his business on decent footing, but after three months the place was still underwater, even with the ice surface being full during the day with Jessica's help. He was at his wit's end. Run down. Ragged.

He leaned over to rub his residual limb.

"Thanks for meeting me," Johnny said to Kyle as he climbed onto the open stool beside him. He made a signal to the bartender and turned his attention to the television overhead. The NHL championships were on, and the place was filled with rowdy hockey fans.

Kyle took a swig from his Coors bottle and waited for Johnny to name his price so he could get home and watch the game in peace.

"Hey." Johnny nudged Kyle. "Look who's here? I got radar when it comes to her. Hey, honey," he called out. He nudged Kyle again. "Isn't she something?"

Kyle followed Johnny's gaze past Carol and straight to Jessica. She was halfway across the room but facing him, sitting at a table with Sebastien, Carol and some other woman Kyle didn't recognize. All he cared about was Jessica, though. She wore a sexy low-cut blouse. Her hair was up and she was wearing makeup.

He stared at her and put his bottle down, nearly choking. She was so damn beautiful, and every time the realization caught him anew.

She gazed back at him, a small smile on her face. She didn't drop eye contact, either.

"Carol asked Jessica to be a bridesmaid,"

Johnny remarked, lifting his beer to his mouth as he turned his attention back to the game.

"She did?"

"A-yup."

Kyle assumed that meant Sebastien would be at Johnny's wedding, too. Jessica's fiancé sat across from her, every hair perfectly placed. Right beside him was that other snooty-looking woman. Standing, talking animatedly to Jessica, was Carol, Johnny's bride-to-be.

Kyle glanced back to Jessica and caught her looking at him, too. She glanced away quickly.

"So, anyway, Carol tells me I have a problem," Johnny said, still fixated on the game. "Oh!" he shouted, as a general roar went up from the bar patrons. "He's a bum. I don't know why they don't trade him!"

Kyle didn't know who Johnny was talking about. He hadn't seen the play. He was staring at Jessica again, who stared openly back at him. Her cheeks were pink and she was smiling.

Sebastien is going to notice, Kyle thought. He looked away, to try and save her, but he couldn't help it, she was like an addiction, so he found himself gazing back at her.

"…so that's why I need you to be a groomsman for me at my wedding," Johnny was saying.

Kyle's attention jerked back to the conversation in front of him. "What did you say?" he asked Johnny.

"I know it's a pain in the ass," Johnny said. "You'll have to wear a tux or a uniform or whatever Marines need to do." He pitched his head back and drained the beer bottle, smacking his lips before continuing. "I'm not one for the big dog-and-pony show, but it makes Carol happy. That's why, if you do it, I figure that the least I'll owe you is to fix your rink machinery for free."

"For free?" Kyle repeated.

Johnny shrugged. "I'm hoping it won't take longer than a weekend to sort out. I'm not promising anything, and I'm not available to do it for a couple of weeks, but—"

"Hell, yeah!" Kyle said. If his residual leg hadn't been bothering him so much, he'd have jumped up, danced and sung. Maybe trotted over and grabbed Jessica to join him.

"You look like the cat that ate the canary," Johnny said.

"That's 'cause I am. This is huge for me. If I can't turn a profit with this place, I'm screwed. That's it for me. I've got nothing…"

He paused, because Johnny was looking at him strangely. Johnny didn't know about his leg.

Jessica did. She would have understood.

Not able to fight it, he glanced over at her. She was probably the one person who would be as excited about this news right now as he was. With each passing day, she was getting more involved in the affairs of the business. Having fun with him. They were building something together.

Jessica stared point-blank at Kyle, a smile curving her lips.

This time, he crooked a finger at her.

Her eyes widened. Her gaze flicked away from his, then back. As he watched, she stood, rubbed her hand over the rear of her jeans and then turned and headed for the back of the room.

The restroom. She was going to the restroom. Sebastien's back was turned and he was alternately laughing with the other woman and staring at the big screen, which was turned up to top volume because of the crowd noise. Sebastien hadn't appeared to notice Jessica's absence.

Kyle slid back his stool.

"Where're you going?" Johnny gestured to the television over the bar. "This is a big play."

Kyle had to go see her. "Give me a sec." He threaded his way to the narrow back hallway.

Jessica surprised him. She wasn't inside the restroom, but leaning in a hidden corner, beside a wall of potted plants.

He fought the urge to kiss her in greeting, and instead sidled up to her casually.

"You were watching me," she said breathlessly.

"And you were watching me." A man passed

close by them, so Kyle pulled her closer. He didn't take his hand from her sleeve when the man left, either.

"I've got news," Kyle said.

"So do I," Jessica whispered, her eyes dancing.

"Do you?" He leaned closer to her ear. "You first."

"No, you first." Her voice was breathy.

"Okay." He grinned at her. "Johnny agreed to take a look at the second compressor. We'll have more ice time to sell now."

"That's great!" She grinned as much as he did. Jumping a bit, she moved so that his mouth brushed the side of her neck. She didn't move away. It was so obvious they were playing with fire. "Your good news is good timing because it goes well with my good news," she said in a low voice.

"Hmm." He rubbed his hand up her arm. Smooth, soft skin.

Her cheeks turned pink. And then she stood on her toes and whispered into his ear. A shot of desire raced down his spine.

"Benjamin's mom called me this morning," she said. "She wants to schedule a private skating session with him as part of his therapy."

Benjamin, the boy with the prosthetic legs?

Kyle's heart was hammering out of his chest. Something was going on here. He just wanted to keep her talking. Wanted that sweet breathy whisper to continue in his ear.

"Great," he murmured. "I'm all in, if you want me to be there…"

"Yes, pleas-s-e." The *s* ended on a breath that nearly killed him. She placed both hands on his chest.

"When?" he somehow managed to ask.

"Two Saturdays from now."

He swallowed, nodding. He didn't want it to happen, but he raked his hands gently up her back to the base of her skull, tangling his fingers in her long, glossy hair.

Sighing a bit, she leaned her head back into his palms. For a long moment, she melted into him, as if testing the waters. She closed her eyes and smiled.

But then she drew her hands gently down his arms, too. And looking as if she was sorry to do it, she stepped a pace back.

Don't push her, he thought. *She'll come back when she's ready.*

He tipped his hat at her and gave her a grin. "See you in two Saturdays."

She nodded. "On the ice with those skates that you gave me."

"You noticed them, huh?" He kept up his careful grin. "I hoped they'd come in handy."

"You're a sweet man, Kyle Northrup," she murmured.

"Hmm." He wanted to make sweet love to her, was what he wanted to do. He just let his gaze linger up and down her body. Shaking her up. *Let her make of that what she wants.*

Jessica gave him a small surprised smile. An interested smile. Backing up, with mischief in her eyes, she waved at him breezily.

And damned if, just a few seconds after she'd turned the corner, Sebastien appeared, headed toward him, giving Kyle the stink-eye and "accidentally" stepping on his prosthetic foot.

"Sorry," Sebastien said with a smirk.

Kyle couldn't be mad. Because Sebastien might have the real thing now, but not for long.

TWO WEEKS LATER, on a sunny, promising Saturday morning, Jessica was thinking of Kyle. Again.

This time because she stood on the hockey ice at the twin rinks, wearing the skates that he'd bought her.

Her new, old skates.

Somehow it made the fact that she was on the ice again, for the first time since withdrawing from the national championships, somewhat palatable.

She glanced over to the corner by the Zamboni

garage where Kyle stood watching her. He hadn't inserted himself into her meeting with Benjamin and his parents, but he'd kept vigilant, as he'd promised her. While he watched, she pointed down to the new skates and gave him the thumbs-up sign.

He gave her back a slow, sexy smile and tipped his baseball cap to her.

She put her hand over her heart. Since that night in the pub, neither of them had mentioned the skates again.

And she hadn't told anybody else that she was lacing up again after so many years. This was just something she wanted to do herself, and doing it for a good cause, for Benjamin's therapy, was the perfect thing for her.

At present, she waited for Benjamin, who was in the men's room with his dad. Her boots felt stiff and new, so she stomped up and down, just to get the feel of being on blades again.

Kyle still watched her. He wouldn't have known this, but she'd tried many brands of boots and blades over the years. Some had been given to her for free, for endorsements and advertisements from manufacturers, but these boots were the result of her first, minor rebellion against her mother, a rare thing in her life back then.

She had liked how these fit best even though her mother had liked the owner of a competing company better. But Jessica had performed better in these boots. She felt best in them.

If she'd been so inclined, she would have broken them in first by skating in them every day for a week until they softened enough to naturally take the shape of her foot and feel more comfortable. Much like a baseball player broke in his glove.

But she had not been inclined, so she stood still and waited. The ice in the rink was especially cold and hard today. Classic hockey ice. The other rink, the second rink, which she hadn't been inside yet and where Johnny was busy taking apart machinery with Mike as his helper, was kept warmer. That ice was typically softer, classic figure-skating ice, easier to hold an edge and dig a toe pick, easier to spin and jump, but not as "fast" as hockey or speed-skating ice.

She saw that her client was ready for her, so Jessica glided back to the boards and stepped onto the rubber matting. Her wet blades made twin parallel tracks as she headed for the bleachers. Today, her mission was to stand up for Benjamin.

The small boy sat on a bench, flanked by each parent. Benjamin's prosthetist fitted his legs and attached them to his skates.

Benjamin was thrilled, grinning ear to ear. He stood on his new skates and loved it as Jessica helped him walk along the mats, but the prosthetist called him back for a readjustment after he observed Benjamin's steps.

Now Jessica watched. Beside her was a plastic assistor contraption, sort of like a plastic walker that could be used on ice for beginning skaters who wanted something to hold on to. Jessica had never believed in them, but in Benjamin's case, she definitely saw the value.

"Okay, you're all set," the prosthetist said, straightening. "Let's get you on the ice for real."

Benjamin grinned again. Without glancing at either parent, he rose and hustled toward Jessica. His gait wasn't smooth and practiced like Kyle's; he was still getting used to his prosthetic legs—and now prosthetic feet inside of skates.

Jessica held open the rink door and reached for his small hand. "Good job, you're looking great," she encouraged him.

"I'm skating, Jessica," he said, as he stood on the ice, a bit wobbly, but balanced.

"You sure are." She grinned back at him. "Would you like to hold onto the assistor?"

"No. I'll skate like you." His big blue eyes were deadly serious.

"Let's take little steps, like this." Jessica faced him so he could see her. She held out her arms and made slight marching steps, moving backward. "Lift up your skate, a little bit at a time."

Hesitantly, Benjamin copied her very slowly, inching forward where she went backward. From the line on his forehead and the way the chin strap of his helmet dug into him, she could tell he was concentrating fiercely. Benjamin wanted to learn this new skill.

And a skill it was. It took hard work, guts and heart. More than talent—because talent only brought a person so far. More than pleasing another person—because pleasing, without heart, was doomed to failure. As she had been doomed to failure.

"You're doing great, Benjamin," she encouraged him.

"I'm skating!" he called to his parents at the boards, who were waving at him through the glass. Jessica glanced at the prosthetist and he gave her a thumbs-up.

In reality, Benjamin had traveled just a few feet. Jessica had planned to get him around the rink in one lap, but she now realized how overly ambitious that was. They would aim for just a couple of dozen feet, instead, for this session.

She glanced up at the clock. The prosthetist had recommended fifteen minutes to begin. That seemed reasonable to her. Then Jessica would see Benjamin privately at a table she'd set up in the closed room she'd been referring to as the "birthday party room." There she would ice and massage his muscles as needed.

Benjamin tumbled, but Jessica helped him back up and then checked his balance. He was well padded, so there would be no bruising.

"Are you doing okay?" she asked him.

"Yes."

Music played in the background, one of the kids' songs from a recent Disney movie, so Benjamin seemed not only happy, but inspired. He had a new bounce in his step.

"Can you lift your left skate a bit higher?" she asked. "Yes, just like that."

Benjamin clapped his hands to a beat in the music. He sang the chorus aloud. Jessica cracked up. The kid was too cute.

"What a personality you are," she told him.

The time passed quickly, too quickly, and Jessica was soon back on the mats, talking with his parents as if she were his skating coach as well as his physical therapist.

She shook her head. For a moment she had an out-of-body experience, the wonder of looking down at herself, in pride, as she'd accomplished something difficult.

She'd come as far as Benjamin had.

She glanced over at the garage door where Kyle had been standing, but he was gone. Instead, Mike was in the Zamboni bay, climbing up on the machine and getting ready to resurface the rink before the middle-schoolers' youth hockey league games began.

Ah, well. Kyle had probably gone back to check on Johnny's progress. From what she remembered of Johnny's work sprees, he probably had pieces of engine and metal parts spread out all over the floor.

She headed over to the bleachers, prepared to change out of her skates. She wiped down the blades with a small towel she'd brought from home, then slipped on a pair of old skate guards—purple and glittery and somewhat scratched up—that she'd borrowed from the lost-and-found bin along with a pair of raggedy terrycloth soakers, so the blades wouldn't rust when she stored them.

She was just about to walk back to her office and change into her sneakers when she turned and bumped into Sebastien.

"Oh!" she said, surprised. "I didn't expect you to stop by."

His nostrils flared like an angry bull's. "*What* are you doing? I looked for you at Wallis Point PT. When you said you were working, I assumed…" He noticed her feet. "And you're in freaking *skates*?"

She clutched her hands in front of herself, determined to stay calm. "Yes. Benjamin, my physical therapy client, wants to learn to play hockey, so I'm teaching him to skate."

"And somebody else couldn't do it?" Sebastien asked incredulously.

She thought for a moment. "No, nobody else could do it. I'm his physical therapist and I have a relationship with him. I also have skating skills."

Sebastien was so furious he was nearly sputtering. "I thought this stuff traumatized you? I thought you wanted to sell this place—get rid of it and give the money to a children's charity, is what I recall you saying to me."

She nodded slowly. "It looks like I've come to change my mind about that." It was surprising to her. But she'd been on a long journey, alone, mostly.

Scratch that, she'd been with Kyle.

"Where'd you get the new skates?" Sebastien asked. "Aren't they expensive? You told me once how expensive your skates were."

Kyle had bought them because he'd thought she would need them, and he was right. Kyle had been on this journey with her, every step of the way.

Sebastien glanced around at the crowd of kids milling about the open area between the ice and the bleachers where their parents sat. Incredulously, he shook his head. "This place is packed. It's been packed both times I've been here."

"Yes, it's been doing much better lately."

"Do you realize what you're saying?"

She nodded. "I think it's important the rink stay open."

"Because Kyle wants it?"

It had started out that way. But now... "I want it. I *like* helping people. I *like* using my creativity and my skills to bring out joy. That's what I want to do with my time."

"Great. You can do that for our family. Just not..." He looked around again and made a face. "Just not *here*."

"But what if our child wanted to play hockey?" she pressed. "Wouldn't you be in the stands, cheering them on?"

He gave her an incredulous look. "My kids aren't getting involved with that."

"Even if they wanted to? Even if they asked to?"

"No. Absolutely not," Sebastien said. "Tennis is fine. Golf, good. Swimming, great." He shuddered again. "Not this."

"But that's..." That's what Jessica's mother had thought, too. She'd thought figure skating had been the one thing for Jessica, and nothing else would do. Jessica's lack of choice had been a big part of her problem.

"I have a whole different philosophy of life than you do," Jessica said aloud.

"Because I don't want my kids to play hockey? As I recall, before you worked at this rink, we were on the same page. Jess, what is going on?"

That was a good question. A really good question.

Sebastien shook his head. "When you figure it out, meet me at home." And then he stalked out.

Jessica put her hands to her cheeks. They were flaming. Treating her kids the way her mom had treated her was nonnegotiable.

She was about to continue into her office to change when Kyle returned. He walked slowly, his face creased with worry.

"Kyle?" Jessica called. "How's it going with Johnny?"

He looked at her and blinked. Then he came over to her, glancing at the room where she'd been working with Benjamin and his team. "Did Benjamin leave?"

"A little while ago."

"I'm sorry I missed him."

"That's all right. You'll get more opportunities to talk."

"He's coming back again?" Kyle sat beside her on the bench and grimaced. "At least that's one good thing," he muttered.

"Why? What happened?"

Kyle shook his head. "The other rink is hopeless. The machinery is too far gone. The estimate for replacement is tens of thousands of dollars." His face looked bleak. "It's impossible, Jess."

"Nothing's impossible," she said firmly. She moved closer to him, her body touching his. She tried to draw his eyes to hers. At the pub a couple of weekends ago, he couldn't keep his eyes off her even all the way across the crowded room.

Now he seemed defeated, and that came from within. She knew a lot about that herself.

She didn't want him to give up. She wouldn't give up either, no matter how Sebastien fought her on this.

Right then and there, she decided to drag Kyle to the very end with her. They would both win. She would make sure of it.

CHAPTER THIRTEEN

ON MONDAY MORNING, Jessica conferred with Kyle and then made an appointment with Natalie's office to review the current financial numbers so they could come up with a plan together.

On Wednesday afternoon at the scheduled time, Jessica finished with her last PT client and drove to Kimball Family Law. The plan was for Kyle to meet her there.

She found a parking spot on the street in front of the entrance. With a feeling of optimism, she checked in with Zena, who led her to the front conference room.

"I guess Kyle's not here yet?" Jessica asked, settling into a chair at the boardroom table.

"No," Zena said. "But Natalie should be in soon. Would you like a bottled water?"

"Yes, please." While Jessica waited, she took out her cell phone to call Carol.

But not a moment later, Sebastien stalked in with a furious look. "I saw your car parked outside. What are you doing?"

Jessica clicked off her phone. "I had some questions for Natalie," she said, flustered. She'd been muddling along with Sebastien for the past few days, not sure how to fix their differences. Discussing anything related to the rink had been like tiptoeing through a minefield. Since he'd been back she'd realized how much her attitudes had changed. For the time being, their disagreement had been shelved while Jessica focused on Kyle.

"I shouldn't be long here," Jessica said to Sebastien. "I'll call you when I'm done."

"Is this about the rink business?" he demanded.

She nodded, feeling tense. She knew what would come next. Another argument.

"May I join you?" he asked quietly instead.

He'd surprised her. What could she say? She would rather he didn't stay. The three of them might need to discuss Kyle's leg, and they couldn't speak frankly with Sebastien present. Not to mention how awkward it would be with Kyle and Sebastien in the same room with her.

But if she asked Sebastien to leave, she doubted that their already fragile relationship could be repaired again.

The babbling of a toddler's happy voice echoed from outside the open doorway. Jessica saw Bruce walk down the hall with little Hannah in his arms. Just a reminder of everything Jessica wanted and what she risked losing out on.

Sebastien sat across the table from her. "What

are you doing, Jess?" he asked gently. He seemed sad and there were dark circles under his eyes.

She put her hand over her mouth. "I can't tell you because everything I feel inside isn't what you want to hear."

"You're here to save the rink, right?"

She nodded.

"Are you pursuing this out of guilt?" he asked.

Her eyes teared up and she glanced down. She did feel guilty—guilty that she felt more allegiance to Kyle than to Sebastien. But that point had been put on the back burner. She was most worried about Kyle these days. He hadn't looked well this morning. He'd been pale and quiet, and he'd skipped skating with his friends. The worst thing was that he'd seemed to have lost hope that they could make the business work.

She just shook her head.

Sebastien slid something out of his pocket, unfolded the slip of paper and spread it on the table.

She leaned over and picked it up. A news article from an Armed Services magazine contained a photograph of Kyle as part of an amputee rehabilitation hockey team.

"Where did you get this?" she asked, alarmed.

"Everything is on the internet, if you know where to look."

She gazed pleadingly at Sebastien. "Please don't hurt him by making this public."

"You *did* know he had a prosthetic leg." Sebastien's shoulders slumped. "You knew and you didn't tell me?"

"I couldn't," she whispered. "It's not my secret to tell."

"Are you in love with him?" he asked her point-blank.

She didn't know. Maybe she was. Was a person in love with another when they thought about that other person all the time? When they couldn't imagine that other person not being part of their lives?

"You're not answering me," Sebastien said.

Because her realization was something she needed to tell Kyle, not him. What was she doing in Natalie's conference room if not to fight for Kyle?

All those morning breakfasts in her car. The times they'd worked together side by side. The sessions she planned with Benjamin.

She didn't want that to end. And Kyle shared many of her beliefs. He treated people with kindness. He didn't force his beliefs where they weren't wanted.

But Sebastien was staring at her now, expecting an answer.

"I care about him very much," she said.

"You can't," Sebastien returned bluntly. She stared at him, shocked.

"I've been patient with the rink thing, Jessica. But this is…this has got to stop. You can't see him anymore. I don't care if you back out of the deal now and leave all the money on the table."

She shook all over. Sebastien was serious. He was sacrificing the money that he cared about and he was making her choose here and now. *Him or Kyle.*

She put her head in her hands. In the hallway, Hannah chattered with her dad. Just more torture for her.

"Jess…" Sebastien sounded tired. "Please just come home with me. Move in. We'll carry all the boxes over this weekend. We don't need the fancy house. We can stay in my rental cottage together."

And leave Kyle? Leave him and never see him again?

A sudden influx of tears blinding her, she reached for her purse. Took out the box with the Tiffany ring, which she had never seemed to find time to get sized for her finger. This should have been a clue to her, but until this moment she hadn't been *sure*.

As she passed the box to Sebastien, she felt a weight lifting from her shoulders. The ring that didn't fit her. The sister who would never think her good enough for her brother. A husband who didn't value her opinion no matter how hard she tried.

"I'm not the one for you," she whispered.

He stared at her for a long time. "He'll never commit to you," he said bitterly. "He's a loner. He's just using you to keep his business."

A sob caught in her throat.

"If you change your mind, I won't be here for you anymore," Sebastien said. "I'm done."

He stood and walked out, and she didn't chase him or tell him to come back. With her hand over her mouth, shaking, she watched him leave.

Bruce stuck his head in the door. "Is everything okay in here? Natalie asked me to tell you that she's been delayed."

Jessica gathered up her bag. "Please tell Natalie that I'm sorry. I have to leave. Please tell Kyle that I'll talk to him tomorrow."

And then she left.

THURSDAY PASSED. FRIDAY DAWNED. Kyle never came back to work.

The wounded warriors continued to meet for their morning skate. Evidently, Kyle had left TJ his rink key. Jessica sat in her office, contemplating stopping by Joe's old house at 18 Linden Lane to see him. She'd called him twice, but he hadn't picked up and his voice mail was inoperable. His phone also didn't take text messages.

She was pacing her office when TJ knocked on her open door. He'd changed back into street clothes, but his hair was still wet from his morning shower.

"How's Kyle?" she asked. "I've been trying to reach him."

TJ gave her a wan smile. "I saw him this morning. He's okay, said he's just feeling run-down and needs to catch up on his sleep. He said he'll see you at the wedding tonight."

"So he *will* be at Carol's wedding," she said, relieved for that at least. "I've been worried about him."

"He'll be fine." TJ's gaze flicked around the room. "Um, I'm supposed to ask if you need anything?"

Did she? "Patrick has the resurfacing schedule and Carol is doing the bills today."

But TJ stared at her because the daily business wasn't what mattered, it was Kyle's peace of mind. "He's worried about losing the rink," Jessica explained.

TJ's lips pursed and he made a slow nod.

"Please tell Kyle that I'll reschedule with Natalie. Tell him not to give up."

"Will do," TJ said.

"COULD YOU DO me a favor and call Johnny to come pick up Kyle's tux?" Carol asked Jessica.

Two days after Jessica had returned Sebastien's

ring to him, she gathered with the female half of the bridal party in the bride's condominium.

Carol sat at a dressing table, having her foundation professionally applied by a makeup artist wielding a brush the size of a drumstick. Jessica already wore her mid-length peach bridesmaid's dress, her hair pulled up in a French roll and decorated with a small beach rose. The Friday evening wedding was only two hours away.

"Is Kyle really okay? I mean, shouldn't he have already picked up his tux?" Jessica asked Carol. "When's the last time Johnny saw him?"

"I'm not sure." Carol held out her hand while her sister—the matron of honor—dabbed polish onto a nail that had chipped. "I don't want to talk to Johnny just now because isn't that bad luck if I do?"

"No, it's only bad luck if he sees you before the wedding," her sister interjected.

"Well, he's already at the Grand Beachfront Hotel, so there's no danger of that," Carol countered.

"Yes, but what if he's in the lobby when the limo drops you off?" her sister added.

"He's meeting the Reverend Ellsworth in the upstairs ballroom," Carol said. "Why would he be in the lobby?"

"In case he needs to go to the bathroom or something? How am I supposed to know?"

Jessica cleared her throat, interrupting the sisters. "I'll, ah, go take the tux to Kyle." Actually, she welcomed the excuse to see him. "Where is it?"

"It's hanging on the hook in the front hallway." Carol took a sip from the flute of champagne at her elbow. "I meant to have Johnny deliver it last night, but in all the excitement it slipped my mind. Do you know where Kyle lives?"

"I do." Jessica had, in fact, driven past his house last night. The lights were off, but his truck had been parked in the driveway. Yes, TJ had told her not to worry, that he was just feeling run-down, but Jessica had a nagging uneasiness about him.

"I'll be back before we leave for the hotel," Jessica said.

"The photographer is coming in an hour. Our group pictures will be in ninety minutes!"

"I'll be there, don't worry about that." Jessica leaned in for an air kiss so as not to smear Carol's makeup. "You look beautiful," she said to her friend.

On the way out, she grabbed Kyle's black tux in its plastic dry-cleaner bag, along with an attached sack containing his shoes. Nearby, she noticed Carol's wedding dress hanging over the back of the door. White, lacy—it looked similar to the dress Jessica had imagined for herself. She sighed, ever hopeful.

But as she sat in her car, motoring down the back roads toward Kyle's house—Joe's old house—on the most inland part of town, she had a bad feeling. Was Kyle really run-down from all the hours he'd been working, or had he simply lost faith?

She parked on the street in front of 18 Linden Lane. Since she'd driven by yesterday, someone had mown the small patch of shaded front lawn, judging by the mower marks and the smell of freshly cut grass. The small Cape Cod-style home was painted a weathered gray and blue, similar to many traditional beach houses in the area. A detached garage was painted in the same colors and Old Glory flew over the door, with a weathervane in the shape of a whale standing watch over the roof.

Kyle's house was quaint and appealing. But she understood now that it wasn't the outer trappings she cared about, it was the people within. She wanted a *home*, not just a house. With love. And family.

But mainly love.

Jittery with anticipation, Jessica followed the sidewalk to Kyle's front gate, opened it and headed up the short walkway. She climbed the steps to the stoop and pressed the doorbell.

Kyle glanced at her through a side window. She gave him a smile and a little wave, then held up his tuxedo. It was heavy. She indicated the shoes, too.

He opened the door just wide enough for her to see he was dressed in a rumpled T-shirt and tan chinos. He passed his hands over his eyes. Had he just woken up? But even though he was pale and obviously tired, he still looked fantastic to her.

"Hi." She lifted the hanger and the shoe bag again. "May I please come in?"

He frowned. "The place is a mess. I've got a housecleaner inside."

"Oh." Jessica did faintly hear a vacuum cleaner running in the background upstairs.

His gaze raked her up and down. Her cheeks felt hot. "Where's Sebastien?"

She gave him a nervous smile. She'd been biding her time, waiting to tell him, but vowing only to do it when he asked. Now that he'd asked, she felt a bit shy.

"I...broke up with him, actually."

KYLE STARED. HIS stomach felt as if it had dropped out.

This was what he'd wanted, for so long. Now that it had happened he felt a surge of terror he hadn't experienced even in combat.

He put his hand to his head.

"When did you break up with him?" he finally asked.

"Wednesday night. He came into the law firm when he saw my car." She cocked her head. "Did Natalie tell you I was there?"

Her eager, upturned face slayed him. He'd fallen in love with this woman, slowly and surely. Now, the moment when he could have taken her, it was too late—it just couldn't be a reality for him. Even without Sebastien in the way, it was impossible for Kyle to build a future with her. Her timing was horrible.

"Kyle?" she whispered. Her face fell, as if she sensed what he wasn't saying.

He couldn't do it. He couldn't disappoint her. She was all dressed up in that strangely hot bridesmaid dress, with the short skirt and the high heels, the lacy flowers in her hair, blowing wisps around shiny pink lips.

He sucked in his breath and forced himself to meet her eyes. "Wait here, Jess. I'll be right back."

Ignoring the confusion in her big brown eyes, he took the tux and the shoes from her, then closed the door and went back into his house.

Rose, the woman TJ had sent over to clean for him, looked at him quizzically.

Kyle wasn't in the mood to talk with anyone.

"When you're finished, could you just lock up behind you? I'm going out tonight."

"Sure, no problem."

"Thank you," Kyle said.

Picking up his cane, he walked gingerly to the staircase. He hadn't taken his pain medication yet because he had wanted to be lucid and feel the soreness when he talked with his doctor about it. Now that he had discussed things with his doctor and scheduled an appointment, he would take his prescribed pill.

Kyle settled into the motorized seat contraption that Joe had installed to get himself up the steep stairs to the second floor. A neighbor had mentioned to Kyle that Joe had installed it after his knee replacement surgery. The irony for Kyle was that the place was completely handicapped accessible.

In his bedroom, Kyle tossed the tux and shoes on the bed. The shoes might be a problem that he hadn't anticipated, but he'd deal with that once Jessica left. His Marine uniform was hanging on the back of the door, just in case the tux hadn't shown up. Kyle was entitled to wear the uniform to a wedding, as he'd been entitled to wear it to Joe's funeral, but the absolute last thing that Kyle wanted to do tonight was to draw attention to his military service, and therefore, to his leg.

He ran his hand through his hair. Progressively,

his leg pain had been increasing, no doubt the result of all the stress he'd been putting on it. Shortly after he'd last seen Jessica—Wednesday at noon, after she'd left for Wallis Point PT—he'd wrenched it hard and the pain had been extremely sharp. He'd been able to mask it enough to make it through the meeting with Natalie, who'd had nothing but bad news for him. They had two months left, true, but there was no way for the numbers to work unless some kind of miracle happened with the machinery in the smaller rink.

He'd been crushed when he'd left. Maybe his mood had made his leg worse, because when he'd wakened Thursday, he couldn't walk at all. He'd phoned his prosthetist in Maryland, then had an internet consultation with his doctor's nurse in the same building. They'd both agreed—they wanted him back in Maryland on Monday. He'd thought they'd been discussing a simple appointment, but then his surgeon had phoned. He'd made Kyle go to the emergency room and have X-rays. Then the nurse had called him back and talked of bringing a suitcase and arranging a leave.

A leave! His heart had frozen. Whatever scrap of faint hope he'd had left had shredded in the face of this news.

His rink dream was dead.

And there was just no point anymore. He was a wounded veteran, his life once more focused on a shattered limb that ruled everything. Yet again, it was slapping him down.

Kyle drew back the blind on the window and gazed down at Jessica. The only good thing in his life. She sat on his stoop, her slender arms wrapped around her knees, waiting for him to go down to her.

At any other time in his life, he would have killed to have this gift. To him, Jessica Hughes was a princess. She would always be a princess, always out of reach.

The timing always wrong.

She wore her pretty dress, dolled up and excited about her friend's wedding. She'd finally ditched the guy that Kyle had known all along was wrong for her. Now was Kyle's time, but yet again, his leg was preventing him from having what he wanted.

And yet, he loved her. He wanted her to have happiness. Eventually, he would tell her everything that had happened this week, but now would be too heartless, not when she was hoping for a romantic evening with him.

She deserved that. Maybe he could give her one good night before it all came crashing down. After the night was over, he would tell her that they'd lost the rink and he had to leave—head back to Maryland to get his leg worked on once again.

Kyle found his medication bottle and took a

dose. Then he made his way downstairs again, and just before he left the house he ditched the cane. With a smile he didn't quite feel, he went outside and sat gingerly on the stoop beside Jessica.

She gathered her satiny skirt and scooted closer to him. "How are you feeling?" She had real concern in her eyes.

"I'm okay now. Just tired."

"I've been worried about you these past two days."

"I didn't want you to. That's why I didn't say anything."

"It is?"

He smiled gently at her. She was still worried— he didn't want her to feel that way. "It's okay, Jess. Natalie told me you had to leave, so I met with her anyway. But you know what? Let's not talk about that right now." He took her hand and ran his thumb along the soft skin of her wrist. "I'd rather focus on tonight. And you."

"You would?"

"Yes, I would."

She put her hands around his neck and pressed her forehead to his chest. "I missed you, Kyle," she murmured.

Oh, Jess. He gently cradled her head against him. Closed his eyes and breathed in the scent of her hair.

She gazed up at him. "I have to admit, I'm relieved you're coming. When you weren't dressed yet, I wondered."

"They told me to be at the hotel at five o'clock," he said, in a mock-indignant manner. "I still have an hour."

She chuckled and shook her head. "The women have been getting ready all afternoon. Then again," she teased, a twinkle in her eye. "I like you as you are."

She had him wrapped around her finger. He couldn't move as she traced her hand along his jaw. "I've grown used to your beard," she murmured, lightly caressing his cheek. "It's softer than I realized."

"I was thinking of shaving it for the summer."

"Really?" She cocked her head. "I'd like to see that."

"Would you?" he asked in a low voice.

She nodded with a breathless sigh, her eyes on his face.

He couldn't stand it anymore. He reached over and kissed her neck beside her pretty, dangling earring, then along her throat and ending, with a sigh, on her lips.

She closed her eyes. Sighing in the back of her throat, she kissed him more deeply, wrapping her arms around him and pressing her breasts against his chest.

He groaned inwardly. He wanted this physical closeness so much, but he couldn't keep it.

Leaning his forehead against hers, he caught his breath. Despite himself, he had to ask. "Did you break up with him because of me?"

She drew back and gave him a playful smile. "Yes and no."

He waited.

She glanced up at him beneath lowered lashes. Her chest was rising and falling. She was so close to him he could smell the scent of her shampoo. "Kyle, there are two answers to your question. The heart answer and the head answer. Which would you like to hear first?"

Frankly, the heart answer scared him. "Let's go with head."

She nodded, her lips pressed together, her eyes dancing. "I'm going to answer that with a question."

He couldn't help smirking. "Of course you are."

"Are you planning to have children someday?"

His smile faltered. That was a dream he couldn't have. Was she kidding?

"You do like children," she said gently.

"Love 'em," he said gruffly.

"Well, what if a child of yours didn't want to follow the agenda you had set for him? What if he wanted to do something different from what you dictated—assuming it's safe, morally ethical and within your family budget?"

"You have to ask that question of Joe Mansell's stepson?"

"Exactly," she said. "You see my point."

"And…Sebastien doesn't think like that?"

"Sebastien was wrong for me for various reasons. But for this case, let's just say I am Hedley Jackson's daughter. And I'm not going to dictate choices to anyone, especially my children."

Kyle laughed. "Yeah, I see where you're coming from."

"Ironically, I really do like working at the rink with you. You're right for me, for every reason." She smiled shyly at him. "I'd like to stay on after August, if you don't mind. I was even thinking of not selling you my share for a while. That way there's no immediate pressure for you to come up with a loan before you're ready."

She doesn't get it. Keeping the rink at all, for either of them, was impossible now. And now the problem with his leg made it even more impossible.

He glanced away, because he didn't want her to read his face and be disappointed. Not tonight.

He checked his watch. "I should be getting ready."

"Yes. And I have to go get pictures taken." She stood and brushed off her skirt.

"Jessica?"

She turned.

"I, ah, fixed the glass in your skating picture. It's hanging in my locker room—you know where the key is. You can do with it what you'd like."

She tilted her head. "Why are you telling me this now?"

He shrugged. "We were talking about pictures. It seemed like a good time."

She nodded slightly, and he watched her walk away.

"Oh!" she said, turning again. "Wait!" She went back to him and whispered charmingly into his ear. "You didn't ask me my heart reason. It's because I'm crazy about you. I have been since you kissed me against the door in Joe's office. Nobody ever kissed me like that, Kyle. That's all I wanted to say."

While he stood there, dumbfounded, she gave him a soft, lingering kiss, her lips brushing against his so sweetly. "Save me a dance, all right?"

She was back in her car before he could think.

Everything Kyle wanted, wrapped up in a bow for him to take.

Tonight was his only chance.

WHEN KYLE ARRIVED clean-shaven at the Grand Beachfront Hotel, Jessica nearly fell over. She leaned against the festive, bubbling fountain where Carol and her bridesmaids were having their picture taken.

"What do you think?" he asked during a lull in the action.

"I think you shocked me." She reached up and caressed his cheek. Though he looked handsome with a clean-shaven face, she adored him with a beard, too. She would take him any way he was. "I love it." *I love you, Kyle.*

He grinned at her. "That's good, because there's no going back."

"I hope not."

"I have a rose for Kyle's lapel!" Carol's mother stepped between them and thrust forward a cardboard tray containing the last of the men's boutonnieres. "Jessica, why don't you pin it on him, dear? When you're finished, join the ladies in the suite before the ceremony begins."

"Of course," Jessica murmured. She already had a bridesmaid's bouquet with red and white rose blooms to match the flower for Kyle's lapel. Her duty was to precede Carol down the aisle to the altar set up inside the ballroom, but she had a few more moments before that would begin.

She stood close to Kyle, her arms grazing his chest as she concentrated on setting the pin through the stem of the rose and the fine woolen material of his lapel. His head was inches from hers. His body heat warmed her hands, and the scent of his shaving lotion lingered on his skin.

She should back away, check that she hadn't pinned his rose on crooked. But she didn't want to stop touching him. Kyle made her feel alive in a way that she hadn't known she was missing until now.

He drew his hand up the outside of her thigh and rested it on her hip. Everything about her body seemed achy and yearning: The nerve endings under her skin. Her taut nipples, rubbing against the lace of her bra. The juncture between her legs, suddenly damp and throbbing.

She melted closer to him. His hand moved to a more proprietary position against the small of her back. They seemed to be in their own bubble. Dimly, she heard the chatter and noise of seventy-five wedding guests arriving for the ceremony, mingling and talking over a DJ's bluesy, aching recording of "When a Man Loves a Woman."

Kyle gazed at her with a contented smile. "If I could stop time, I would do it."

"Why?"

"Just to keep you near me like this."

She hugged him closer, squeezing his waist, her hands beneath his unbuttoned suit jacket. *I'm in heaven,* was all she could think.

"Kyle?" Johnny nudged him. "You want to head in and help my brother with the ushering duties?"

Kyle gave Jessica an apologetic glance.

"Save me a dance later," she whispered.

"I'll save all of them."

TWO HOURS LATER, after the wedding ceremony, a break for more pictures, an open bar, a champagne toast, the introduction of the bridal party and parents of the bride and groom, and a sit-down dinner, Jessica finally got her dance.

The lights were dim. The music loud, especially the bass, which vibrated to her bones.

Within moments, she and Kyle were making out like teenagers, or the teenager Jessica had never had the chance to be.

It felt exhilarating. If she and Kyle were alone, clothing would definitely have been discarded. As it was, they were touching each other all over—hands, arms, little nipping kisses on the earlobe, deeper kisses on the lips.

"Should we get a room?" she murmured to Kyle.

His glazed-over eyes seemed to wake up. He pulled back, searching her face.

Carol danced by them. "You two are causing a scandal at my wedding," she said cheerfully.

"I'm sorry," Jessica replied.

Carol laughed it off. "I was just teasing. I love it. Everybody should be in love." She grabbed a disposable camera from a nearby table and quickly snapped their photo. "I'll save this for when you two are married."

Stop, Carol, Jessica automatically thought, because Kyle's eyes were wide, and she could see how, of course, he would be worried about such talk. *Marriage?* This was too much, too quick.

Kyle, looking pale, stepped back from Jessica.

At the same moment, an exuberant woman, her enthusiasm lubricated by the contents of her champagne glass, no doubt, went crashing past them, bouncing against Kyle like a wayward ball in a pinball machine.

Kyle faltered and fell to his knee. A look of intense pain crossed his face.

Jessica knelt to him. "Do you want to sit down for a while?"

"Yeah." He stood, and for a split second his prosthetic was in view as his tuxedo leg rode up.

He paled, then shoved the pants leg back down. Jessica didn't know if anybody else saw. She knew how intensely important it was to Kyle that nobody did.

Someday she needed to have a conversation with him about becoming public about his prosthetic. Now wasn't the time, though. Worried about the pain he was feeling, she sat beside him at a reception table. "Will you show me where it hurts, Kyle?"

"No."

"But, I can massage—"

"Never. That's never happening."

Confused, she stood.

"But I thought we were moving toward a relationship," she said. "I thought things had changed with us?"

"Not in that way, Jessica," he said sharply.

He wouldn't let her help him with his leg. That's what he was saying.

"But that *has* to change, Kyle. Let me help you. If there's going to be something between us, you *need* to let me in."

"We don't have a future. I wish we did, but that's just the hand I was dealt."

She gaped at him, shocked. "What do you mean?"

"I have to leave," he said. "Please don't come after me—that's not what I want." He turned and Jessica watched him make his way to the men's room. Soon after, he left for the exit to the street.

Her bridesmaid flowers clutched in her hand, Jessica wavered on her feet. His reaction didn't make sense. But for the time being, she didn't know what to do.

So she, too, made her way home alone.

CHAPTER FOURTEEN

WHEN JESSICA WOKE, it took her a moment to orient herself because she was in her new summer quarters in a one-bedroom apartment above Natalie's law offices.

Her bridesmaid dress from last night was draped over a chair, her shoes kicked off beside the bed. Her bouquet was propped in a glass of water.

She sat up, her head buzzing with the aftereffects of too much champagne, which she'd followed with a short bout of crying herself to sleep. Everything had gone so well until Kyle had fallen. Then, faced with showing her his leg, he'd said that they didn't have a future. It just didn't make sense based on his earlier behavior.

In her view, he'd been retreating into his fears again. If she could get him to feel more comfortable with being in a relationship as a man with a prosthetic leg, then maybe they stood a chance. That was all she could think of that made sense.

How to do it, she wasn't sure. The only solution that stuck out to her was that maybe she could try a more gentle approach. She had so many connections in the medical community. Surely she could find someone local to help him—and her.

It was worth a try. She would go and sell him on the idea now. She wanted to make sure he was okay, anyway.

She showered quickly and dressed in a short summer dress and a pair of flat sandals. Her Volkswagen was parked in the back lot. The seats were scorching from the intense sunlight, so she sat on her sweater to protect her thighs.

Beach traffic already wound through the center of town. A ten-minute drive took her nearly an hour. The air conditioner in her old car wasn't working, so she rolled down the windows in an attempt to find relief.

She was sweating and nearly frantic by the time she turned onto Kyle's street. Unfortunately, there were no open parking spaces near his house.

She couldn't believe it. This part of town wasn't even near the beach—it never got busy. But as she idled in front of his blue and gray Cape, she smelled barbecue in the air. Hotdogs, hamburgers, steak tips. It served to remind her that she hadn't eaten yet.

She pulled into Kyle's driveway behind his pickup truck. Her car was small enough that it didn't block the sidewalk too much. She gathered her purse and headed up his front walkway.

As he had yesterday, he answered the door with a pained expression.

"Kyle, I—"

"What are you doing here?" he interrupted.

She steeled herself. His anger hadn't dissipated since last night. "I'm checking on you," she said.

"Thanks, but I'm fine."

She crossed her arms. Even though it was sweltering hot, he still wore long pants and sneakers. He just wouldn't allow anyone to see his prosthetic leg. The stubborn, stubborn man.

"Where are you parked?" he asked her quietly, as he gazed beyond her, into the driveway. "Come with me, I'll walk you to your car."

"Kyle, you don't have to do this."

"I'm sorry, but I do." He headed toward her car and she had no choice but to follow. He reached to open the driver-side door for her, but she blocked him with her body.

"It's okay for you to tell people in Wallis Point about your prosthetic. You're among friends. Nobody will judge you."

He shook his head. "That's not why I'm doing this."

"What *are* you doing? Sending me away like Joe sent you away?"

It was a low blow, and Kyle winced. But she'd reached him with her point, because he became thoughtful, and suddenly he was talking to her instead of strong-arming her to stay away from him.

He crossed his arms. "Don't you think you deserve better than a life like this with me?"

"I don't care that you have one good leg, if that's what you mean. It's not your legs that I love. Maybe you think you're protecting me from that, but I don't need you to."

"I've lost the rink, Jess," he said softly. "I didn't want to tell you yesterday because I wanted you to enjoy the wedding."

"But…how could you lose the rink? It's not August yet. We still have time to make it profitable."

"That's impossible without the second rink up and running. But the situation is worse than that, because I woke up Thursday and I couldn't walk without pain. I called my doctor, I showed it to him with pictures, and he's concerned. I have to leave for Maryland on Monday morning. I don't know how long I'll be gone. Bottom line, I have to forfeit the terms of the will. Don't you see? The terms of the will demand that I be present every week, so it will be over anyway. Done."

Her heart ached for him. So this was what had been going on with him. At least he trusted her enough now to discuss the problem.

"I'm sorry, Kyle. Don't worry about the rink. And I can help you find a—"

"If I've failed at this, then there's nothing else I can do," he said grimly.

"You can't say that! You aren't—"

"Jessica," he said tiredly, "I'm not up for the fight anymore. I'm sorry. I need to take care of my leg in Maryland, and you need to go home. Please."

"I'll go with you to Maryland," she said stubbornly.

"No." He said it with such harshness that tears came to her eyes. She stepped toward him.

He used the opening to reach for her car door handle. He was letting her know that there was nothing left for her here, nothing more to be said, and that she should just step inside and drive away.

"You are so stubborn and prideful," she whispered to him. "That hasn't changed about you."

He stepped back, his smile twisting on his face. As if he *did* care about leaving her.

He wobbled on his left foot, visibly, and his face went white.

Cursed, prideful man. So unwilling to ask anybody in Wallis Point for help. Why? Because he needed so badly to be seen as strong and capable?

Sometimes we all need to ask for help! she wanted to yell after him. She sat in her driver's seat and rolled down the window, intent on telling him just that.

But then the squeaky screen door of his Cape house opened. Down the stairs came a slender, young blond woman, her pretty summer sandals deftly stepping over the cracks in the walkway.

"Kyle!" the blonde called. "We're ready for you out back! I've fixed you a plate."

Jessica felt the ache of betrayal. And while she watched, Kyle nodded at the blonde, following her through the latched gate and down a side pathway to what Jessica presumed was a backyard.

Was *he* the neighbor hosting a barbecue? Was everything that she'd assumed about him—a protective loner, not trusting people in Wallis Point—an outright lie?

She swallowed, stunned. Jealousy stabbed at her. What was going on with him?

She forced herself to stay calm, to think rationally.

Kyle had told her he cared about her last night. That wasn't a line. She'd seen it in his eyes. Had felt it in his touch.

These past weeks, she'd allowed herself to be open and honest and expressive with Kyle, and he had responded in kind. They had a real basis on which to build a relationship. He just needed to trust her to share in the hard parts, too.

Protecting her from unpleasantness wasn't a heroic action on his part. Not to her. She considered them a team of equals, who helped each other according to their strengths.

"I'm a medical professional, and he's going to listen to me," she muttered to herself.

Tearing open her car door, she strode back up the sidewalk.

Now that she was paying attention, she noticed that one of the trucks lining the sidewalk belonged to TJ. She spotted Oscar's SUV farther down the block. Maybe Kyle was hosting a party or a barbecue for his wounded warrior friends? Maybe the blonde was part of that group?

If so, Jessica was being incredibly nervy barging in on his party like this. Perhaps she *should* just drive away. It was what Kyle had asked her to do. She paused, debating.

But all of a sudden, the rickety gate at the side of Kyle's house opened. A toddler—about two years old judging by his jerky gait—with spiky blond hair and clear blue eyes, staggered onto the sidewalk and headed away from the house as if he knew exactly where he was going.

Straight onto the street. Potentially into oncoming traffic.

Jessica half strode, half ran after the boy. "Hi," she said to him when she caught up. "Where are you going?"

"Kitty," he said. And pointed his chubby finger across the street in the direction he was moving.

"Okay," she said, taking his hand, warm and sticky from whatever he'd been eating—a cherry Popsicle judging by the red smears on his chin and cheeks. "Let's go see your mom and ask where the kitty went to."

He gazed up at her with big blue eyes, nodding. She stooped over and walked with him at his pace back to the house, then unlatched Kyle's side gate and followed the flagstone path around the corner and into a large, open backyard that was filled with music, laughter and the splashing of water.

Kyle had a swimming pool? She felt dumbstruck, as if she was seeing a side of him that she'd had no idea existed.

She'd never been to this house when Joe had lived here. Like Kyle, Joe spent what seemed to be his entire life at the twin rinks. But this backyard was a pleasant world of its own. A group of people sat at two tables shaded by an umbrella. They all appeared to be enjoying a pool party.

"Reed!" a woman exclaimed to the little boy holding Jessica's hand. She turned from adjusting a young girl's inflatable water wings to gesture him over to her.

"He got out through the gate," Jessica said. "He's a smart boy."

"Kitty," Reed said to his mother.

"Oh, I think he was looking for Kyle's cat."

"I didn't know Kyle had a cat," Jessica said.

"He does, even if he doesn't acknowledge it." TJ handed Jessica a paper plate with a perfectly cooked hotdog on it. "Hey, Jessica. Why don't you grab something to eat and join us?" With his chin he acknowledged an aluminum fold-up table that looked to be groaning with the weight of summer salads, pasta salads, hot baked beans in a crock pot, a plate of cheeses and a gathering of condiments: mustard, ketchup, relish and salad dressings.

Her stomach rumbled. "I am hungry," she admitted.

"Come sit here." A woman patted a folding chair next to her. "Hope you don't mind getting splashed."

A little kid plugged her nose with her thumb and finger, then closed her eyes and jumped in a half cannonball into the pool. She made a decent-sized splash.

Jessica laughed. "I'm having a hard time picturing Kyle with a cat. Or a pool." *Or friends with wives.* She took a big bite of the hotdog.

The woman leaned forward. "Kyle said that the cat came with the house." She knelt before an azalea bush, just about to lose its red blooms, and called for the cat to come out. A small, orange tabby peered warily out.

"Was he Joe's cat?" Jessica asked, wiping her lips with her napkin.

"I don't know," the woman answered. "TJ mentioned that he showed up after Joe's funeral. I guess he stayed the winter inside the back porch, at first. Kyle left food for him. He called the traveling vet—Martha—and checked him for an embedded chip. He didn't have one, and none of the neighbors had seen him before, even though he was fixed. The kitty had lots of ticks and worms, too, so the vet gave Kyle some medicine that cleared them up. Kyle doesn't say much, but I think he likes that Simba chose him as his human. I think they're good for each other, even though Kyle would never admit it."

"Simba? Is that what Kyle named him?"

"My daughter named him. He looks like Simba from the *Lion King*, doesn't he?"

Jessica nodded. "You're TJ's wife, aren't you? I know TJ from the twin rinks."

"I'm Sarah. And you're Jessica Hughes, right?"

Jessica stiffened, automatically preparing herself.

"You run the rink with Kyle," Sarah said simply. "I need to thank you. His morning hockey sessions mean a great deal to us."

Jessica glanced over at TJ. He was lowering himself from a wheelchair into a hot tub on the porch. Unlike Kyle, he wasn't wearing his prosthetic.

"It's much easier for him to swim without it," Sarah said.

The men present were wounded warriors like Kyle. "You're all close, aren't you?" Jessica asked.

"We've known Kyle since TJ was in rehabilitation. Kyle's a great guy, but you already know that." Sarah smiled at Jessica. "I've heard a lot about you at home lately."

"All good, I hope." She glanced around. "Is Kyle coming outside?"

"Well, he's not feeling well. I've been checking on him—I'm a registered nurse."

"I didn't know that. I'm a physical therapist," Jessica added.

"That's great." Sarah caught Reed and set him back in his chair. "I'm sorry that our weekend here was poor timing. TJ organized it weeks ago. Kyle was reluctant because the house wasn't ready, but TJ gathered everybody together, and we came yesterday and cut the lawn, cleaned the house, things like that. We got the hot tub running, cleared out some of the brush. The house looks small, but did you know it has four bedrooms and three baths?"

"No."

"It's also outfitted with ramps, and the whole thing is wheelchair accessible."

"That makes sense," Jessica mused. "Joe had double knee replacements. I helped him with his physical therapy."

"Well, TJ, Oscar, myself and Claire are here for two nights with the kids. We sort of invited ourselves." She laughed. "It's sandcastle weekend, and there will be fireworks later tonight. At dusk we're going to bring the kids down to the beach. I'm told the sandcastles are amazing."

"They've been holding the sandcastle competition for years," Jessica said. "The sand sculptors come from all over the world. There's even one ballot where kids get to vote on their favorites. The contest organizers give all sorts of prizes."

"You should come with us. I brought our single neighbor, Rose, but Kyle doesn't seem to be interested in her."

So that's who the blond woman was.

"Sorry about that," Sarah confided. "When Rose asked to come, I didn't realize you and Kyle were an item. But I do now."

"You think we're an item?"

"Well, you were kissing…"

Jessica sighed. It just occurred to her how much she really needed to confide in another woman. That Sarah knew Kyle and was a medical professional could be really helpful. "He's pushed me away, I'm afraid. I think he feels that his prosthetic is too much of an obstacle. I don't feel that way, though."

Sarah nodded. "It'll help to have patience. Right now he's not feeling well—he's been sleeping much of the day with painkillers."

"He met me at the door. We talked a bit, but I know he's upset about the rink. And about going to Maryland."

"That's good that he's told you." Sarah thought a moment. "We're leaving tomorrow afternoon at three. That might be a good time to talk to him again before he leaves."

"You're right," Jessica said. "Thank you."

"Would you like to come to the beach with us and the kids later? We have room in the truck."

Jessica was grateful for the invitation. And the new friend. "I appreciate it. I think I'll come back tomorrow, though, and see you before Kyle leaves."

"I'll look forward to it," Sarah said.

THE NEXT DAY at three o'clock, Jessica again parked in front of Kyle's house. This time, she went around to the back and let herself in through the gate.

The yard was quiet. The pool still.

She went through the porch, opening the screen door. "Hello? Is anyone home?" No one answered.

She'd come this far—might as well keep going. She stepped into a large eat-in kitchen. Immediately it struck her how much the place reminded her of Joe. The clutter of the appliances and knickknacks were reminiscent of Joe's office at the rink. It was clear that Kyle hadn't settled in here yet.

"Kyle?" she called.

Jessica headed through the kitchen and out another doorway. She'd expected maybe a dining room, but it was a television room. The house looked like it had started as a small Cape, but over the years, rooms had been added.

She came to a staircase leading up. Against the inner railing was a seat and a mechanized contraption that a mobility-challenged person could ride to the second floor. Jessica didn't think Kyle needed it, but she could see where it would be helpful for others.

She climbed the stairs, determined to find him, knowing she shouldn't be in his home uninvited. If anyone had done that to her—anyone other than Kyle—she might have been upset. She hoped Kyle wouldn't be upset with her.

She faced a long hallway lined with doors. All were open... It looked as if kids had been staying in one, adults in another, and a third was neatly made up and spotless. The last two doors were closed. She chose the door on the left. Rapped softly. "Kyle?"

After a moment, the door cracked open. "Jessica, what are you doing here?" he asked quietly.

Obviously, she'd come too early. Sarah, TJ, Reed and the others hadn't returned from the beach yet. "Sarah told me that now would be a good time to stop by before you leave. I'd like to program my number into your phone so you can call me from Maryland and give me an update as soon as you can."

Kyle just nodded. He seemed too tired to argue with her. His face was drained.

"Are you okay?" she asked. "Really?"

He looked at her sharply.

Oh...maybe he wasn't alone. It was strange how he wasn't opening the door wider, wasn't letting her in.

"Is somebody in there?" Jessica asked. *Rose, perhaps?*

An angry line appeared on Kyle's brow. Before he could answer her, there was the sound of water running in the room across the hallway, behind her.

She turned. In a moment, the door opened and Rose appeared from a bathroom, smoothing her hair. When she saw Jessica and Kyle standing there, her smile faltered. "Oh! Hello."

Jessica tried to speak, but her throat was dry.

"Hello," Kyle murmured.

Rose glanced quickly from Jessica to Kyle. "I'll...be downstairs. Everyone will be back soon. I promised to help tidy up."

"I need to lie down for a while," Kyle said to Rose. "Tell the others just to let themselves out when they're ready."

Rose gave a short nod. She was making a heroic try at smiling, Jessica could tell.

After Rose's footsteps faded down the staircase, Jessica turned to Kyle. "Is there anything going on with her? Am I complicating matters?"

"No," Kyle said flatly.

"Are you sure, because I—"

"I'm not involved with anyone. Not besides you."

"*Are* we still involved?" she whispered.

He glanced away. "You don't give up, do you?"

"You've got a good heart, Kyle. A strong, loving heart, and you've been waiting for somebody to see it, and I do."

Kyle suddenly grimaced. He backed up and sat down hard on the bed. Leaning over, he rubbed both hands below his knee where she guessed the top of his prosthetic leg was.

Please let me help. But she bit back the words. He'd made his wishes known. She stood where she was, absolutely still.

The room was silent. All she could hear was

the sound of her own breathing. *Please, Kyle, let me in.*

He glanced up at her. His face was twisted in pain. "The medication will kick in soon. Beyond that, nothing has changed with me. I will never, ever show my leg to you. It's the one thing I can't do, no matter how much I love you. So please, don't ever ask me."

"You…just said you love me," she said in wonder.

He closed his eyes. "How could I not?"

He loved her. Her heart sang with the joy of it. She clasped her hands and pressed them to her heart.

The door downstairs opened just then, and children's voices and laughter drifted toward them. Sarah and TJ and all the others were back.

"Oh, I wanted say good-bye to them," Jessica said. "I'll be right back."

In the kitchen, she said her good-byes. Sarah went to the bedrooms to pack up her family's weekend belongings and then to check on Kyle. Jessica heard them inside Kyle's room talking, but she didn't interrupt. Her heart pumping, she played with Reed and Simba until Sarah returned.

"He'll be okay," Sarah murmured to Jessica, pulling her aside. "He may be away for a few weeks, but I'm sure he'll be back." She programmed her number into Jessica's phone.

Jessica stood on the front stoop waving at them until their truck drove away. When she could no longer hear the engine, she went back up the stairs to Kyle's room.

He lay on his back, on top of the covers. His green eyes settled on hers. "I'm powerless when it comes to this."

"Not to me," she said quietly. "I see a take-charge person. You're confident, and you know who you are. You believe in the same things I do. And you're so gorgeous. Every woman was jealous of me dancing with you at that wedding—"

He pulled her down with him. It happened so suddenly that she made a small squeak, until he put his finger against her lips.

And then softly, gently, kissed her.

CHAPTER FIFTEEN

ALL SHE'D WANTED was to give him encouragement to love her, and it seemed as if she'd broken through the dam he kept locked tight—at least, for now. She had no idea how long it would last. Kyle was determined to keep himself strong, determined to keep her emotionally at arm's length, while she was just as determined to breech that defense.

Jessica kissed him back. It was easy to kiss him, just as it was easy to love him. There was a sweet, vulnerable side to Kyle that was incredibly sexy to her.

A moan escaped from her throat and he seemed emboldened by that, because he flipped her over, resting her head on his pillow. She turned and caught the comforting smell of his unique scent. Putting her arms around his neck, she pulled him closer.

He tugged on the buttons at the top of her dress. As each button slipped free, exposing her hot skin, he dipped his head and pressed a kiss there, making a trail of pleasurable sensations down her chest. She sighed and squirmed, hoping that he wouldn't stop.

"Do you still want to do this, Jessica?" He nudged aside the lace of her bra. The cool air rushed to peak her nipple, and a delicious shiver passed over her body.

"You know that I do." She moaned again, and he drew her nipple into his mouth. Kissed her puckered skin with his hot mouth. A tight line shot from her breast to a spot between her legs and she cried out. His hand pushed up her dress, his palm rough over her thighs, under the elastic of her cotton underwear. She drew up her knees. So long she'd waited for him. She sifted her hands through his silky brown hair. She would know him by touch alone, by the shape and contours of his face.

"I'm not going to stop, Jessica."

"Good. Don't." She sighed as his head went lower, to where she'd felt such need for him. Her mind was losing focus. Thinking stopped. She lost herself in him as he gently made love to her with his mouth and his hands.

It was as if she'd never known her body at all. Was just now seeing what it was like to be so close to a man as lovers. True lovers. Not only a physical connection—a soul-deep one.

He gazed into her eyes as she soared over the edge. Tremors shook her and she threw her head back. Kyle gathered her close to him, his clothed hips pressed to her. Bucking and pulling with her, he kissed her as she cried out.

She lay still for a time, her hips raised, toes curling and uncurling, a wide smile on her face. As she shifted, she felt him settle on top of her.

Kyle was still fully dressed. *Now this is just wrong,* she thought. She reached for the button of his pants.

He gasped and sucked in his breath. "Jess, I don't want you to see my…"

My residual leg, she finished for him. *Yes, I know, Kyle.* "I won't look at your leg until you ask me to."

"That'll never happen," he muttered.

"Then it will be hard to make love." And as she said so, she pressed her palm against his rock hard abs and then slid her hand beneath the loose waistband of his jeans.

"Jess," he hissed.

She wasn't anywhere near his leg. Instead, she gently touched his swollen erection. While a look of pleasure crossed his face, she caressed the length of his smooth strength. She slid her fingers beneath his testicles.

He gave a sharp gasp. His body twitched in her arms. "Jess—"

She hid a smile. "Yes?"

He glanced at her, hissing out a breath. "You're going to make me…"

"I hope so." She stretched sensuously, shifting her hips to rub against his. "I've wanted to touch you for so long. You feel so good. Please give me that pleasure."

He let out a guttural gasp as she slowly stroked the length of him. His skin felt like silk. He was so hard and thick…

She let her palm linger on the head.

He cursed. "Jessica…"

"You don't have to hold on. You can let go." She stroked him again. And again.

And again.

With a gasp, he gave up fighting her. His clenched teeth turned to a deep groan. She felt him pumping inside her hand, the warm fluids running over her skin. It felt so erotic—Kyle wasn't a man who easily ceded control.

He cried out and lay spent in her arms, breathing heavily.

She nuzzled her head against him. She loved this man so much.

Turning his head on the pillow, he kissed her tenderly. "You never stop surprising me."

"Good." She could stay right here in his arms and forever be happy.

"I hate that I have to leave you," he murmured.

"When do you leave?"

"Tomorrow. Early."

"Please just don't kick me out before then," she whispered.

He laughed softly, as if she'd just said the most absurd thing. "No. I won't kick you out of my bed, Jess. Not ever."

"Thank you for that, at least."

He reached over and lifted the rest of her seersucker dress off her. Then he unclasped the front of her bra and the let the thin cups drop to the side. He laid his cheek between her breasts, just resting there.

She caressed his hair, his brow. He seemed calmer now, more pain free, and she said nothing to disturb that peace for him. She just lay with him, the windows open and the afternoon shadows lengthening, the sun moving to the other side of the house and leaving his bedroom darker.

"I'm scared, Jessica," he whispered, his eyes still closed.

It surprised her that he'd confessed it. She kept softly stroking his brow, sifting her fingers through his hair that felt so baby fine and soft. Quite a contrast, considering how pumped full of testosterone he was.

"I don't think I can take another operation," he said.

I'm sorry, she thought, but didn't say it. Though she ached to ask him questions, she knew that if

342 THE SECRET BETWEEN THEM

she spoke, she would break the spell between them that allowed him to speak truthfully. She remained silent for him.

"April nineteenth was my anniversary date. Do you remember April nineteenth? It was the day your skates came in the mail. I always know when it's coming, but this year, I forgot. I only realized when I saw the postmark on your package."

She leaned down and kissed the top of his head.

"I was driving and I hit an IED. That's how it happened. I knew right away my leg was gone. I knew my life would never be the same."

She slipped her hand down the back of his T-shirt and gently rubbed his muscles.

"Thank you for listening." His lips were muffled by her bare breast. "Thank you for…getting it."

"Thank you again for not kicking me out of bed," she replied jauntily.

He laughed, as she'd known he would. Deep, mirthful laughter that made his stomach muscles shudder against her.

After a while he turned his face to her. Propped his head on his elbow. "I have some pills that help me sleep through the night. They tend to zonk me out if I take them though."

"That's good," she said. "If it helps you to sleep, then by all means, take them."

"It's not even dark yet."

"That's fine. I didn't sleep much last night, so I'm tired myself."

He smiled at her. "I'll be right back."

"Okay."

She lay wrapped in his sheets, watching as he walked into an attached bathroom. This was the master bedroom to the house, she realized. Kyle shut the door behind him, but as with many older houses, the door didn't quite close all the way. She heard water running inside.

The water ran for a long time, it seemed.

Quietly, barefoot, Jessica left the bed and approached the gap between the door and the jam. She peered through the slit, barely daring to breath.

Kyle sat on the edge of a tiled platform tub. He wore just his T-shirt and a pair of boxer briefs. The water flowed from a big silver faucet. He was bent over, washing his residual leg.

The sight pierced her heart. It *pained* her. Not for his injury or the discomfort he was going through, but for the fact that he'd chosen to bear it alone.

He bathed alone. He traveled alone. Tomorrow, he would leave her alone.

She crept back to bed. Put her cheek to his

pillow, which smelled like him. A comforting smell. From somewhere in her memory, long ago, she remembered she'd had a father in her house. Men's pillows always smelled different from women's pillows. It might have been the shaving cream or the aftershave, but it was comforting to her. She wrapped her arms tightly around Kyle's pillow.

He was a long time coming back to bed. The daily care of an amputated limb involved careful washing, drying, lotion application. The gel sleeves that amputees wore also needed to be carefully cleaned and kept sanitary, due to the risk of infection. Jessica had learned much from working with young Benjamin. She could easily find patience and respect for what Kyle needed to go through each day of his life.

When he lifted the sheets and crawled under them beside her, she saw that he'd put on his pants and his prosthetic limb again. She didn't say a word about it. Stripped out of her own clothes, she padded into the bathroom across the hall and washed her face and rinsed her mouth.

Now she was naked, under his crisp, soft sheets. With a grunt, Kyle sat up and stripped off his T-shirt. He lay back down and pulled her against his hard chest, and she wrapped her hands around his arms.

She was careful to avoid brushing against his lower extremities. He wasn't ready for that yet.

The drugs did, indeed, knock Kyle out. For a long time, she lay listening to his breathing until she, too, fell into a deep sleep.

When at last she woke, the sun was shining in her eyes. She patted the sheets beside her, but they were cool, and Kyle was gone.

CHAPTER SIXTEEN

IN THE END, Kyle had known he would have to leave.

He'd put his phone alarm on vibrate and had left it under his pillow so he wouldn't miss his taxi. He woke while Jessica was still sleeping. His bag was packed and ready downstairs. He had the boarding pass for his plane ticket inside his wallet. His phone held the reservation for the hotel he'd be staying at down in Maryland.

But despite all his planning, Kyle hadn't expected this uneasiness at leaving Jessica.

Why had he confessed to her? She hadn't needed to hear that stuff about him. The only excuse he had was that he was freaked out over the possibility that he might not skate—or walk well—again. That fear had obviously affected his judgment.

Kyle sat on the chair beside his shower stall and laced up his shoe. The other shoe, the one he kept attached to his prosthetic, was always tied, but he checked it just in case.

He wasn't looking forward to going through

the airport check-in. Even though he was out of uniform, it was still a humiliation. He would have driven to Maryland if he'd felt at all well enough to do so.

He caught his reflection in the mirror. He looked terrible. Pale, gaunt cheeked. It was crazy—he was combat hardened. He'd tended other guys' wounds, talked to them, kept their spirits up until the medics arrived. And here he was worried about a little operation?

On his way out of the room he glanced at Jessica, still asleep in his bed. The rawness hit him hard, straight in the gut. He felt tenderness for her. Protectiveness. She'd been through so much drama in her own life, she didn't need to be bothered with his.

She thought she knew what his recuperation had been like, but she didn't. He'd had four operations. Four bouts of being in a wheelchair, of feeling helpless. Rehab hadn't been a cakewalk, either.

Even after everything they'd said to each other, he loved Jessica too much to put her through that.

He grabbed his duffel bag and limped downstairs. Bypassed Joe's stair-climber gadget and just felt depressed all over again. Living in this house definitely didn't help him. The rink he'd felt alive in, but in Joe's house… Well, it was just all about Joe. Not a shred of anything belonging to Kyle had been found in the house, not the stuff from his childhood room, not his sports equipment in the garage, not his baseball cards in the attic.

His mom's things he'd found. Joe had kept her memories around. Her clothes in one of the upstairs bedroom closets. Her small jewelry box on the dresser in his bedroom.

Kyle rubbed his hand over his face and said a silent good-bye to the photo of his mom hanging on the wall at the bottom of the stairs.

Simba was fed. TJ had his rink information. Kyle intended to tell him to have Patrick, Mike and Carol keep the place running until Natalie sold it.

Kyle opened the fridge and grabbed a bottle of water. He was ready to sit outside until the car service came.

"Kyle?" Jessica said behind him.

Closing his eyes and silently cursing himself for not bolting when he'd had the chance for a clean getaway, Kyle turned. Jessica's arms were crossed. She was dressed in his robe. Probably wearing nothing beneath, just his flannel against her bare skin.

"I'm sorry. I didn't want to wake you," Kyle said.

"So you were just going to sneak off?" Her

eyes were bloodshot, and Kyle realized with a start that she was deeply upset.

"Please don't be angry," he murmured.

"I'm your friend. I'm more than your friend, and you still shut me out."

"Jess, I can't give you what you want. Don't you see that?" His voice had risen, and that made everything worse.

"I see what you're doing," she said with emotion. "You *think* you're protecting me, and I don't like it at all. Because what you think of protection, isn't. I'd rather you risk hurting me by telling me the truth." She drew in a breath. "If there's one thing I've learned in my life, it's that I can't expect people to know what I want if I don't tell them. You already know I want to go with you to Maryland. But what I'm also telling you is that no matter what your doctor says you need for course of treatment, I'm here to go through it with you. Nothing about that will ever scare me away or make me think less of you. So stop pushing me away."

He stared at her, not knowing what to say. He'd heard her argument, but he didn't believe in it.

He'd been at Walter Reed, surrounded by other wounded warriors and their families. At a visceral, emotional level, Kyle just didn't believe in putting a loved one through that.

He stood, breathing heavily. As did Jessica.

She crossed her arms, her fingers worrying the faded plaid fabric of his robe, looking as though she was going to cry at any moment.

He softly exhaled. "Good-bye, Jessica."

She exhaled. "That's it?"

He nodded and headed for the door, intent on waiting by himself in the early morning dawn.

But outside, the car was already idling on the street at the end of his front walkway. Kyle slowly made his way down. The driver loaded Kyle's bag, opened the door for him.

Kyle got inside.

He'd almost made a clean escape, too. But Jessica came flying out the door, still dressed in his bathrobe. It was so big on her, the ties dragged past her knees, but she held it closed.

She had something white in her hand. She knocked on his window and he had no choice but to roll it down.

"I found this in the bathroom drawer," Jessica said. "You never even opened it. You never even gave him a chance to explain himself to you."

It was the letter from Joe.

Jessica's chin was set and she was angry with him. Without a word, Kyle reached to take the letter from her.

She held it back. "No, wait. Here's the deal. You *won't* call Natalie," she said to him. "You let me do that. You give me that."

"Jess—"

"If you don't agree," she threatened, "then I will open this letter and read it aloud myself, right now."

"Fine," he said quickly. "You tell Natalie what's happened."

Jessica handed him the envelope. Kyle took it from her, then unzipped his jacket pocket and stuffed it in there.

Her hand reached for his, but something had turned off inside him. Something was making him numb. He just felt disappointed in himself— angry and bitter and full of regret.

Tears rolled down Jessica's cheeks.

I'm sorry, he should have said. But it just seemed like yet another admission of failure.

He rolled up his window and got on with it. Headed toward the airport and then Maryland. The fear and the terror of having something major wrong with his leg, changing his life for the worst, all over again.

ON TUESDAY AT six o'clock Jessica was dressed and parked in her habitual spot at the twin rinks parking lot. She had her breakfast in hand, and she also had a plan.

She sipped her coffee and debated what to do about Kyle's empty parking space next to her. The one weak spot in her plan was that Kyle's truck wouldn't be parked at the rink and Natalie might notice.

And then TJ's truck—the same make and model as Kyle's—turned into the lot from the main road, and Jessica had her answer.

Now that Kyle had New Hampshire plates, TJ's truck could definitely pass as Kyle's. Maybe it would be enough to fool Natalie on those days that Natalie came around.

Not that Natalie was a fool, by any means, but Jessica knew that outright telling her what she was doing was probably a no-no as far as the legal profession went, and Jessica wasn't going to risk that.

Before Carol came in for the day, Jessica opened her desk drawer and took out the sign-in notebook that Natalie had left for her and Kyle.

Natalie would be coming by to pick up the sheets on her monthly visit. Jessica planned to call and ask Zena if Natalie could meet with her while she was here. Jessica had a lot of questions she needed answers to if she was going to figure out how to make this rink successful.

Keeping the business open was the one thing that she could focus on, the task that would keep her going and give her purpose while Kyle was gone.

Jessica opened her office door and immediately saw the skates Kyle had bought her, sitting on her desk. Down the hall in Kyle's now-empty locker room, her repaired photograph hung.

She decided to leave it there. Kyle would be back.

AFTER LUNCH, JESSICA met with Patrick, Mike and Carol. "Kyle is getting some personal business taken care of," Jessica explained, keeping as much of a straight face as she could. "You won't see him around as much, but don't worry. He's still a partner with me. We're open, we're in business, and if there are any questions send them my way."

Before anyone could speak, Jessica turned to Patrick. "Are you all right with taking charge of the ice maintenance during the day?"

Patrick perked up. Riding the Zamboni was his favorite thing. "Awesome. Yeah."

"Carol, are you still good in your job?"

Carol shook her head. "Kyle didn't say anything to Johnny about this. What kind of personal business is he attending to?"

Jessica smiled as easily as she could. "Nothing to worry about. Just something down in Maryland. He'll be back soon."

No matter what, she was determined to downplay Kyle's absence. With the staff, she would treat it as "business as usual." With Natalie, she would have to rely on subterfuge.

Jessica took the old sign-in sheets inside her

office. She took a slip of paper and traced Kyle's initials. She had no idea how long he would be gone—he surely didn't either—but as Jessica understood Joe's will, both she and Kyle needed to be present for thirty hours per week. If she had to forge his initials to keep the terms active, then she would do it.

Luckily, Carol had only a vague understanding of their deal, anyway. Without comment, Jessica replaced the notebook inside the drawer in the main office.

Carol was humming at her desk.

"Did you have a good honeymoon weekend?" Jessica asked.

"The cabin at the lake was wonderful. Next month, though, we're planning to take a full week at Niagara Falls. That's okay with you and Kyle, isn't it?"

Jessica could only hope he would be back by then.

If he came back.

She crossed her fingers behind her back. "Of course," she said, smiling at Carol.

Natalie arrived at one o'clock, wearing another of her skirted business suits.

"How's Hannah?" Jessica asked, as she pointed Natalie toward the couch inside her office.

Natalie sat, crossing her legs. "She's doing great. Bruce's parents are watching her today.

They actually have a tea party planned. Hannah was quite excited when I dropped her off this morning."

"I can imagine. She's adorable."

"I'll tell her I saw you today." Natalie smiled. "She talks about you. Calls you her friend."

"Thanks. Maybe...she'd like to learn to skate in the fall? She'll be four then, won't she?"

Natalie nodded. If she looked surprised by Jessica's offer and optimism, she didn't show it.

"Where's Kyle?" Natalie asked.

"He stepped out for a while. He knows I'm talking with you, though."

"Okay."

"Well, here's our sign-in book for the month." Jessica passed the binder to Natalie. "I was wondering if you could fill me in on our financial reports. Like how much more money we need before we'll be showing a profit."

"Have you talked with Kyle? I reviewed the numbers with him."

"Of course." Jessica feigned an easy confidence she didn't feel. "Still, I'd like to take some steps to surprise him. You told me that Joe included me as part of Kyle's inheritance in hopes that I would contribute to the success of the figure-skating rink, right? Well..." She took a breath and faked an easiness she didn't feel. "I wasn't ready to do that before, but now I am. I'd like it to be a surprise for Kyle. In order to succeed, I need your advice."

Natalie clasped her fingers and studied Jessica. Whatever she saw, Jessica must have passed the test, because Natalie opened her leather folder, withdrew a notepad and wrote down a figure for Jessica. "This represents the revenue you need over the next two months."

She passed the notepad to her without a word.

Jessica gazed at the figure, her stomach sinking. It was much worse than she'd thought.

"If you can get a figure-skating club with deep pockets to commit to renting the second ice surface," Natalie said, "and they're willing to purchase that large of a block of ice time, then I can absolutely guarantee that you and Kyle will be keeping ownership of the twin rinks."

"And if we don't?" she whispered.

Natalie smiled sadly. "I'm afraid you already know the answer."

She did. Kyle would be on the street, job-wise, and Wallis Point would have another condominium development.

Natalie stood. Jessica couldn't seem to summon the energy.

No wonder Kyle had given up.

For two days, Jessica mulled over her options.

The problem was, she didn't really have any.

There was only one regional figure skating club with the kind of money available that Jessica needed. She not only needed the figure Natalie had calculated, but also an additional amount to repair the rink machinery. And Jessica wasn't exactly their favorite person.

She asked Carol if she, by any chance, had a contact at the Ice Captains Figure Skating Club.

They sat over morning coffee and Toll House cookies. Jessica tried to keep the conversation as relaxed as possible. The famous New England club, one of the oldest and most respected in the country, had been the club that both Jessica and her mother were affiliated with during their competitive careers. Pretty much all the locals who knew Jessica and had followed her career back in the day knew that.

"Why don't you ask your mother?" Carol suggested as she poured another shot of cream into her coffee. "Johnny says that she knows everybody in the sport. If someone could find a rich skater who needed to buy private ice, then it would be Hedley. You wouldn't need to talk to anyone at Ice Captains."

Jessica's heart was pounding. She gazed into her coffee, not meeting Carol's eyes, because while Kyle knew about her estrangement from her mother, Carol and Johnny didn't.

"I suppose I could ask her," she murmured.

"She was talking about you on TV," Carol said. Jessica looked up. "When was that?"

"During the world championships."

"I missed that. What did she say?"

"Just that she's proud of you. She mentioned you're a physical therapist on the East Coast and that you excel at working with children. I wish she'd mentioned Wallis Point, but maybe she wants to help you keep your privacy. Everyone knows how important your privacy is to you." Carol took a sip of coffee.

Jessica felt stunned that her mother said those positive things about her, especially on the air. She hadn't thought her mother ever mentioned her.

"Well," Carol said, "I suppose if you're going to stay with the rink after August, then you really can't expect to have much privacy anymore, can you?"

"That's true." Maybe the inevitable was at hand. Jessica took her cell phone. She went out to her car and then drove to her favorite place to walk on her favorite beach.

Parking across the street, she had little choice but to pass by Sebastien's house on the way to the remote end of the point.

She trudged down the sandy path, glancing at his house only out of curiosity. She didn't feel anything anymore when she thought of him.

Even if Kyle never came around, she'd done the right thing.

Holding her breath, she dialed the only phone number of her mother's that she knew.

The phone rang and rang. No one picked up. Jessica almost hung up, not even sure this was still her mother's number, but when the phone went to voice mail, Hedley Jackson's trademark, gravelly voice said, "Please leave your name and number, and I'll get back to you as soon as I can."

Jessica inhaled a breath of salty fresh air. She hadn't heard her mom's voice in so long, her hands shook. She hadn't considered the possibility of leaving a message and was caught unprepared.

She tried to concentrate on the ocean, on the waves, large from the high tide, rolling in gently on the beach.

"Mom?" she said. "This is Jessica. I wonder if you could call me back? I'm…in Wallis Point. Joe Mansell died and I inherited his rink. I need some advice and I…thought of you." She inhaled and exhaled. Did she dare to say it? "I'd really like to talk with you," she said softly.

Then she left her cell phone number and hung up.

Jessica put the phone in her pocket and stood watching a seagull flying low over the surf. This was the most daring thing she'd done in a long time. For too long, she'd been too fragile. As Kyle refused to show people his leg, she had refused to deal with her old world—her old wounds.

But somehow over these last few months, she'd rediscovered her strength. Much of that had to do with Kyle. And now, in truth, the only reason she'd even phoned her mother had been to help Kyle—she never wanted him to feel like a failure. He was anything but.

Please, Mom. Call back.

She was still standing before the ocean ten minutes later when her mother returned her call.

"Jessica? This is Mother."

"Thank you. Thank you so much for calling back."

There was a pause. "You said that Joe Mansell died?"

"In February. I was…his physical therapist for a knee injury. I didn't expect to inherit his rink at all…"

"Are you skating?" her mother asked.

The number one priority in Hedley Jackson's world. It had always been so, but Jessica found that she didn't feel bitter about it anymore. "Yes, I've been on the ice. I have a young client who I'm teaching to skate with two prosthetic legs."

"That's actually quite interesting," her mother said, in a drawn-out tone that told Jessica she was considering how best to capitalize on that angle.

Jessica bit her lip. Her mother was still the same. But Jessica took a deep breath, ready for a change. "I miss you, Mom."

There was a short silence. Then she heard a softer, "I miss you, too."

"If you're ever on the East Coast, I'd love to see you."

"Actually," her mother said, "I'm coming out in August to visit Ice Captains."

"That's…wonderful. I could meet you there."

"Jessica, are you looking for their number?"

"That would help, yes. I'm really trying to make our ice rink into a success."

"Then you should call Heather Wellesley in their main office. Do you have Heather's number? No, I suppose you don't. I'll wait while you get something to write it down."

Jessica took out a pen and copied the number that her mother gave her. She promised to catch up with her in August.

"Tell Heather I told you to call her," her mother said.

Kyle sat in yet another waiting room on yet another day, waiting to get the results from yet another diagnostic test.

He felt restless and irritated. By paperwork. By uncertainty. But the absolute worst feeling was missing Jessica. Thinking of her left an emptiness inside him that nothing seemed to fill.

Nearby was a veteran in worse shape than Kyle was. The young guy wore a pair of shorts and a tank top, and Kyle could see that he had an above-the-knee prosthetic and an above-the-elbow "bionic arm" similar to Oscar's.

He saw Kyle looking at him. "You want a Coke or something when my wife comes back? I'm gonna ask her to grab me one. I can have her get you one, too."

"No, thanks," Kyle said.

The guy smiled at him anyway. "I'm Travis. You?"

"Kyle." He braced himself, figuring Travis wanted to talk. Kyle wasn't up for conversation. He felt out of sorts and ticked off in general. It was turning out to be a bad day. A "why me?" kind of day, as a counselor he'd once been forced to sit with had termed it.

Travis took out his phone. A sign in front of the reception desk said "Show consideration—turn off your cell phones, please," so Travis got up and made his way toward the door.

He walked slowly. Painfully slowly. He obviously wasn't adept with the leg yet. But Travis's expression showed that he was okay with that.

Travis had made it about six feet when the door opened and a pretty redhead scooted cheerfully inside, holding the door for a girl who looked about six or seven.

"Hi, honey," Travis said.

"We brought you a Coke, Daddy," the girl chirped.

"That's funny, you must have read my mind."

Travis's daughter ran over and hugged him.

Kyle sat still. The two were directly in front of him, so close he could reach out and touch them if he wanted.

Travis turned to Kyle and winked. "Best thing about recovery is that I get to be with my wife and daughter all day."

Kyle didn't say anything. He tried not to watch Travis as his daughter walked him slowly—always slowly—back to his chair. Travis's wife smiled briefly and nodded at Kyle on her way past to take the chair on the other side of Travis. All three put their heads together, talking quietly and giggling over something.

During his initial recovery, he'd been surrounded by lots of guys who had their families with them. To Kyle's mind, that was the worst thing possible. How could anybody subject their loved ones to this? It sickened him to think of Jessica being here. She wouldn't bat an eye, of course. She'd be just like Travis's wife, supportive and happy. Knowing Jessica, she'd probably be making conversation with Travis's daughter, too. She was like that. So sunny in her disposition.

He was the grouch about it. Didn't see how that could be any different.

The desk clerk at the window called Travis's name and held out a clipboard. Travis's wife skipped up to retrieve it for him.

Kyle had already filled out a ream of paperwork. He hoped his turn to see the doctor was coming soon, because he was sick of waiting.

"Excuse me?" It was Travis's wife, leaning over Travis and talking to Kyle. "Do you have a pen we could borrow? The one they gave me is out of ink."

"Yeah. Sure." Kyle reached into his jacket pocket where he always kept his pen.

He found the pen, but he also found Joe's crumpled letter. He gave Travis's wife the pen, then glanced around for a wastebasket to throw the letter out, but there wasn't one.

Kyle should have disposed of the letter a long time ago when he'd had the chance. After the lawyer meeting, when Natalie had given him the key to Joe's house, Kyle had gone inside and tossed the letter on the counter. It had ended up in the drawer upstairs and he didn't even remember how. He just remembered thinking that Joe didn't own a shredder, and that Kyle wasn't going to risk throwing a legal document into the trash.

Except…through the plain white envelope, now that Kyle studied it, he could see the blue of a ballpoint pen and words written in cursive. A more formal document would have been typed, not written—and this letter had a lot of writing. Strange, because Joe was a man of few words.

Kyle tapped on the envelope, wondering.

A nurse came and got a man who was sleeping in the corner. She actually had to shake him awake. Looking around now, Kyle realized there were at least two more people in front of him in line.

He tapped at the letter some more. Held it to the light.

Rows and rows of Joe's scratchy handwriting. What could he possibly have to say to Kyle that would take so many words? Joe had usually berated him in one sentence.

Travis's wife walked the pen back to Kyle. "Thank you," she said.

Kyle nodded. The door opened and another guy walked in. He had two kids with him—boys— and one of them was Reed's age. He toddled over to Kyle and crouched, staring at him.

Kyle put a finger in the envelope and tore it open. He put the lined notebook page up in front of his face as if he was reading a newspaper. Maybe the kid would get the hint.

Stop being like Joe.

Jessica had asked him to do just that, in so many words.

He exhaled, long and hard. Concentrated on what Joe had to say to him from beyond the grave.

Dear Kyle,
I bet you've been wondering why I left the rink to Jessica Hughes as well as to you.

No, Kyle thought crossly, *I haven't been wondering.*

I thought long and hard about it. And to answer your question, no, it has nothing to do with you losing a leg in the service. Don't think that for a minute. You're capable of the work no matter what, rest assured about that.

I was harsh on you as a boy. I see that now, and I should not have been. I did badly by your mother. She would not have liked the way I treated you. It was a terrible, terrible thing when she died, for both of us. I wanted so badly to save her but I could not. I brought her to every doctor, I spared no expense as you know. But she was taken from me anyway. I know it is no excuse for my actions. Little good it does you now, you are probably thinking.

Kyle, it is not your fault you remind me of her. It is not your fault I pushed you away. Please do not make the same mistakes I made. I'm giving you the opportunity to right old wrongs with Jessica. I see her life here and I see she is not happy.

It grieves me. I remember the two of you at the rink together and I know you were sweet on each other. Do not blow it now! If you can achieve any of the happiness that your mother spread to me, then you will have the best life possible. Enjoy it now! Don't push her away, as I pushed you away. A woman can be the best of companions. In my life, your mother was mine.

Be kind and help her. Allow her to help you.

That is all.

Your stepfather,
Joe

CHAPTER SEVENTEEN

JESSICA WALKED INTO the one place she never imagined she would see again: the Ice Captains Figure Skating Club.

Home of many Olympic champions, including her mother, the facility was surprisingly small, squeezed as it was into a crowded Boston neighborhood. Therefore, it had been tradition for years that many of the club's skaters practiced on ice at facilities farther afield. As Jessica had done, for instance.

She opened those familiar double doors. Everything inside looked smaller. She felt as if she were seventeen again.

She paused for a moment, rubbing her arms. The air outside was humid and she'd left her sweater in the car. In here, it was cold. She headed past the single ice surface where a pairs team was skating a program to music by a female pop vocalist, and then she turned into the bank of offices.

Jessica had never met Heather Wellesley before. "Jessa," the middle-aged matron said warmly, peering closely at Jessica over the tops of her eyeglasses and holding out her hand in greeting. "It's lovely to meet you."

"Thank you." Jessica took the chair that Heather offered. She'd tried to talk to her over the phone about recommending some skaters whom Jessica could call, but Heather had insisted she come to the club offices in person.

"Your mother tells me that you've been skating," Heather said.

Jessica felt her jaw locking. "Actually, I'm here for business reasons."

"Oh, yes. You're running the Wallis Point Twin Rinks."

"Not quite. I'm representing the person who will be, though."

"Jessa, we don't make those kinds of arrangements anymore. All of our club members skate either in this facility or in our satellite location."

"Then why did you—"

"Why did I ask you here?" Heather smiled. "Because we would like to extend an invitation for you to skate in our annual televised festival this September."

"I'm sorry, I don't do that kind of thing anymore." Jessica rose.

"Please consider it," Heather said. "While it's true that the proceeds from the ticket sales and the television contract are earmarked for charity, we do make allowances to pay our skating talent. And we pay very well."

"Would you excuse me?" Jessica stood and tucked her purse under her arm. "I think I need to leave." Blindly, she walked as fast as she could to the ladies' restroom.

Inside, she sat on a couch in the lounge area and clutched at her stomach. She felt nauseous. She hadn't expected to be blindsided. She could barely skate, never mind perform for an audience. And a televised audience! The yearly Ice Captains Festival was broadcast all over the country. All the big names in the sport, past and present, skated in that show. Her mother had appeared several times herself.

For Jessica to perform at all on the public stage was out of the realm of possibility.

The door to the restroom opened, and two women walked in. One of them looked at Jessica and did a double take.

Jessica rose to her feet and left.

Outside in the hallway, Heather waited.

"I'm sorry," Jessica said. "But there's been a misunderstanding. I don't skate anymore, for anybody."

"I know." Heather smiled and handed Jessica a document. "But please read this. It's the contract we're offering. Review it with your agent and then get back to us."

"But I don't have an..." Jessica saw the dollar sign at the bottom of the page and she inhaled sharply.

"Yes, it's quite a bit of money. You're worth it to us because there's a demand to see you. Everyone remembers Jessa Hughes. Think of it as an opportunity to end your career on a highlight this time."

Jessa was still fixated on the amount of the payment. It was more money than she needed to keep the rink profitable for Kyle.

She couldn't think straight. The blood had seemed to drain from her head.

"Think about it and call me," Heather said.

WHEN JESSICA GOT back to the twin rinks an hour later, she felt overwhelmed.

Carol met her at the door. "So what happened?" She studied Jessica's face and sighed. "Not good, huh?"

"They lured me on false pretenses. They don't want to buy ice time from us."

"Then what did they want?"

"This." Jessica handed Carol the contract then went into her office and put her head down on her desk.

She'd failed. She'd wanted so badly to find a way to secure ownership of the rinks for Kyle.

She covered her face with her hands. There

was nothing left to do. She might as well let Natalie know that they'd failed. Best case, she could ask her to contact Kyle and check up on how he was doing at the doctor's in Maryland.

Defeated, she headed into the main office.

Natalie was already there. She and Carol were paging through the contract Heather had given her.

Natalie glanced up when Jessica walked in. She had an excited gleam in her eye. "This is an answer for you."

"What do you mean?" Jessica asked cautiously.

"If you're willing, it's even possible to structure this deal so that the Ice Captains pay the twin rinks and not you personally—if that's what you really want." Natalie laughed. "It seems like an awful lot of money for three minutes on camera followed by a ten-minute interview for print media."

"They want an interview, too?" Jessica steadied herself by placing a hand on the counter. "No."

"Not even to save the twin rinks?" Carol asked.

Both women looked expectantly at her.

Kimmie arrived for her noon skate. She waved at Jessica as she walked down the hallway to the hockey rink.

Kimmie was counting on the rinks being open, as were a lot of people.

Jessica wasn't just fighting for Kyle, she realized. A lot of other people were depending on her, too.

Benjamin. The retired ice dancers. Kyle's wounded warrior friends. "But I vowed I'd never perform again in public."

"You won't have to," Kyle said.

Jessica whirled to face him. "Kyle!"

He was home.

KYLE GAVE JESSICA a long embrace before walking them both to her office so they could have some privacy.

"I'm so glad you're here," Jessica said.

"Me, too. I came back as soon as I was finished at the doctor's office. I've decided I'm staying in Wallis Point and finding a doctor here." He took a deep breath. "Will you help me, Jess?"

"Yes! Of course I will."

"Thank you." He wrapped his arms around her and held her close. "I don't need this rink in order to be happy. I just need you."

"What changed your mind?" she asked, teary eyed.

He chuckled under his breath. "Would you believe Joe? He told me in his letter not to be like him. And then I looked around me in that doctor's office, and I saw myself as I saw him—the only guy sitting there without a family surrounding him." He took Jessica's face in his hands. "Can you forgive me? I was an ass. I should've asked for your help to begin with."

"Would you like to get out of here?" she asked.

"Yeah. Take me to your apartment."

"I warn you, it's very small."

"Good. You're all I want to see, anyway."

He drove with her in her tiny car, walked up the two flights of stairs. He must have been extremely motivated, she realized.

Once safely inside her homey two-room apartment, he gathered her in his arms and kissed her as she'd never been kissed. Then he drew back. "Tell me how much time I have. When are you due at the physical therapy clinic?"

"Today's a day off, actually."

He grinned. "Perfect. I love you, you know. I've always loved you. I promise I won't let you alone again."

"Even if we don't have the twin rinks?"

"Even if we have nothing besides ourselves," he said tenderly. He thought of Travis back at the doctor's office, injured worse than Kyle was and yet thrilled because he was with his wife and daughter. "It's you that makes me strong, Jess."

He kissed her until she was breathless all over again.

And then he led her to bed. He made love to

her with all the tenderness and passion she'd grown to see he was capable of.

Afterward, lying in his arms, she realized that while he'd removed his pants, under the sheet he still wore his prosthetic.

He noticed her thoughtful expression. "I can show you now, if you'd like," he said quietly.

"I'm honored that you trust me."

"I do, Jess."

Still, his hands were shaking as he drew back the sheet that covered him. Leaning over, he removed his prosthetic. She placed her hand on his back, showing him her love and support.

His face ashen, he removed the gel sock and then tentatively gazed up at her.

With her hand she gently touched the scarred, angry skin. Then she gently kissed him on the lips. "I love every part of you."

He bowed his head, exhaling. "Thank you, Jessica."

AFTER THAT, JESSICA decided that he'd inspired her to take a big risk herself. The one thing she'd never thought she could do.

But as long as she had him—and Kimmie, and Carol, and Patrick, and the lunchtime ice dancers, and Kyle's wounded warriors and Benjamin—to cheer her on, then maybe she could skate in the Ice Captains Festival, after all.

She had two months to prepare. The music selection was easy. She chose to perform to the first song that she'd danced with Kyle to, at Carol's wedding.

The costume was a bit more difficult, but Jessica had longed to design and sew her own costumes as a girl. Looking on the bright side, she'd finally received her chance.

Harder was learning to figure skate again. She needed to choreograph a simple yet effective program for the music—something that she could actually execute.

But it was a shock to Jessica that skating really was like riding a bike. The rhythm seemed to be embedded in her muscles. Her body, with all the years of prior training, had kept the memory of what she needed to do to stay upright, to glide effortlessly, to spin on one foot and to interpret music with her arms and facial expressions.

It was true she didn't have the fitness to execute triple jumps, but that wasn't the point. Neither were excessive speed or difficult tricks.

She wasn't competing with anyone, not even with herself. She was presenting a story with her performance, a gift to those who watched.

As part of her contract, she secured guest tickets for Benjamin and his parents on the evening of the event. Kyle, of course, went backstage with her that September evening. As her name was called, preceded by a heartfelt introduction from her mother, Jessica's entrance received a standing ovation. In those seconds before the music started to play, her knees shook and her legs felt like rubber, but with the audience's support, she quickly acclimated.

Jessica skated through the emotional choreography. Her first spin centered perfectly and felt effortless. The moving piece into her loop jump flowed, and the audience's response seemed to make her float longer in midair. Then she glided across the ice in a beautiful spiral, the wind in her face—she felt exhilaration, as she remembered from when she was young and loved to skate. Dare she think it?—she was enjoying herself.

Then, before she knew it, the music was over and she was taking her bows on a surge of euphoria.

She skated from the spotlight to the corner door and into Kyle's embrace. He had tears in his eyes.

"What did you think?" she asked.

"That I had better ask you to marry me now, before all your new admirers see you on TV and beat me to it."

She laughed and put her head on his chest as she hugged him. "Who knew you were a flatterer?"

"I've waited a long time to do this." He smiled

at her and then leaned over and murmured into her ear, "Jessica Hughes, will you marry me?"

"Yes, please," she whispered back. "Can we do it right away?"

He smiled, moving a wisp of hair from her eyes. "As soon as we pick out an engagement ring for you. Any one you want."

"Really? I'd like that."

Kyle nodded. But then he glanced up as a group of people, including a man carrying a television camera on his shoulder, approached their private corner. Jessica noticed that her mother was at the head of the line.

"We'll talk later," he murmured in her ear. "At dinner."

"Please stay." She held onto his hand. "I want you to stand with me."

He gave her a special, private smile. And he didn't leave her side.

"Jessica?" Her mother stepped before her, tears in her eyes. Blushing, she waved the camera-man aside, then turned to Jessica and gave her a hug. "I'm so proud of you," she whispered, for Jessica's ears only. "You're beautiful, and I know how hard that must have been."

Jessica nodded, a lump in her throat, her arms around her mom.

"Well." Her mom cleared her throat. "I'll let

you finish up here." She stepped back, but looked longingly at Jessica.

"Would you like to join us for dinner?" Kyle asked, completely surprising Jessica.

"I would…yes, I would." Her mom brightened. "Thank you, Kyle."

Jessica smiled up at him. This wasn't easy for Kyle, either, she knew.

But he took them to a nice dinner in the North End of Boston. Their conversation focused on the present—nothing difficult—and Jessica relaxed with happiness. Everything seemed to be falling into place. Jessica had faced her fears, she was starting a new relationship with her mother and she was headed into the future with Kyle. What more could she want?

It wasn't until Kyle had walked her mom outside to a waiting taxi and then returned to the table with Jessica, relaxing over the last of their wine, that she found out.

"Now I can tell you the rest of my news," Kyle said, leaning forward to clasp her hands. "I put Joe's home on the market. I'm thinking we can use the money to choose something just for us."

"Oh, I like that idea!"

"Excellent." He leaned forward and kissed her. "And you realize that," he said, in a serious tone, "with your performance back there, we're able to keep the twin rinks in the family."

"Is it official?" she breathed.

"It is." He grinned. "Natalie called me before you went on tonight. The check was deposited and the title transfer approved."

"So that's it? We own a rink?"

"We indeed own a rink. You and me. Team Northrup-Hughes."

"I think I'd like to be called just plain Team Northrup," she said. "I don't want to confuse our children."

He leaned his head back and laughed. "Remind me how many children we're gonna have."

"Oh, I don't know," she said breezily. "Enough to form a hockey team? How many is that?"

"As many as we want it to be." And then he kissed her again as if they were the only two people who mattered, and she knew that she had found her happiness where she'd least expected it to be.

* * * * *